A team of hardmen sprinted toward the shattered hut

Mack Bolan dropped into a fighting crouch and let the grenade launcher rip, the HE round looping toward his mobile targets. The leader saw it coming, tried to veer off course, but he collided with one of his gunners. A heartbeat later the blast pitched him head over heels through a cloud of smoke and dust. Two other men went down, their four companions staggering on weak legs, shaking their heads and trying to get a fix on the source of their torment.

The Executioner took them out with short bursts from the rifle, dropping each man in turn. Other hardmen were finding the range now, bullets whispering around Bolan's ears and snapping at his heels. He started to run for the nearest cover, sliding in behind the generator shed.

In another moment they would have him pinned, and Bolan still had work to do. He had caught a glimpse of Hans Erdmann in the distance, gaping from the open door of a bungalow before he slipped from view.

If Erdmann was left alive, the Executioner knew the mission would be a failure.

MACK BOLAN®

The Executioner

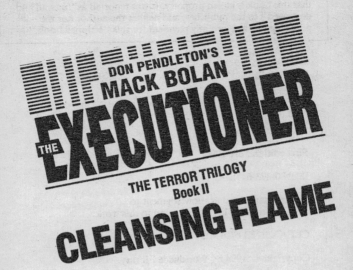

DON PENDLETON'S
MACK BOLAN
THE EXECUTIONER

THE TERROR TRILOGY
Book II

CLEANSING FLAME

A GOLD EAGLE BOOK FROM
WORLDWIDE.

TORONTO • NEW YORK • LONDON
AMSTERDAM • PARIS • SYDNEY • HAMBURG
STOCKHOLM • ATHENS • TOKYO • MILAN
MADRID • WARSAW • BUDAPEST • AUCKLAND

First edition July 1994.

ISBN 0-373-61187-0

Special thanks and acknowledgment to
Mike Newton for his contribution to this work.

CLEANSING FLAME

Honor is like a steep island without a shore: one
cannot return once one is outside.
—Nicolas Boileau

What, then, is your duty? What the day demands.
—Goethe

Today, honor and duty demand an extra sacrifice.
Whatever is required, I will see that duty done,
regardless of the cost.
—Mack Bolan

1

The mountain highway due west of Viacha is a winding, two-lane track, its hairpin curves constructed to accommodate the rugged landscape of Bolivia's Cordillera Central. It is the only serviceable road between La Paz and Guaqui, on the southern shore of Lake Titicaca. Across the border, in Peru, the snow-capped Andes march a thousand miles northwest to Ecuador, and on from there into Colombia.

Mack Bolan's prey would never get that far.

From Guaqui, they would seek a quiet point along the lakeshore, someplace far enough from any village that they wouldn't be observed or interrupted at their work. The prisoner would scream himself hoarse before they finished with him, and no one would be close enough to hear, or brash enough to intervene. When they had done their worst and finished with a point-blank bullet to the brain, the lake was deep and cold enough to hide their secret for a hundred years.

It wouldn't be the first or last time that a corpse had disappeared beneath the slate-gray surface, weighted down with cinder blocks and chains. Drug murders, highway robbery, Indian vendettas, human sacrifices—take your pick. The border region was a kind of lawless no-man's-land, where anything could happen to unwary travelers, no questions asked.

But not tonight.

The Executioner had other plans.

He didn't know the targets or their hostage personally, but he knew enough to place him on the slope above a blind curve in the highway, midnight coming on with nothing but a quarter moon to light the killing ground.

With any luck, he thought, it just might be enough.

Bolan was dressed to take advantage of the night, his face and hands darkened with combat cosmetics. The jet-black nightsuit fit him like a second skin, elasticized for ease of movement, pockets custom-tailored for garrotes, stilettos and assorted other killing gear. A Beretta 93-R semiautomatic pistol with custom silencer attached was slung beneath his arm in fast-draw leather, while a Desert Eagle .44 Magnum rode his hip on military webbing. Extra magazines were slotted into pouches circling his waist, and a sheath holding a razor-edged Ka-bar fighting knife was buckled to his calf.

The warrior's head weapon was an M-16 A-1 assault rifle, complete with an M-203 grenade launcher mounted underneath the barrel. The bandoliers that crossed his chest held surplus magazines for the rifle and 40 mm high-explosive rounds for the launcher.

He shifted in the darkness, checking his watch to verify the time. There was an outside chance his information had been wrong, but Bolan didn't think so. He couldn't afford to dwell on the alternative, if his intended prey slipped past him now.

A failed beginning was the kind of blow that often doomed campaigns before they started, but the Executioner trusted his information, secure in the combination of greed, fear and loyalty that kept his source honest. The informer in La Paz had been well paid for his disclosure, and he knew exactly what would happen to him if he lied, if Bolan managed to survive a hasty trap.

Above all else, his source despised the very men whom Bolan planned to kill. It was a private matter, understood between them, never spoken of in any detail. Family honor was a part of it, and ancient pain. If Bolan was successful, his connection in La Paz would feel a measure of relief, and that had almost been enough to cut his asking price.

Almost.

Money talked in Bolivia, from the presidential palace to the urban slums and rural villages where peons lived from hand to mouth, surviving on their wits and willingness to tackle any job, no matter how distasteful, with a payoff waiting at the other end.

Business and pleasure. A convenient mixture of revenue and revenge.

A flash of headlights brought the Executioner to attention, studying the highway. Still a mile or more away, just visible on looping curves, two vehicles were running close together in a miniconvoy, high beams burning yellow tunnels in the night.

He waited, scooped up the rifle and let it rest across his knees. There was no hurry, when the prey was moving toward him of its own accord. He had only to wait, to be certain of his target when he squeezed the trigger. In the midnight darkness, on a narrow mountain road, there would be no room for mistakes.

And while he waited, there was time for calling up the images of friend and enemy alike, the living and the dead.

MACK BOLAN'S JOURNEY to Bolivia had started in Los Angeles thirty-six hours earlier. It was a lifetime for some, and far too little time for others.

Payback.

He had blown into the L.A. action on a slender lead from Stony Man Farm, a California neo-Nazi dead in Jordan, one of nineteen gunners wasted when the men of Phoenix Force surprised a black-market Iraqi convoy and left it smoking in a mountain pass. Washington was worried by the prospect of a link between Iraq terrorists and native bigots, all the more so when a German skinhead was identified among the other corpses.

Phoenix Force had drawn the German gig, while Bolan caught the next flight out to Southern California, gunning for a paramilitary outfit called the Aryan Resistance Movement, who were involved in violent crimes against minorities, gun-running and the importation of Bolivian cocaine. Where familiar, old-line racists still paid lip service to "traditional morals," the new breed had opted for strategic compromise to fatten up its bankroll.

That was progress, and it gave the Executioner a target he could shoot for when the L.A. campaign started to un-ravel. It had cost his contact's life, a lady Fed working un-dercover before she was burned, and while Bolan had wreaked havoc on the Aryan Resistance Movement in her name, the leader had escaped. He had flown south, in fact, to find a cooler, more forgiving climate.

Better luck, next time.

It had been relatively simple, running down the travel agent: some strategic pressure, turning up the heat, and on his third try Bolan had the name. Three dead, before he got it right, and it was cheap at half the price.

Ross Mueller—"Rocky" to his redneck friends—had dropped out in his freshman year of college, when he found out forging drivers' licenses and other documents paid bet-ter than the job he had in mind when he enrolled at USC. It started out with fake IDs for thirsty friends whose birth-days seemed intolerably far away, progressing into firearms permits, travel documents and such when Mueller found a new home in the youthful neo-Nazi movement. Private ar-mies like the ARM were always moving stolen hardware, shuttling fugitives from one point to another, and convinc-ing paperwork made all the difference when the chips were down.

Take passports, for example. When the leader of the ARM blew town with charges pending for the murder of a federal agent, it was necessary to disguise his passing with the sort of first-rate bogus documents that wouldn't draw a second glance from immigration. Visas would be called for, at the other end, and documents to verify a new identity.

No sweat.

With friends at the receiving end, a mediocre job would probably have been enough, but Rocky Mueller had his pride. He also had an ego suited to a member of the self-styled master race, which sometimes set his tongue wagging in celebration of a particular assignment.

As in this case, for example.

Three stops down the line, a gut-shot Nazi pointed Bolan to the travel agent, and a quick call to the FBI confirmed Mueller's link to the upper echelons of the ARM. It was a short drive to Mueller's Culver City home and workshop, catching the man in the sack with a cute little fascist groupie who might have been sixteen without the fake ID Mueller provided in return for services rendered.

Short and sweet with the grilling, a knee shot to get Mueller's attention, and downhill from there to a full confession, complete with names, dates and destination. The Nazi's only hope to salvage something from the situation was a bonehead move in the direction of a pistol he kept hidden in the nightstand. Bolan let him get there, touching-close, before he put a bullet through the man's skull and finished it.

La Paz was Bolan's destination when he left Los Angeles, duplicating his quarry's flight with a timely assist from Stony Man Farm, smoothing the way for a transfer of military hardware. No time would be wasted shopping for replacement items when he hit the ground.

In La Paz, he would rely on other contacts, lined up in advance, to help him sort the local action out and find his way. The change of scene meant brand-new players in the game, new stakes and longer odds. Instead of butting heads with misfits in Los Angeles, he would be running up against the faction that controlled a major portion of Bolivia's economy. He couldn't count on the police or military if it fell apart, and Bolan knew his enemies could come from anywhere, at any time.

Strike one was when he tried to reach his contact in La Paz and found out that the man had disappeared that very evening. A neighbor spoke of strangers she couldn't describe, young men who kept their backs turned toward her window for the most part, even when they helped the poor, sick man next door into their waiting vehicle. Of course, she hadn't bothered to record the license number, and her eyesight had been getting worse with age.

In fact, eyewitnesses weren't required. A tip from Bolan's stateside contact put him next to the informant—one who nursed a grudge and cultivated an encyclopedic knowledge of the local underworld, including drugs, fringe politics and other realms where strange bedfellows abound. The informant had known Bolan's contact by name, and he described the hit team chosen for the pickup.

If the crew ran true to form, they would interrogate their hostage prior to execution, maybe torture him for fun while they were at it, make the prisoner a grim example. When they were finished, with or without the optional head shot, they would weight his body down and feed it to the fish in Lake Titicaca.

There was something to be said for tradition, after all. It kept your adversaries running on familiar tracks, unconscious of the danger gaining from behind . . . or waiting for them out in front.

It gave the Executioner a killing edge.

Like now.

He watched the headlights drawing nearer, lost around the curves each time but always reappearing, that much closer. Still sitting with his shoulders braced against a slab of stone, the warrior raised the Starlite scope and focused on the highway. The scope wasn't an infrared device, instead relying on the ambient light of moon and stars to maximum advantage, giving the user a cat's-eye advantage in near-total darkness.

He caught the lead car just emerging from a hidden curve, its headlights muted by the Starlite's tinted lenses. Bolan did his best at counting heads, four showing, but he was more interested in the glint of metal showing just above the dashboard as they cleared the curve.

A gun barrel?

The second vehicle rolled into view, and there was no doubt this time. In the off-hand seat, the shotgun rider had his stubby automatic weapon resting on the dash, plainly visible through the windshield.

Contact.

There was no sign of the hostage, but it figured they would keep him hunched down on the floorboards, maybe tucked inside the trunk. Which car? Would he be riding point, or bringing up the rear?

It made no difference, either way, to Bolan's plan.

There were inherent risks to stopping any vehicle with troops inside, the hazards multiplied with two cars spotted on a narrow mountain road, a sheer drop on the driver's left. A hostage further complicated matters, limiting the shooter's options off the mark.

He had a plan, but if the action blew up in his face, all bets were off. The captive had no hope at all if Bolan drove his targets off the mountainside. He might be lost regardless, shot on reflex by his captors when the trap was sprung, or tagged by one of the Executioner's rounds, possibly trapped inside a burning car.

There were at least a dozen different ways to die within the next few seconds, but with Bolan's plan, at least the hostage had a fighting chance. The same couldn't be said if the warrior left him to his fate and turned away.

Picturing the torment that his captors had in mind before that final bullet brought relief, it came to Bolan that the hostage might prefer a sudden finish on the highway, even blazing down the cliff with jagged boulders waiting for him far below.

It was a devil's choice. No choice at all, in fact.

One final curve remained before the vehicles approached his sniper's nest. Bolan laid the Starlite scope aside. He didn't need it now, with target confirmation guaranteed.

The warrior broke the M-203 launcher's breech and thumbed a fat cartridge into the firing chamber. Moving out from his position on the slope, he edged down closer to the highway, taking up his place behind a boulder he had spotted coming in. His car, a rented compact, was concealed a hundred yards behind him, backed into a scenic turnout that faced south.

The target cars were running twenty yards apart, an estimated thirty miles per hour. The headlights of the point car swept toward Bolan's position, casting distorted shadows on the slope behind him and the pavement at his feet.

Decision time. He had five seconds, give or take, to focus on the move he had in mind.

The lead car straightened out into its run toward the next curve behind him, and Bolan was ready. He edged around the boulder, braced the rifle's stock against his hip and flexed his index finger on the launcher's trigger, taking up the slack.

Three seconds.

Two.

The launcher let loose a muffled popping sound and spit the high-explosive round downrange. A smoky thunderclap devoured the point car's grille and blew the hood back toward the windshield like an unhinged jaw.

Bolan hit the pavement running, firing on the run.

NO MATTER HOW HE TRIED to turn it upside down, it was the worst night of Ernie Gallardo's life—and damned unlikely to be rivaled by another, since it was his last.

, He had no illusions on that score. If the hit team had merely intended to rough him up, let him off with a warning, they would have beaten him senseless by now and dumped him in a gutter somewhere.

Of course, things didn't work that way around La Paz. There were no warnings, nothing in the way of second chances where a drug-enforcement agent was concerned. The day you lost your cover was the day you died, and if they only smoked you in a simple drive-by, you were points ahead.

Ernie Gallardo didn't have that kind of luck. Not anymore.

He couldn't really bitch, at that. In eight years working for the DEA, with six of those in South America, it was the first time he had been this close to death with no way out.

But once was all it took.

He had been close, this time, no doubt about it. He'd spent six months soaking up the local color, learning everything he could about his targets. His reports would be a gold mine for the agent they assigned to follow him. They'd save loads of time for the poor bastard who'd be dropped into La

Paz to pick up where Gallardo left off. Ernie knew where the bodies were buried, and now he was about to join them.

He didn't like the poor, dumb bastard's chances, but they wouldn't let it go in Washington. Not now.

Gallardo's death would guarantee a vigorous response.

He thought about the pain to come, the first time he had let himself consider his impending fate beyond a vague acceptance of the fact that he was soon to die. He had time now, during the long drive out of town, bound hand and foot with copper wire, hooded with a cotton pillowcase.

It wouldn't be an easy death, Gallardo understood that much. There would be questions, and he wondered how much pain he could withstand before he cracked.

Not that Gallardo had any great secrets to share. He reported to the American Embassy in La Paz, and any smuggler worth his salt would know the DEA's resident agent on sight. There had to be other agents in the field, but Gallardo didn't know their names, wouldn't have recognized them if they passed him on the street.

Small favors.

They would torture him regardless. If nothing else, he would be useful to his enemies as an example, the kind of object lesson that made other agents hesitate, thinking twice before they did their jobs.

How long until they reached their destination? Gallardo estimated that they had been driving for at least an hour since the pickup. It would be a rural setting, somewhere short on nosy neighbors and telephones.

Someplace they could work in peace.

It was amazing, Gallardo thought. When you got scared enough, your skin really *did* crawl.

If only he could crawl the hell away from where he lay, bound hand and foot, with someone's heavy boots wedged tight against his spine. . . .

The blast came out of nowhere, bringing the point car to a screeching halt, smoke billowing. His captors were cursing a blue streak in Spanish, the car stopped dead after one last hard jolt, and all Gallardo could think about was getting out of there alive.

He heard the doors swing open, with no glare from the dome light, which told him the battery was gone. A boot heel scraped across his ankle, painfully, and he cursed and tried to squirm away, a hard fist thumping him behind one ear before the gunners bailed out in confusion.

It had been a careless, glancing blow, but it was more or less on target, and his world went gray. It was hard to tell anything for sure inside the hood, but he could feel the dizziness and nausea that told him he was on the verge of blacking out.

Hold on, goddamn it! If the car was burning, and he lay there like a witless side of beef, then he would fry.

He started pushing with his feet, as awkward as it was, worming his body over the hump in the middle of the floorboard. The doors were still open, he knew from the clarity of outside noise, so there would be no problem fumbling with the latch. As for the rest of the maneuver...

Gallardo reached the open doorway, gave a final wriggling lurch and felt empty space below him. Falling. His forehead stuck the pavement with sufficient force to stun him.

Keep going.

It was all he had, but one more kick succeeded in propelling the DEA agent from the car. He huddled on the asphalt, cringing at the sound of automatic weapons hammering the night.

And realized that he had nowhere left to go.

BOLAN CAUGHT the point car's driver spilling from his seat on rubber legs, a veil of fresh blood drawn across his meaty face. A burst of 5.56 mm tumblers took the wheelman in the chest and slammed him backward, sprawling on the blacktop in a boneless heap.

One down, and three more bailing from the shattered lead car, jerky silhouettes in the high beams coming up behind. Bolan lobbed another HE round in the direction of the second car, already tracking with his M-16 before the grenade went off, catching one of the back-seat gunners with his guard down and blowing him away.

The second car was stalled and burning, bright flames licking out from underneath the buckled hood. Bolan left the second-string gunners to their own devices for the moment, mopping up. He circled toward the rocky hillside, moving warily, the assault rifle braced against his hip.

A burst of aimless fire erupted from behind the point car, bullets striking sparks against a boulder on the warrior's left. He saw the gunner rising from a crouch, charging into the open, driven by a combination of fear and anger to confront his enemy head-on. If nerve was any guarantee of victory, he would have had it made.

Tough luck.

Bolan met him with a dropping burst that stitched his target from the Adam's apple to the paunch that overhung his alligator belt. Explosive impact drove the thug back against the compact's crumpled fender, airborne, and he lay there like a bloated hunting trophy, with his feet six inches off the ground.

One shooter from the point car remained. A burst from his machine pistol fanned the air above the warrior's head, Bolan jackknifing into a crouch that saved his life. The first rounds from his M-16 were off the mark, a line of holes across the hood, but then he got it right, the second burst taking his adversary's head off and dropping the corpse beyond the warrior's line of sight.

Bolan came up running, ditching the rifle's spent magazine and reloading on the move. Four gunners spilled from the second car, disoriented by the blast that had disabled their vehicle, none of them spotting their target as yet.

A figure huddled on the pavement captured Bolan's full attention for a moment. He noted the bound wrists and ankles, a crude hood concealing the face. The hostage was moving, but feebly. There were no visible wounds, but for all Bolan knew he could be dying from internal injuries.

No time to check, in any case.

He went to meet the four surviving gunners, picking off the shotgun rider first, a quick burst fired across the crippled compact's bow to drop him twitching in his tracks.

The driver hunched behind his open door for cover, reaching wide around to fire a pistol with his left hand, missing Bolan by at least a yard. The warrior stitched a figure eight across the door, full-metal-jacketed projectiles drilling through. He saw the wheelman go down on his back, short legs and outsize shoes protruding from beneath the door.

The last two gunners broke in opposite directions, one dodging into the street while his companion scrambled up the rocky slope to Bolan's left. It was an awkward course to follow, loose shale sliding underneath his leather soles, and the warrior left him scrambling for a moment, concentrating on the closer threat.

He faced the runner from a range of twenty feet, firing his assault rifle from the hip as the shooter broke stride, trying to find a mark with his compact Walther MPL machine pistol. The guns went off together, Bolan's swarm of 5.56 mm bullets plucking the shooter off his feet and spinning him around, the Walther spewing jagged spurts of flame into the darkness, well off the mark. The dead man collapsed on his face and lay there, unmoving, as Bolan turned to bring his final target under fire.

The shooter on the hillside was still having trouble with his balance, trying to compensate with one outstretched arm while he steadied a semiauto pistol in his other hand.

Too late.

The final burst from Bolan's M-16 was dead on target, crimson spouting from the gunner's chest before he sat down hard, the pistol sliding from his lifeless fingers. The Executioner watched him for another moment, making sure, then turned back in the direction of the wriggling hostage.

"Take it easy."

He lifted off the makeshift hood, revealing a battered face, blood crusted at the nostrils, one eye swollen nearly shut. He spent a moment on the wire and released Gallardo's hands before proceeding to his ankles, waiting while the federal agent flexed his fingers, bringing circulation back.

"We haven't got a lot of time," he said unnecessarily.

"I'm out of here," Gallardo answered him.

"My car's this way."

"Who are you? Should I ask?"

"We'll talk about it on the road," the Executioner replied.

2

"I didn't catch your name," Gallardo said again, when they had traveled several miles in the direction of Viacha, running smoothly through the night.

"Let's start with yours," the Executioner replied. "Gallardo, Ernest T.—for Timothy, I think it was. You've got eight years in with the DEA, most of it in Latin America. How am I doing so far?"

"I never cared for 'Timothy.' You know more than you ought to, man."

"I'm on your side. If I wasn't, I'd have left you with your friends back there."

"No friends of mine," Gallardo stated emphatically.

"Who were they?"

"First things first. Before I spill my guts, I like to have some vague idea of who I'm talking to."

And that was fair enough, though Bolan saw no need to jeopardize himself beyond a certain, predetermined point.

"My name's Belasko," he informed the federal agent. "Mike Belasko."

"I don't see you working for the same folks I do. Not with all that hardware and the rough approach."

"Somebody had to lift you out."

"I'm not complaining, man," Gallardo hastened to explain. "Don't get me wrong. It's just not how we do things, if you get my drift."

"We're on the same side of the fence. Some different rules—"

"I'd say."

"But similar objectives," Bolan finished, keeping both eyes on the road.

"Speaking of objectives, maybe we should clear that up. It's obvious you know your way around my personnel file, but you're not from DEA. The Bureau would have sent a hostage rescue team, if anything, but this is way to hell and gone beyond their jurisdiction, right? You feel like Langley, but I can't imagine anybody from the Company would give a shit about what happens to a narc down here."

"It's none of the above," Bolan replied. "That's as far as I'm prepared to go."

"More need-to-know, I guess?"

"You called it," Bolan said. "Is that a problem?"

"Not for me. I'm like a mushroom, as it is. They keep me in the dark and feed me bullshit half the time."

"I'm not about to run your ass in circles," the warrior said. "I need your help, the way you needed mine a while ago."

"I can't imagine you need help from anybody."

"Guess again. I'm looking for a needle in a haystack, and I'm running out of time."

"Okay, I'm listening."

"This time the day before yesterday," Bolan began, "I was in Los Angeles. Strictly a domestic problem, on its face. Drugs were involved—cocaine, specifically—but it wasn't the primary focus."

"I'm with you so far," said Gallardo.

"There were problems at the finish, and a friend of mine went down. A federal officer. I tried to balance out the books, but the big fish got away. Word is, he caught a flight out to La Paz, where he feels safe among his friends."

"You mean the big-time dealers?"

"Maybe, maybe not. I ought to tell you there was politics involved."

"Specifically..."

"The Nazi kind."

Gallardo whistled softly, shifting in his seat. "Your rabbit's one of those 'white power' guys who pop up on the talk-show circuit?"

"Right. They call themselves the Aryan Resistance Movement," Bolan said. "My information is they've been importing powder from Bolivia for sale through middlemen to ghetto dealers. The cash goes for guns or whatever, and the drug sales constitute official policy. A new Final Solution."

"Terrific. Holocaust Two, coming soon to a neighborhood near you."

"That's about the size of it. Anyway, I've thrown your game off schedule."

"I believe it, brother."

"But I can't afford to let the top man walk."

"Who is this flake?"

"At home he's Justin Arthur Pratt. The night he left L.A., he used a passport in the name of Joseph Peeler."

"I don't know anything about your Aryan Resistance people," Gallardo said, "but we've got Nazis up the butt, and then some. Never mind your haystack. In Bolivia, where Nazis are concerned, it's more like looking for your needle in a sewing shop."

"That's what I heard."

"Believe it. Do you know your local history?"

"Bolivian?" The warrior shook his head. "Not even close."

"No sweat. You're in with the professor, now." Gallardo smiled and settled back to tell his tale. "You know the Germans pumped all kinds of money into South America, before and during World War Two?"

"That much, I do know," Bolan said.

"Okay. They also founded colonies—no other way to say it—German enclaves in the countries of their choice, supporting friendly governments with multimillion-dollar bribes. The friends you buy down here stay bought, at least until a bigger spender comes along. Perón in Argentina was the prime example in the postwar years, but you had Stroessner down in Paraguay, similar juntas or strongmen in Chile, Peru, Venezuela, Brazil."

"Bolivia?" Bolan prodded.

"More of the same. They've had a thriving Nazi enclave in La Paz since 1930-something. Hitler's number two, Martin Bormann, was here from 1958 to '62. He skipped out to Paraguay after the Israelis grabbed Eichmann from Buenos Aires—felt safer, I guess—but he came back in 1973 and stayed in La Paz the rest of his life."

"I've heard the Bormann rumors."

"Have you heard about Klaus Barbie?"

"Sure. The Butcher of Lyon."

"You win the silver swastika, my man. Around La Paz, he called himself Klaus Altmann, but his real ID was an open secret. France petitioned for his extradition in the early seventies, and Peru was after his lily-white ass for some crimes over there...including murder, I believe. Bolivia refused his extradition for another decade, using Barbie and his crew to train their death squads in the fine points of genocide. At the same time, the government was clearing forestland to make room for another crop of racist refugees—Rhodesia, this time. It took the junta's resignation in October, 1982, to finally pull the plug on Barbie, but I'm telling you, he was only one apple in a big, rotten barrel."

"Even so," the Executioner suggested, "these SS fugitive types have to be on their last legs by now. We're talking fifty years. Nobody lives forever."

"You're right, as far as it goes. If the old guard hung tough with their own and let it go at that, you could write them off. No more Mengele, no Franz Stangl, no Hans Rudel—the old boys are gone or going, like you said."

"But they didn't hang tough with their own?"

"Not a chance. Your basic Nazi is like a religious fanatic. He recruits for the cause, trains his children and grandkids, spends a fortune on slick propaganda. Did you ever hear of something called the Kameradentwerk?"

"Can't say I have," the Executioner replied.

"I'm not surprised. In the old days, it took over on this side of the Atlantic where the ODESSA escape network left off, finding homes and jobs for Nazis on the run, putting them in touch with other fugitives, you name it. The leadership was tight with Perón and Evita through the coup in

'76, and they put out feelers all over the continent. There's a whole new generation of Nazis in South America these days, my friend. I figure half of them have never seen the fatherland, but they still wear their armbands and reminisce about the good old days with Adolf and the camps. Every year they get together for a combination beer bash and beauty pageant on Hitler's birthday. 'Miss Nazi,' they call the winner. She gets clothes, a car, a college scholarship. They might have started off with loot from Europe, but they've got fifty years of smart investments to support them now, and that includes Wall Street, by way of some strange bedfellows at Langley."

"You think so?"

"Common knowledge, man. Remember, it was the Bolivians who bagged Che Guevara in '62, when Castro was still busy trying to export his revolution. You think the Barbie exposé surprised anybody in the Oval Office?"

"How does the cocaine fit in?" Bolan asked.

"Simple. Drugs are money, and plenty of it. Copper and tin go down on the books as Bolivia's chief exports, but I don't believe it for a minute. Twenty-five percent of the coca leaves grown for illegal cocaine production are cultivated right here, with most of the balance grown in Peru. Both countries used to ship the coca paste and cocaine base to Colombia for final processing into pharmaceutical-grade cocaine, but in the past ten years or so, Bolivian dealers have started refining cocaine hydrochloride on their own, for direct shipment to wholesale markets. Phase out the Colombian middlemen, you quadruple the profits at home."

"And the new-wave Nazis are involved?"

"From day one. Coca farming was legal in Bolivia until July of 1988, unless the leaves are used for legitimate medical production or—get this—for chewing by the Indian laboring class. Maybe that loophole explains why so many Indians work in the mines for an average two dollars per day, I don't know. Whatever, large-scale landowners have been growing coca forever, and the new law is full of holes. DIRECO—that's the government agency in charge of coca reduction and alternative development—has to negotiate with the growers on their own terms, compensate them for converted acreage, the whole nine yards. Foreign 'donors' are supposed to pay the growers two thousand dollars for each hectare removed from production. You tell me where the profits are.''

''No contest. And the Nazis own land,'' Bolan said.

''They own land, they own labs—hell, they own politicians. Does the name Luis Arce ring a bell?''

Bolan shook his head, a terse negative.

''He was a colonel in the Bolivian army for years, doubling up as minister of the interior in the early 1980s. Brother Barbie helped him organize the death squads, but another coup left Arce out of work, and he split for the United States. Bolivia tried to extradite him for trial on human rights violations, but the colonel had friends in high places, if you follow me.''

''I'm with you,'' Bolan said.

''Anyway, come January, 1991, he took a fall in federal court, Miami. They convicted him of conspiracy to smuggle drugs. Turns out his buddies used to call him the 'Minister of Cocaine.' Some joke, eh?''

''I'm not laughing.''

''Neither was the DEA. We bust our asses getting evidence on slugs like Arce, and half the time we get stonewalled by our own people. Same thing from Vietnam, the lifers tell me. At least that was before my time.''

''I'm interested in here and now,'' the Executioner informed him.

''Right, okay. You're looking at second- and third-generation Nazis in La Paz—hell, all over the country—and they're up to their eyeballs in dope. That doesn't mean they've lost their edge for hating Jews and anybody else who isn't white enough to pass the litmus test. Far from it. If I had to guess, I'd say the new breed are more rabid than the guys who got things rolling in the first place.''

''Politics.''

Gallardo shrugged. ''Since autumn '82, you've had a democratic congressional government, at least on paper.

The military still has plenty of muscle, but it doesn't make a lot of difference. Money talks in La Paz, just like Washington, and today's politicians have grown up with Nazis in their own backyard. It's nothing new, you see? Officially the government is helping fight the drug war, but their buy-back program is a farce. The DEA calls its cooperation with the Bolivian narcotics police 'encouraging,' but I'm here to tell you it's an uphill battle, all the way."

"I need a handle on the players," Bolan said.

"No problem, but I couldn't guarantee that they're connected to your boy."

"I'll take my chances."

"Right." Gallardo thought about it for another moment, marshaling his thoughts. "The biggest dealer in La Paz is one Bernardo Gomez. Actually he lives a few miles out of town, your basic *rancho grande*. No coca on the homestead, understand, but he's got major plots of land all up and down the cordillera. Laboratories, too. But somehow the Bolivian narcotics cops can't find them. Should I act surprised?"

"I take it he's connected?"

"Coming and going," Gallardo replied. "Colonel Hector Rivera is the new interior minister. He didn't exactly take over where Arce left off, but he's well on his way. A nice, fat bank account in the Bahamas, getting fatter by the month. Third-generation army, and he's cozy with the German enclave."

"Meaning the Kameradenwerk?"

"Or its modern-day equivalent. You called it. German training is the backbone of the military hereabouts, the same as Argentina, Paraguay and half a dozen other countries I could mention. Even today, you see the Wehrmacht mentality cropping up in everything from crowd control and counterterrorism to the so-called Indian problem."

"Does he have a specific Nazi connection?"

"That's affirmative," Gallardo said. "Hans Gustav Erdmann, sixty-something, living in La Paz. His father was Waffen SS in the old days, assigned to Buchenwald in 1944 and '45. He came through the ODESSA pipeline six weeks after V-E Day and settled in with relatives at Sucre. Hans is a chip off the old block, let me tell you.''

"Foreign connections?" Bolan asked.

"Besides the dope, you mean? Hell, yes. He keeps in touch with Aryan types in the States, and back in Germany. Some other parts of Europe, too, I guess. I've even heard some talk about a group in Russia, but it could be bullshit."

Bolan wasn't interested in Russian Nazis at the moment. The Bolivian subspecies would keep him busy for the time being . . . along with Justin Pratt.

"I take it you've been working Gómez," Bolan said.

"I thought so, anyway," Gallardo said. "The way it went tonight, it looks like they've been working me. The only thing I know for sure is that my cover's shot to hell."

"You're going home?"

Gallardo thought about it, nodding to himself. "Unless I get a better offer, yeah."

"It seems a shame to waste six years of groundwork."

Something like a smile was tugging at the corners of Gallardo's mouth.

"So, what's the plan?" he asked.

FOUR THOUSAND MILES due north, among the scenic Blue Ridge Mountains of Virginia, Aaron Kurtzman occupied his seat at the computer command console of Stony Man Farm. Two screens in front of him were blank, two others crawled with block-set paragraphs of information scrolling in and out of view, while yet another offered detailed maps at the stroke of a key.

At the moment, Kurtzman was plugged into sensitive data sources on three continents, sifting the harvest for workable clues and coming up damnably short.

The California blowup was yesterday's news. The FBI and LAPD were picking up the Executioner's leavings, and the Aryan Resistance Movement—or its Southern California branch, at any rate—was in chaotic disarray. Drug-enforcement agents were scouring the city for pushers who dealt with the Nazis and palmed off their crack in the ghetto.

It was the next best thing to a clean sweep, except for Justin Pratt... and therein lay the problem.

Kurtzman himself had arranged Bolan's transportation to La Paz, Jack Grimaldi handling the charter flight, with a CIA contact in Bolivian customs finessing the delivery of military hardware to a waiting car. They had the name that Justin Pratt had used to cover his escape, a local contact from the DEA on tap to help coordinate the strike, and yet...

Things have a tendency to fall apart, despite the best-laid plans. The first word from La Paz was reassuring, Bolan and Grimaldi right on schedule, ready to proceed. Within the hour, though, came word from Grimaldi that their contact from the DEA had been abducted, possibly assassinated. Bolan had a lead, but if he couldn't find the missing agent and retrieve him, they would have to wing it on their own.

And the rest was silence.

The word from Phoenix Force, in Germany, was no less fraught with complications. Yakov Katzenelenbogen's team was still on schedule, orchestrating rapid-fire attacks on neo-Nazi cells around Berlin, with the surprise addition of an Israeli Mossad agent from Tel Aviv. The unscheduled alliance was shaky, at best, but at least it appeared to be functional.

Still...

Six days into the game, Kurtzman still had no clear fix on the Middle East connection that had started it all in the first place. Nineteen dead in Jordan, two foreign Nazis among them, and the Stony Man crew was still scrabbling for answers. What had lured two young fascists, one American and one German, to the no-man's-land of the Iraqi-Jordanian frontier? Why were they traveling armed, with a convoy of black-market Iraqi merchandise bound for distribution in Amman? Did the presence of fanatic foreigners among die-hard Arab guerrillas indicate some new and sinister terrorist clique in the making?

"Damn it!"

"Trouble?"

He hadn't heard Carmen Delahunt approaching from behind him, caught up as he was in private reverie, his eyes locked on the bank of glowing monitors. He turned to face her, easily maneuvering the wheelchair that had been his mode of transport since a sniper's bullet took his legs away.

"Nothing new," he replied. "Nothing, period."

"It takes time," she reminded him, settling into a nearby swivel chair. "It hasn't been two hours since we heard about the missing agent in La Paz."

Two hours. Anything could happen in that length of time, and they might never hear from Bolan again. He was off in pursuit of a presumed hit team, enemy strength unknown, leaving Grimaldi behind as his sole link to the outside world. For all Kurtzman knew, the Executioner could be dead by now, vanished forever without a trace.

"Two hours, right," Kurtzman said, trying for a hopeful tone and missing by a mile.

Delahunt shifted in her seat, crossing her legs under the long, white smock she wore on duty. Hal Brognola had lured the redheaded woman away from the FBI National Crime Information Center at Quantico, Virginia. Thus far, Delahunt had meshed well with the other Stony Man staffers, despite a temper befitting her fiery red mane.

"Striker knows what he's doing," she told him. "Don't sell the man short."

"I never have. But we've got people spread out from Bolivia to Germany, all chasing different leads, and I can't get a handle on the bottom line to save my life."

"It's not your life that has you worried, am I right?"

Hell, yes, she was, and Kurtzman didn't have to tell her that. She knew him well enough by now to read his moods and know what he was thinking when the job began to get him down. It didn't happen often, but the raw uncertainty of everything about this mission had his nerves on edge.

"So, I should just sit back and let it go?" he asked.

"You're doing everything you can from this end. When it breaks, we'll be there."

Too damned late, he thought, and settled for "I hope so."

"Maybe you should get some rest."

"I'm working on it."

Delahunt raised an eyebrow, checking out the bank of active monitors. "I see that." She sounded faintly mocking, but she wasn't on his case.

"Hal's waiting up. I ought to tell him something?"

"Such as?"

"That's the problem, right? In a few more hours, we'll have been on this gig a week, and all I've got is what we started with."

"Not quite," Delahunt said. "There's La Paz. When Striker gets a handle there—"

"That's *if* he gets a handle," Kurtzman interrupted her. "The shift from L.A. to Bolivia is one thing, but he's lost his contact going in."

"We don't know that, for sure. He still might pull it out."

"And if he does, then what? In California, Striker started off with the advantage of surprise. The ARM didn't know he was coming, or where he'd strike next once he got the ball rolling. Now, we've got Pratt on the run, maybe expecting a tail, and Striker thinks the bastard got a fair look at him when the nasty hit the fan. Down south, his contact's either dead or compromised across the board. That's not a lot to build on, Carmen."

"Such an optimist, you are. What happened to the man of steel?"

"I'm having trouble with the phone booth angle, lately," Kurtzman told her, putting on a crooked smile despite his mood.

"You could have fooled me."

"Stunt doubles, Red."

She let the nickname pass, this once. "We haven't lost it yet," she said. "If you can get around the unexpected for a second, things look pretty good."

"And while we're at it, you've got all this beachfront property in Arizona, am I right?"

"No jive. When Striker gets his balance—and he will— smart money says he comes out swinging. Even if his contact's blown for working under cover, he'll be sitting on a load of vital information."

"If he's still alive."

"And if he's not, they'll find another way. Believe it."

Kurtzman wished that it could be that easy, wiping out his doubts and their potential losses with the simple power of belief. But the world that Aaron Kurtzman occupied was bound by rules of logic, even if he sometimes lost that focus with the crap he had to wade through, slogging toward solutions for the problems life kept dropping in his lap.

In younger days, he had enjoyed assembling puzzles, but the game was always simply that: a game. If Kurtzman lost a piece or tried to fit one backward in its proper place, no lives were lost. These days, his game pieces were flesh and blood, often precious friends. One slip, one careless move, and he could kiss those friends goodbye forever.

And they still might die, no matter what he did on their behalf. No matter how he tried to help them, even if he got it right. Unlike the games of childhood, there was so much here beyond his personal control. Those early puzzles came complete with color photographs of how the picture ought to look when he was finished, giving him a leg up on the competition with himself. This time around, he couldn't even glimpse the end result in any kind of detail.

Doubt and indecision, damn it, with no end in sight.

Delahunt seemed to read his mind. "You're working on the Middle East connection?"

"If you call this working. I've got nothing to show for it, so far."

"I'd still put my money on Baghdad," she told him. "There's no percentage in it for the Jordanians, on their own."

"They make a nice commission trading with Iraq."

"Granted. But what have crackpot outfits like the Vanguard and the ARM got to offer?"

"So, we're back to subsidized terrorism?"

"That would be my educated guess, if anybody asked."

"I'll note that, for the record."

She ignored his light, sarcastic tone. "The good news, if I'm right, is that we caught them in the planning stage, before they got a lot of points up on the board."

"They did all right with Asher Blum," Kurtzman reminded her.

The Israeli cultural attaché in Berlin had been assassinated three days earlier, by members of the neo-Nazi National Vanguard. That was before Phoenix Force had arrived on the scene, and while the German fascists were now on the defensive, they were far from down and out.

"So, we've got work to do," Delahunt stated.

"You got that right," Kurtzman said, as he turned back toward the bank of monitors.

It might be hours yet, before he found a chance to sleep. And when the time came, Kurtzman prayed he wouldn't dream.

3

The cocaine lab had been erected in the mountain forest west of Achacachi, roughly forty miles northwest of La Paz. A spacious campsite had been cleared by hand, with camouflage netting strung in the trees overhead to defeat aerial surveillance.

Within the clearing, several sheds had been constructed out of corrugated metal, lean-to style, each structure with an open side in lieu of doors and windows. The central feature of the compound was a long pit, lined with plastic tarp, filled nearly to the brim with gray sludge that gave off an odor reminiscent of a sour-mash distillery.

Mack Bolan recognized the sight and smell of coca leaves dissolving in a bath of spring water seasoned with a dash of sulfuric acid. After three or four days' time, the heady soup would be drained off and processed through a series of plastic mixing buckets—lime water, gasoline, more acid, potassium permanganate and ammonia. The end product, a reddish-brown liquid, would be filtered through denim until it dripped clear. Another application of ammonia would produce the ivory-colored granules of cocaine base, seventy-five percent pure, that was known as *la merca:* the merchandise. Further refinement—using acetone, ether and hydrochloric acid—produced the crystalline powder known as cocaine hydrochloride, up to ninety-eight-percent pure, ready for cutting and sale on the street.

Bolan understood the global economics of cocaine. An acre's yield of leaves produced around four hundred grams of cocaine base, with a given acre ready for harvest each thirty-five days. Refinement into pure cocaine reduced the haul by some sixty percent, but the payoff increased astronomically. In a nearly bankrupt country, where fully half of the Indian miners were now unemployed, the lure of "easy" money from the drug trade was an often irresistible attraction. In the Chapare region alone, at least 200,000 natives earned their sole living from cocaine production and smuggling. Bolivia's annual take of $400 million to $600 million from cocaine easily dwarfed the $75 million provided in legitimate foreign aid from Washington.

There were five young men in the camp, all mestizo, dressed in faded khaki and denim. As Bolan watched, one of the men, barefoot and wearing cutoff blue jeans, waded into the slime pit, treading the coca leaves underfoot and stirring the sludge with his hands for perhaps ninety seconds. Climbing out, he crossed to one of the open sheds where a water trough stood waiting, and scooped water out with a metal cup to rinse his legs clean.

According to his information from Gallardo, the cocaine lab was owned by Bernardo Gomez, one of ten or fifteen hidden bases where the harvest from his mountain acreage was converted into powdered gold. If the agent's background research was correct, the Gomez labs produced some eighty thousand tons of cocaine base per year, refined to twelve or thirteen thousand kilos of ninety-eight-percent pure cocaine.

That kind of operation demanded protection, from the bribes paid in La Paz to guns on-site. In the latter department, he counted three automatic rifles, third-world AK-47 knockoffs, leaning in a corner of the open shed directly opposite his hiding place.

The Executioner had seen enough.

He emerged from the shadowy tree line in camo fatigues, covering the five mestizos loosely with an Uzi submachine gun. It took a moment for the first of them to spot him, then the young man blurted out a warning, four heads snapping into line with narrowed eyes and tight-lipped mouths. A whisper passed among them, Spanish Bolan couldn't translate. He let his weapon do the talking, waggling the Uzi's muzzle to herd them away from the shed with the rifles, toward the eastern perimeter of the camp.

When it began to fall apart, it happened in a heartbeat. One of the mestizos spun and bolted for the shed, his nearest colleague breaking off to Bolan's right and digging for a nickel-plated handgun in his waistband, covered by the hanging shirttail.

The Executioner took the *pistolero* first, a burst to lead his target, squeezing off a quick half-dozen rounds. The runner seemed to stumble, his momentum carrying him through an awkward dive into the coca pit. His splashdown sent a wave of acrid fumes across the open ground to Bolan's nostrils, stinging his sinuses.

He turned in time to see the second runner reach his destination, groping at the stack of rifles, coming up with one and fumbling back the cocking lever as he turned to face his enemy.

Too late.

The Uzi stuttered, stitching a line of holes across the gunner's chest as parabellum manglers did their work. The impacts punched his target backward, taking down the stack of rifles as he fell, a wild burst from his AK-47 punching through the tin roof of the shed.

The three unarmed survivors watched him, rooted in their tracks, apparently prepared to die. He could have mowed them down, but it would be a waste of time and ammunition. All of them were shirtless, none with any weapons visible. Their only means of contact with the outside world was a walkie-talkie hanging on the wall above their fallen comrade in the shed. Instead of killing them for who they were and how they earned their living, Bolan flicked his Uzi toward the tree line.

"*Vamos. ¡Pronto!*"

There was no need to repeat himself. The three mestizos raced out of sight in seconds flat. He heard them crashing through the forest undergrowth for several moments, sounds that faded out of earshot as he stood there in the clearing, alone with the dead.

The rest was cleanup, two mags from the Uzi sprayed around the camp in short, strategic bursts, exploding glass and plastic jugs of ether, acid, other chemicals employed in the production of cocaine. Incendiary sticks were next, one to a shed, and Bolan waited for the fuses to run, watching the sparks catch, flames start to spread.

He had no fear of touching off a forest fire, where the yearly rain average of 110 inches kept the earth and foliage perpetually damp. If metal sheds didn't contain the fire, it would burn out on open ground once it devoured the flammable materials and stock of processed coke on hand.

It was a long walk back to the access road where his vehicle waited. Bolan put the forest lab behind him, heading south. The acrid, gratifying smell of smoke pursued him, clinging to his camouflage fatigues.

It smelled like a good beginning.

FRANZ KALTENBORN was ready when the beeper sounded from beneath his jacket. He didn't look around the lobby for a telephone; the signal was familiar, part of his daily routine, which indicated Dieter Gerstein was preparing to descend, his private elevator dropping from the penthouse to the street.

Kaltenborn crossed the spacious lobby, shouldered through the glass revolving door and snapped his fingers at the doorman. There was no need for a spoken order. The doorman knew his business well enough to signal for the limousine to carry Gerstein off to luncheon at the restaurant of his choice. He kept no schedule, alternating spots from day to day, but Gerstein only dined in gourmet restaurants with maître d's and menu prices that would keep the common riffraff at a distance.

Kaltenborn admired Gerstein's material success, but he was more enraptured by the old man's strength of character. It was close to half a century since Gerstein served his fatherland at Oradour, a young lieutenant graduating from the cleanup detail to a post as captain of the guard before the Russian army swept it all away. He had been brave and wise enough to outrun Communist assassins, swap ID with one of the lamented Wehrmacht dead and make his way to South America by 1947. With support from members of the gallant Kameradenwerk, he had become a multimillionaire in real estate and mining. The lessons from Oradour had served him well in handling his Indian laborers, another triumph for the master race.

If Franz Kaltenborn felt any overriding emotion toward Dieter Gerstein, aside from admiration, the emotion would have been envy. At twenty-five, Kaltenborn was the proud grandson of a veteran gestapo officer who took advantage of the postwar ODESSA network to flee occupied Germany in 1946. Cancer killed Harv Kaltenborn eighteen years later, but not before he had resettled his family in La Paz, producing a son who had followed in his father's political footsteps, teaching his own offspring the hard realities of waging war against the World Jewish Conspiracy.

His present situation, as a bodyguard for Dieter Gerstein, was a stepping-stone for Kaltenborn. He liked the guns, the sense of power that accrued from traveling in moneyed circles, standing close to men of power, guaranteeing their security. In time, though, he would prosper on his own. At some point in the future, five or ten years down the road, he meant to stand in Gerstein's place, have young men like himself to stand on guard and take the risks for money he could easily afford to throw away.

But this was now, and he had work to do.

Kaltenborn reached inside his tailored jacket, checked the stubby Heckler & Koch MP-5 K machine pistol hanging in its shoulder rig. Spare magazines were positioned on the right-hand side, if it came to that, but so far he had never fired the gun in anger. Twice-weekly practice sessions at a basement firing range in suburban La Paz kept his hand in, but he sometimes longed for an opportunity to prove himself against flesh-and-blood targets.

Not that he wished any harm to his employer; far from it. Kaltenborn had confidence enough to think that he could deal with any danger that arose. He wanted an opportunity to show what he could do, impress the old man with his personal disdain for non-Aryan, subhuman life.

The limousine was pulling up outside, its driver scrambling from behind the wheel, his jacket unbuttoned for easier access to the pistol in his fast-draw shoulder holster. Nothing was left to chance.

Two gunners would be coming down with Gerstein in the elevator.

Thirty seconds later, when the car arrived, its doors hissed open and both men stepped out and to the sides, like bookends. They checked out the lobby for themselves, no insult to Kaltenborn—and they would have caught hell from Franz if they hadn't—before proceeding with their charge in lockstep toward the glass revolving door.

Kaltenborn preceded them, feeling perspiration ooze from his pores in the humid afternoon air. At least the limousine was air-conditioned, and the restaurant would be a sanctuary from the heat that was Bolivia's main drawback in Kaltenborn's mind.

Still, without the climate, there would be no coca forests, no cocaine to underwrite Herr Gerstein's real estate investments and provide a narrow margin of survival for the failing tin and copper mines. Perhaps, if they could implement strategic SS tactics with their native labor force, the mines might struggle back to solvency, but there were limits even to the influence of Gerstein and his ranking cronies in La Paz.

The world was watching, more or less, and if the Red Cross winked at shipments of contaminated blankets airdropped into jungle villages, the damned United Nations would undoubtedly investigate reports of slave labor in the Bolivian mines. Someday, when the party's influence and honor were restored, the UN would have nothing left to say about the disposition of inferior minorities.

When that day came, Franz Kaltenborn would know he had it made.

Kaltenborn stood beside the limousine, waiting with his fingertips grazing the door handle, ready to open the door for Gerstein when he was halfway across the sidewalk. He was emerging now, one bodyguard in front of him, the other hanging back in case some undiscovered threat suddenly materialized in the lobby.

It was a textbook execution, poetry in motion...right up to the moment when it all went wrong.

Herr Gerstein's driver was the first to die, his passing signaled by a loud, wet, ripping sound that spattered Kaltenborn with something warm. Glancing down before he turned to check the driver, Kaltenborn was startled by the crimson flecks that stained his shirt, more streaked across his fingertips as he reached up to wipe his cheek.

He swiveled toward the driver then, and saw his nearly headless body draped across the fender of the limousine. He would have been facedown, if there was any face remaining.

The rifle shot was audible a heartbeat later, and it was amazing how the action seemed to stall, shifting into slow motion as if the key players had suddenly been immersed in molasses. Kaltenborn swung back toward Gerstein and his guards, shouting the alarm as he reached for his weapon, frantically trying to calculate the firing angle, find a target he could isolate, pin down, annihilate.

Impossible, with only one shot, but the second wasn't long in coming. Gerstein's guard on the left was reaching for his gun and tugging his charge back in the direction of the lobby when his head snapped back and seemed to keep on going, crimson spouting at the jawline as if an invisible hinge had sprung open, allowing the rest of his head to fly back like the lid on a hope chest. Momentum took him down, still clutching Gerstein's sleeve with force enough to shred the fabric at its seam and leave the old man's shirtsleeve on display.

How many seconds had elapsed in the attack so far?

Kaltenborn ran to throw himself in front of Gerstein, duty winning over common sense. The other bodyguard was already dragging Gerstein back toward the revolving door. The echo of the second shot had just reached Kaltenborn when number three came in six feet in front of him, the second guard lifted off his feet and slammed directly into the revolving door. A scarlet flower bloomed between his shoulder blades, and there was more fresh blood as heavy plate glass shattered, cleaving through the tissue of his face and throat.

Impossible to beat the sniper now, thought Kaltenborn, but he would have to try. It was his duty, hence his life.

He launched himself into a flying tackle, bent on toppling the old man from his feet at any risk of minor damage from the fall. Herr Gerstein would forgive him minor cuts and bruises, even broken bones, if Kaltenborn could only save his life.

The runner's fingertips grazed Gerstein's custom-tailored jacket, clenched for leverage . . . and the old man's head exploded like bursting melon in his face. Franz Kaltenborn was blinded, plummeting on top of Gerstein's flaccid corpse, the impact driving lifeless breath from the stump of Gerstein's neck in a windy sort of belch.

Kaltenborn was nearly overcome by a rush of mixed and powerful emotions.

First, a rush of burning shame, the product of his failure to protect the great man he was hired to serve. Before his very eyes, in seconds flat, Franz Kaltenborn's whole world had been destroyed with four swift rifle shots.

Survival, next. If there was nothing he could do for Gerstein, no way to return effective fire, the best that he could hope for was to break away. More shame at that, a failure *and* a coward, but he estimated that his death would serve no purpose to the cause. If someone in authority decided, later, that his failure merited an execution, Kaltenborn would present himself to the firing squad without complaint or pleas for mercy.

Later.

Pushing up on hands and knees above the headless corpse, he almost lost his balance in the spreading pool of blood, but caught himself before he fell back onto Dieter Gerstein. Standing up would be more difficult, if only by a fraction, but he got his feet under him, rubber soles digging in for traction on the wet pavement.

In the fraction of a second that remained, Kaltenborn knew that he was helpless, standing with his back turned toward a ruthless enemy whose marksmanship was proved four times over, with as many shots. It came to Kaltenborn that he was dead, but he couldn't just stand there waiting for the ax to fall. He had a chance, however marginal, to reach the lobby and conceal himself.

As he began to run, Kaltenborn was wondering how it would feel to die.

And then, he knew.

THE OFFICIAL RESIDENCE of Colonel Hector Rivera was a sprawling estate on the northern outskirts of La Paz. Five acres overall, with two of those in manicured grass out front, the rest in woods that ringed the great house on three sides. Sporadic threats from isolated malcontents and left-wing guerrillas entitled Bolivia's minister of the interior to a full-time military guard, and he took full advantage of the perk, turning his home into an armed camp, habitually traveling with a dozen uniformed killers to keep him safe and sound.

Rivera wasn't at home this afternoon, a fact determined with a simple phone call to his office in La Paz. He wasn't in the office, either, but Gallardo had elicited the information that El Excelensio was booked for a full day of meetings pertaining to government business.

That business might or might not involve cocaine, but Bolan was indifferent to Rivera's speaking schedule. He was more concerned with demonstrations at the moment, well on his way to rattling the major players in La Paz. As Rivera was the military honcho coordinating illicit drug traffic and covert Nazi politics, Bolan had saved the man for last on his first round of strikes.

A friendly—meaning honest—contact with the Bolivian narcotics police had briefed Gallardo on the security trappings in place at Rivera's estate. An eight-foot wall of cinder blocks was more for show than anything, but it was topped with strands of gleaming razor wire, each strand imbedded with a fiber-optic core that would set alarms shrieking in the big house if a single strand was cut.

There were no ground motion sensors on the property, according to Gallardo's source, but closed-circuit television cameras had been mounted every forty yards along the wall. The cameras were mounted on pivots, powered by electric motors, each lens performing a 180-degree rotation at thirty-second intervals. Alternating cameras were positioned to face in opposite directions, so that every camera facing toward the grounds of the estate was flanked by others scanning the approach outside the wall.

Inside the stout perimeter of brick and razor wire, there would be well-armed sentries, some of them supposedly on horseback, allowing them to cover more ground at great speed. No dogs, reportedly—the colonel had a phobia for canines, dating back to childhood—but the men and guns could be enough.

With the colonel away from home, Bolan guessed that the active guard force would be reduced. Some of the household gunners would follow their boss on his daily rounds, while others let themselves relax a bit, believing that the threat had briefly passed them by.

It was the kind of overconfidence that got men killed . . . and sometimes saved a savvy warrior's life.

The approach was critical, with all those cameras watching him, but Bolan found a kind of blind side, wriggling on his belly through a weed-choked gully, suffering the ant bites and buzzing, bloodsucking flies in silence, working his way toward the fence. A twisted old tree sprouted out of the gully's mouth, gray and haggard now, but once freely nourished by a flowing stream that had been cut off by Rivera's wall of privacy. The branches had been trimmed to deal with overhang, but not within the past twelve months or so.

If he could climb that gnarly giant unobserved, select a limb with strength enough to carry him and length enough to let him clear the wall . . .

Too many *ifs*.

He had to take the problem one step at a time, Bolan knew, as he paused against the thick roots of the witch tree, catching his breath and listening to the soft whir of the cameras.

From this point on, at least until he cleared the wall and touched down on the other side, timing was everything. Once inside, there was a built-in snafu factor, no way he could calculate or compensate for the erratic movements of unseen guards.

One step at a time.

The warrior checked the nearest cameras from his place among the weeds, and watched them through a full rotation, left and right. They were approximately synchronized to offer constant coverage, but rough triangulation showed him that the drooping branches of the tree would screen him, more or less, from the surveillance camera on his right, if he was climbing while the camera on the left was turned away.

So be it.

Bolan timed his move precisely, scrambling up the trunk until he reached a point twelve feet above the ground. He froze there, stretched out on a limb the thickness of his thigh, and hoped that there were lapses in efficiency among the crew assigned to watch the indoor monitors. If he was spotted now, by chance...

The cameras started tracking, Bolan counting off the seconds that remained until the lenses on his left and right were pointed toward the empty land beyond the wall. He moved out, creeping, offering a silent prayer to let the fat limb hold his weight until he cleared the wall and razor wire below.

Another gamble now. The drop was nothing, if he did it properly, some fourteen feet, allowing for the sloping ground below. There should be no problem if he bent his knees, perhaps a gentle shoulder roll to eat up the momentum of his fall. But dropping in without a twisted knee or ankle was the least of Bolan's problems.

He saw no sentries anywhere within a hundred yards, and that was good, but there were still the interlocking, inner-facing cameras on the wall. No help for that, once he was on the ground. The best that he could hope for was a slow re-

sponse from the defenders, ranks depleted by extraction of
a traveling security detachment.

If they spotted him at once and fielded any kind of major force, he was in trouble.

But there was no such thing as turning back.

He counted off ten seconds. The drop was vertical, with
impact on a sloping surface that would help him roll downhill on touchdown. Coming out of it, he had to be prepared
for anything, the automatic rifle ready in his hands.

He made the drop and managed it without a roll, twisting the M-16 around under his right arm, releasing the
shoulder sling in seconds flat. He had no way of telling
whether anyone inside the house had spotted him oncamera. No sirens blared to greet him; there was no immediate response of any kind.

He started to move toward the house, an easy double time
that stopped short of a sprint, alert for sentries tucked away
behind the trees and shrubbery ranged in front of him.

The sound of hoofbeats over grass reached Bolan from
his left, one horse or two, he couldn't tell. He found a sturdy
tree and ducked behind it, risked a glance around the trunk
and saw two horsemen bearing down on his position, long
guns braced across their saddle horns.

So it began.

He switched the M-16's selector switch to semiautomatic, steeping out to the right of the tree with the rifle's
butt tight against his shoulder, sighting down the barrel as
they advanced.

The rider on the right had seen him, shouting to his sidekick in Spanish and veering toward Bolan's position. One
shot from twenty yards, and the Executioner saw his target
jerk back in the saddle, drop his weapon, both hands rising
toward the crimson blossom on his chest. A second round
drilled through his open mouth and slapped him backward, rolling off the horse's rump in a somersault that
would have pleased any Hollywood stuntman.

The survivor tried to save himself by reining in and veering to his right, looking for safety among the trees. Bolan
shot him through the armpit, knocking him sideways from

the saddle, but the rider's foot got tangled in its stirrup. The frightened horse took off at a gallop, trailing a boneless rag-doll figure in its wake.

Two were down, but their appearance meant he had been spotted from the house. No further time to waste. He came out running hard, the M-16 held across his chest and ready to confront the opposition. The belt pouch, with its hand grenades and can of jet-black spray paint, slapped against his left hip as he ran.

Fifty yards from target, a sniper tried to drop him, coming through the trees. Bolan missed the first muzzle-flash, too busy dodging for cover, but he made the second, emanating from behind a sculpted hedge. The M-203 launcher mounted beneath the M-16 held a 40 mm high-explosive round, and Bolan let it fly from forty feet, trusting the impact fuse to do its job.

The blast came right on schedule, Bolan going wide around the tree that sheltered him, running in a crouch. The launcher was reloaded, and he had his finger on the automatic rifle's trigger, ready for a mop-up burst, but none was called for. In the middle of the hedge, a smoking gap had opened like a makeshift gate, as if some automated mower had been left to run amok. The sniper's twisted legs protruded from the gap, unmoving.

He found three hardmen waiting for him on the lawn, their submachine guns angled vaguely toward the tree line. The M-16 was on full-auto this time, and even with the smoke of battle rising from behind him, Bolan managed to surprise them, charging out of cover like a wild man.

Firing on the run, he took the middle gunner first, with a swarm of 5.56 mm tumblers that swept the target off his feet and spun his body in midair before he fell. The others saw it happen, one man breaking for the cover of the house in sudden panic, while his friend stood fast.

The tough guy was his first priority, and Bolan dropped him in his tracks, a short burst to the chest that left him stretched out on his back, his submachine gun spitting useless bullets toward the sky.

The runner came next, three rounds between his shoulder blades to help with the momentum, and he went down on his face in an awkward slide across the fresh-mown grass.

The warrior had to reach the house, or it would be a wasted gesture, his intended message undelivered. Bolan came across the lawn full-tilt, alert to any flicker at the windows that would mean a gunner lining up his shot. No sign of opposition, but he could not take the chance. He fired an HE round in the direction of the big house, dropped it through a six-foot ornate window, and was crouching when the blast sent glass and mangled furniture spewing onto the lawn.

His next grenade was angled toward the porch, a bid to keep any remaining gunmen safe inside the house for a few more moments. The blast sheared off a white supporting column, littering the steps with plaster rubble.

Bolan hosed the nearest windows with a quick burst from his M-16, stepped in too close for gunmen in the windows to spot him without exposing themselves. He palmed the can of spray paint, shook it hastily and went to work writing the same message he had left behind him in Los Angeles, trusting the new enemy to translate on their own: Scorched Earth.

Someone tried a long shot as he reached the tree line, but it was wasted. They would soon be mounting a pursuit, when they regained their nerve, and Bolan wished them well. He wouldn't be there when they got around to scouring the grounds.

The strike was still on track as he retraced his steps in the direction of the wall.

4

It was a ragged group of warriors that collected at the Sylter Hof Hotel on Berlin's Kurfurstendam. None of them was wounded, but their faces showed the strain of combat spanning the nocturnal hours and a range of several hundred miles. Their points of contact with the common enemy included Hamburg, Frankfurt, Kassel and Berlin itself. Behind them, dozens of the enemy lay dead, with property worth several hundred thousand marks in ruins.

And they weren't finished yet, by any means.

From his position on the sofa, with a glass of vodka settled on the coffee table at his knee, Yakov Katzenelenbogen listened to the various reports, all victories, but he was still dissatisfied with the results. He saved his own story for last, spelling out the bare facts, offering a postscript with the approximate body count.

"Uri thinks he tagged Lauck."

"There's no thinking about it," said Uri Dan, a temporary Phoenix Force ally from Mossad, in Tel Aviv. "I recognized the bastard from his photographs."

"In any case," Katz said, "there was no sign of Gerhard Kasche."

In other words, the leader of the neo-Nazi National Vanguard had managed to slip through their net so far, and the hypothetical loss of Bruno Lauck, his second in command, wouldn't derail the group's fanatical ideals or terrorist activities.

"So, we keep trying," Katz declared, as if there were no question in his mind. Around the circle, heads were nodding, only one refraining from unanimous assent.

Katz turned to Rudolf Wetzel, their associate from GSG-9, the crack German counterterrorist unit based in Berlin. Wetzel had joined Katz and Uri Dan for their most recent strike, against a Vanguard training camp north of the city. Katz wondered if special dispensation for the illegal move had been granted by Wetzel's superiors. In any case, the agent had obvious misgivings about proceeding with the covert campaign.

"You're troubled," Katzenelenbogen said. It didn't come out sounding like a question.

"I went along the last time on my own," Wetzel stated. "I'm not sorry, mind you, but it's not the sort of thing that I can make into a habit, either."

"Understood," Katz told him. "If you'd rather not participate—"

"I didn't say that," Wetzel countered, leaning forward in his chair. "You run a calculated risk, regardless of the marginal cooperation from my government. The army and police aren't involved, you understand? Berlin has—how would you say this?—minimized its losses."

"Where have I heard that before?" Calvin James asked.

"The same old story," Rafael Encizo groused.

"It's up to you," Katz said to Wetzel. "We're not holding it against you if you want to stand aside." He turned to Uri Dan, including the Israeli in his comment. "We don't have that option, gentlemen. There is a job in front of us we haven't finished yet."

"For me, as well," the young Israeli said, his face set in a grim expression of defiance. "I was sent to punish the National Vanguard. The scope of that punishment is within my discretion. I opt for the destruction of an enemy who threatens me, whenever possible."

"So, it's unanimous," James said. "We keep on kicking ass."

"One difference," Katz replied. "We need to change our focus. Lashing out at any target we can find takes too much time in terms of positive results. We can't afford another week while the police and military get their act together."

"Let's cut to the chase," Gary Manning suggested. "Kasche and Buhler are the men in charge. Let's take them out and get it over with. Whoever follows them will have to start from scratch, with all the headaches we can leave behind."

"We'll need more information," Encizo said. "Right now, they're burrowed deep."

"Long gone, for all we know," David McCarter added, looking sour as he sipped a cup of ink-black German coffee.

"I can help you there, I think," Wetzel said, putting on a cautious smile.

"How's that?" Katz asked.

The German crossed his arms and said, "There is a man..."

DIRK SIEBERT STOOD before the full-length mirror, straightening his tie. The Windsor knot was perfect, as immaculate as every other detail of his suit and grooming. Even with the pale gray frosting at his temples, Siebert could have been mistaken for a model in a rich man's fashion magazine.

In fact, he was a well-known lawyer, specializing in the kind of cases normally described by court reporters as "political." One day, he might be in Hamburg, arguing a challenge to the seating of German National Party representatives in the Bundestag; the next, his clients might be skinheads charged with toppling Jewish headstones in a Frankfurt cemetery. His clients were invariably right-wing activists of one sort or another, many of them branded by the press and the police as neo-Nazis.

Siebert's critics didn't know—though many might suspect—that he had joined the National Vanguard shortly after its creation, rubbing shoulders with the likes of Gerhard Kasche and Bruno Lauck. Officially he represented members of the Vanguard for a fee when they were hit with civil suits or charged with crimes, but every citizen was equally entitled to first-rate legal counsel, weren't they? If Siebert now and then addressed gatherings of the German National Party, no one was surprised. The party's overall philosophy was mirrored in the speeches Siebert had been making for a dozen years, before the GNP was even organized. His views on economics, third-world immigration and the rest of it were all well-known.

What Siebert hid from his detractors most assiduously was his hatred for the Jews and anyone who took their part, from Tel Aviv to Washington, D.C. In Siebert's view, the Jews were parasites who fattened on the blood of decent working men and women, Aryans, who daily sacrificed their birthright in the grinding struggle to survive.

One day, the parasites would be eliminated, as would all the traitors to the fatherland. It would be done correctly, next time, when the Fourth Reich started cleaning house.

He had an early dinner date this evening to discuss the recent troubles with a pair of spokesmen from the GNP. No members of the Vanguard would be present—they were running for their lives—but Gerhard Kasche would be informed of their discussion, the decisions that they made.

Siebert didn't know who was responsible for the attacks his fellow Aryans had suffered in the past few days. The names were unimportant, in the last analysis. At heart, he blamed the Jews, their lackeys in the media and international finance. Whatever happened in the world, if it was detrimental to the interest of the master race, a diligent search would find Jews lurking in the background, waiting for their chance to sabotage the workings of a civilized society.

He finished with his tie, selected a carnation for his buttonhole and started to fill his pockets with the items he would need for a successful evening out. His wallet with the credit cards, a handkerchief and comb, the compact tube of breath spray. He wouldn't require a briefcase for this meeting, as no records would be kept, no transcripts generated. Everything that passed between them would be off the record, buried.

He checked the stylish apartment on Schonhauser Allee, making sure he had forgotten nothing in his haste. It wouldn't do to keep the others waiting, but he still had time.

Outside, he double-locked his door. With the scum that one found around Berlin these days, it paid to take no chances, even in the best of neighborhoods. Subhuman trash was everywhere, stealing anything they could lay their hands on to finance drug habits or bizarre sexual perversions.

He rode the elevator down alone, disembarking in the underground garage. His footsteps echoed in the cavernous enclosure, the sounds of a phantom army on the march. He reached his car, a gray Mercedes-Benz, and had his key inserted in the door lock when a voice addressed him from the rear in flawless German.

"Herr Siebert?"

Turning, Siebert stiffened as he saw the pistol with a silencer attached, its muzzle on a level with his stomach.

"Yes?"

The stranger smiled, without a touch of humor or compassion.

"Come with me," he said. "We need to take a ride."

"HERR SIEBERT NEEDS to spend some time at the gymnasium," Rudolf Wetzel announced, slipping on a pair of tight, black leather gloves. "He's getting soft."

The GSG-9 agent spoke in English for McCarter's benefit, both men aware that Siebert understood his every word. The right-wing lawyer was fluent in English, French and Spanish, facilitating his negotiations with clients outside the fatherland.

"A little thick around the middle, aren't we, Dirk? The women can't be too enchanted with that flab."

Siebert muttered something unintelligible. He was blindfolded and seated in a straight-backed chair, buck naked for intimidation purposes. His hands were bound behind him, ankles lashed tight to the front legs of the chair. He couldn't move, except to squirm and wriggle.

"Don't worry, Dirk. We haven't brought you here to talk about your love life, dubious as that may be. We're interested in your political associates."

"Are you security police?" the lawyer asked.

"We're not police at all, Dirk. The authorities are hamstrung by rules and regulations, you know that. It's how you keep your clients on the street, eh? The police would have to offer you a phone call, the attorney of your choice, all manner of accessories."

"And you?" Dirk Siebert's voice was strained, an apprehensive tremor clearly audible from where McCarter stood.

"We have a different set of rules," Wetzel replied. "I ask questions, and you are free to answer or refuse. Of course, refusal has its price."

"I don't—"

Before the lawyer could complete his statement, Wetzel stepped in close and hit him with a right hook to the solar plexus, cutting off his wind. McCarter knew the feeling well enough, like drowning on dry land, and he could almost sympathize.

Almost.

He thought about the victims, then, and the potential stakes, feeling the first twinge of sympathy evaporate.

"You understand me now, I think."

Siebert needed several moments to compose himself and find his voice. At last he said, "I am a practicing attorney. I have not committed any crime."

"We're interested in your clients, Dirk."

"That is confidential infor—"

Wetzel hit him with a solid left this time, and left a scarlet ribbon trailing from Siebert's nose.

"Not good enough!" the German agent snapped. "I've told you we are not police. Your rules are shit. To save your life and spare yourself great pain, your must consider the priorities."

"I cannot—"

Wetzel struck Siebert twice with gusto, rocking the lawyer's head from side to side. The blindfold was askew, but Siebert had his eyes clenched tightly shut. He made no attempt to glimpse Wetzel as the GSG-9 agent readjusted the cloth on his face.

"Allow me to clarify matters," Wetzel said. "We want Gerhard Kasche and Josef Buhler. Neither one of them is presently at home, nor in their usual haunts. I have good reason to believe you know their whereabouts. If you provide us with that information, you might yet survive. If not..."

"How would I know where they have gone?"

A backhand, this time, was followed by a looping blow to Siebert's gut. The lawyer doubled over as far as his bonds would allow, retching violently. Nothing came up, but it took the best part of five minutes for the man to bring his vocal cords under control.

"Please... please, no more...."

"You begin to understand the situation, Herr Siebert?"

"Please..."

"Gerhard Kasche and Josef Buhler. Where have they gone?"

"I—"

Wetzel slapped his hostage lightly, just a love tap, but the lawyer flinched and started to weep.

"Kasche and Buhler."

"They have gone to Zurich. There are matters to discuss with colleagues from the East."

"Where, East? What colleagues?"

"From Iraq and Jordan. Names are not my province. I do not participate in these negotiations."

"It would sadden me if I thought that you were lying, Dirk. I would be forced to harm you grievously."

"I swear to you, I was not given any names."

"Should I believe him?" Wetzel asked McCarter, putting on a crooked smile.

The Briton shrugged. He reckoned it was fifty-fifty, but he had no doubt that Siebert was terrified. "It's worth a look," he said at last. "But what do we do with this guy in the meantime?"

"Do not worry. I'll handle it."

MEYER LEVIN WAITED for the telephone to ring a second time before he lifted the receiver to his ear.

"Shalom."

"I'm on an open line."

He recognized the voice of Uri Dan at once, knew his top agent was calling from somewhere in Germany. Scrambler devices wouldn't be available on Dan's end, and he would have to trust the operative's skill at delivering reports in oblique language.

"Proceed."

"You have been following the news?"

"I have."

Levin knew about the raids in Germany—or some of them, at any rate. It stood to reason that reports were running well behind events, but he was satisfied with Dan's progress in the field, so far.

"Two of the individuals we hoped to interview have gone abroad. According to the information I've obtained, they went to Zurich."

"Ah."

The Israeli spy master knew exactly what was coming, but he had to hear it for himself.

"Our colleagues will be leaving soon," Dan said. "I hope to join them and conclude our business by tomorrow."

Switzerland was neutral territory, but the state of Israel recognized no boundaries in pursuit of terrorists and other enemies who threatened national survival. Execution teams had been dispatched to Europe, Argentina, even Russia, when the need arose.

"The contract must be finalized without adverse publicity," he said.

"Of course. And there is one more thing."

"I'm listening."

"It is reported that our contacts will be meeting Eastern representatives of their concern. No names, unfortunately, but I hope they may be highly placed."

The trip to Germany by Uri Dan, avenging Asher Blum's assassination, had been Levin's plan. So far, despite the initial surprise of Dan's collision and collaboration with a Western hit team, all had gone smoothly. Their targets—the National Vanguard and the German National Party—had suffered heavy casualties, and more would doubtless be recorded in the next batch of reports.

It would have been a simple thing for Levin to derail the mission, cancel any further action by his agent and allow the foreign team to carry on alone. He might have done so now, except that Dan's mention of the "Eastern colleagues" sparked his interest.

Arabs.

German Nazis killing an Israeli diplomat was bad enough, with its pervasive echoes of the Holocaust, but if the Germans were involved with Arab terrorists, Levin wanted to know about it. More to the point, he meant to disrupt any such liaison, inflicting the maximum damage on all concerned.

"Should I proceed?"

Levin pondered for another moment, weighing options, making up his mind.

"It seems a shame to waste the opportunity," he said at last.

"My thoughts exactly," Dan replied.

"You will observe the usual precautions." It wasn't a question.

"Certainly." There was a hint of mirth in Dan's voice. "The board of directors should not be concerned."

"Very well."

In fact, Mossad's "board of directors" wouldn't be informed. Meyer Levin had made the decision on his own, and he would cope with any fallout from potential failure. As for victory, he had no interest in the plaudits of a thankful state. His one reward would come in the form of suffering inflicted on his enemies.

In that respect, thought Levin, he wasn't so very different from the men he hunted.

And the similarity, perhaps, would be what let him track them to their deaths.

THE HEADQUARTERS of Germany's prime antiterrorist unit, dubbed Grenzschutzgruppe 9, is a nondescript building on Potsdamerstrasse, in Berlin. Once situated in Bonn, the unit's central command was moved as a consequence of reunification in 1991 to maintain a strategic position in the geographic center of the country.

Rudolf Wetzel phoned ahead, and they were waiting for him when he reached the fourth-floor office, having passed the checkpoints where his pistol was retained, his ID scrutinized by men in uniform with nothing else to do. He felt the cameras tracking him along the corridor and knew there would be guns to back them up if he made one false move.

Gert Lochner didn't bother rising from behind his desk as Wetzel entered. There was no smile on his face, and acrid smoke from his cigar hung in a cloud around his head and shoulders, like fog around a brooding mountain peak. From all appearances, the colonel's face might easily have been a sculpture, chiseled out of granite.

"So, you've come back home," Lochner said.

"Am I late for supper?"

"You are pleased to joke," the colonel muttered. "Should I be amused by what has happened in the past twelve hours?"

"I was ordered to assist the foreigners."

"Yes. With information only. You have gone beyond your orders."

"I used initiative."

"A dangerous commodity in today's political climate."

"I'll take that chance."

"You jeopardize the unit, all of us, with any reckless action. If your role in these activities was recognized . . ."

"It won't be."

"You might not control the circumstances. None among us is immortal, Rudolf."

"I'm still working on it."

"Such a funny boy, you are."

"I have to go to Zurich," Wetzel told his boss.

"Zurich? Why?" Suspicion darkened Lochner's face.

"Pursuing leads. Kasche and Buhler are off to meet the Arabs they've been flirting with behind our backs."

"You know this for a fact?"

"The next best thing. I have a source of known reliability."

"And if this source should turn up dead tomorrow, or the next day, what am I to think?"

"That Nazis turn upon their own. Should anyone be startled by the fact?"

"And Zurich?"

"Layers of insulation," Wetzel said. "The Israeli will be suspect, first, if anything goes wrong. It is the sort of operation Tel Aviv would sanction after Asher Blum. If anyone looks further, there are five more foreigners to choose from."

"And if something should happen to you?" The colonel's expression didn't change as he pronounced the theoretical death sentence.

Wetzel was ready for the question, having thought it out beforehand. "I am not on file with Interpol or Swiss security. You know this. Even if by some fluke I should be identified, I trust your staff to sanitize the files."

"It would be easier, less risky, for you to remain at home."

"Less productive, also," Wetzel answered. "We have a chance to roll up Kasche and Buhler, plus their Arab contacts. There might never come another opportunity."

"Is it our problem?" Lochner asked.

"If the Iraqis and Jordanians have sponsored murder in Berlin, you know it is."

"We have no brief or jurisdiction for a raid in Switzerland," Lochner pointed out.

"There would be no raid, officially. Whatever happens, GSG-9 will not be implicated. You have the ultimate in plausible deniability."

"And you," said Lochner, "have vacation time left over from the spring, I think, when you returned to work on the Tunisian matter."

"As you say."

"Perhaps you should relax and take it easy for a few days, Rudolf. Shall we see you in a week or so?"

The smile felt warm on Wetzel's face.

"A week should do me nicely, sir."

YAKOV KATZENELENBOGEN used a public telephone to
contact Stony Man Farm. He kept it short and cryptic, in
consideration of the open line, but got his point across—the
shift to Zurich, Kasche and Buhler running, contacts from
the Middle East expected on the scene. Five minutes saw it
done, and Katz walked back to the Sylter Hof to pack his
things.

The mission was about to come full circle, as it seemed.
From Jordan, they had tracked their targets to Berlin, and
now the Arab link was coming back to haunt them. It was,
perhaps, too much to expect that they could wrap the mission up in Zurich.

Then again there was a chance they might get lucky, but
experience had taught Katz to expect the worst and plan
ahead for all contingencies. The Arab element could be a
wild card, but at least they weren't flying blind.

It would be good to put Berlin behind him, leave the federal police to finish cleaning up the scattered remnants of the
Vanguard. Stopping the German National Party was another problem, but recent events would turn a spotlight of
publicity on Josef Buhler's covert neo-Nazi ties, and Katz
had faith enough in German voters to believe that most of
them would turn their backs on any replay of the Holocaust. And if the men of Phoenix Force were quick enough
in Zurich, Buhler would be history before another day was
done.

Perhaps he would have time to chat with Hitler and the
other brown-shirted psychopaths in hell.

Katzenelenbogen would be standing by with a pocketful
of one-way tickets for all concerned.

But first, they had to find the bastards.

Dirk Siebert hadn't been able to name the Zurich hotel
where Kasche and Buhler were lodging, so Katz had farmed
the problem out to Stony Man. Computer linkups, airline
records and the rest of it could all be accessed from a distance, scanned and correlated, served up in a matter of
hours to the men of Phoenix Force. At the same time,
Kurtzman and mission controller Barbara Price would be
cross-checking air traffic from the Middle East, with em-

phasis on flights originating from Amman, in an attempt to spot the Arab team.

Another hour and a half would spell goodbye to Germany, and it was none too soon for Katz. He didn't blame the modern government or German people for the madness of another generation, but he still felt morbid vibes this close to Dachau, Nuremburg, the rest of it. The smell of death was still too strong, the everlasting memories too fresh and painful for anyone who had lived through that era or lost relatives to the camps.

It would never be over, and that was the hell of it. Not as long as memories and diaries, films and photographs survived, not as long as members of the would-be master race still preached their filth and sought to recreate the nightmare from another time.

Never again.

Groups as diverse as the Israeli "Wrath of God" and the American-based Jewish Defense League had adopted that motto to signal their determination that the Hitlerian evil would never have another opportunity to put down roots and grow.

If Katz and Phoenix Force could strike a blow against that evil in Zurich, it would be worth any risk, any price.

5

Sucre, with some seventy thousand inhabitants, is the constitutional capital of Bolivia, but La Paz, with close to a million residents, has been the de facto seat of government for generations. It is in La Paz where laws are passed and sometimes winked at in the interest of free enterprise, where multimillion-dollar drug deals are consummated in plush offices and the still-fresh memories of paramilitary death squads linger in the streets.

And it was in La Paz that Bolan came to stalk his enemies.

The strike against Hector Rivera's estate had dissuaded the colonel from going home, but it wouldn't prevent the players from convening to discuss their common misery. A watch on Hans Erdmann's suburban rancho, east of town, had noted the arrival of two chauffeured limousines, passing through the guarded outer gate an hour apart. One limo was registered to Colonel Rivera, the other to Bernardo Gomez.

Vultures coming home to roost.

Erdmann's estate covered a sprawling six hundred acres, butting up against the foothills of the Cordillera Oriental. Bolan approached from the north, on foot, making himself at home in the forest with his war paint and camouflage fatigues. The weapon slung across his shoulder was a Walther WA-2000 sniper rifle, chambered for the .300 Winchester Magnum cartridge. The rifle's bullpup design reduced its overall length to roughly thirty-six inches, its fluted barrel designed for maximum cooling and pinpoint accuracy. The Schmidt & Bender telescopic sight would let Bolan tell the color of his target's eyes at any range within a thousand yards.

The estate wasn't surrounded by walls: there were no boundary markers to tell Bolan when he had entered the enemy's domain, but he could feel it, like a sixth sense guiding him on to his destination. Alone in the forest so far, he followed his instinct and the compass in his hand.

His progression toward the Erdmann estate was assisted by the memory of aerial photographs snapped by the DEA, delivered to Bolan by Ernie Gallardo. No coca was grown on the six hundred acres, but Erdmann's association with Gomez and other narco traffickers was well-known in Washington, and the terrain had been scouted against the day when fugitives might be sought under Erdmann's roof.

No one at DEA headquarters had ever anticipated a mission like Bolan's, at least no one had ever openly discussed such an action, but the preliminary spadework was useful, regardless. The warrior knew from certain landmarks when he had closed the gap to within a quarter mile of the great house, and he slowed his pace, alert to any sign of lookouts or security devices in among the trees.

The trees within eight hundred yards of Erdmann's Spanish-style house had been clear-cut, replaced by spacious lawn and tennis courts, a covered swimming pool, a topiary, flower gardens. On the north side of the building, a flagstone patio was fitted out with wrought-iron furniture, a deep-pit barbecue and bright-colored umbrellas for shade. The umbrellas would hide any loungers from aerial surveillance, but they did nothing to cover the patio from Bolan's slightly elevated viewpoint, just inside the tree line.

The warrior picked his spot, well covered by a stand of ferns, and stretched out prone, the Walther's stock against his shoulder, its truncated muzzle supported by a built-in bipod. The magazine inserted in the stock, behind the pistol grip, held six Winchester Magnum rounds, and Bolan carried five spare magazines. It should be more than he would need, his side arms adequate to deal with anyone who turned out in pursuit.

Implacable and stoic, Bolan found the eyepiece of the telescopic sight and settled in to wait.

JUSTIN PRATT WAS disappointed when he heard about the wetbacks coming over for a parlay. They weren't really Mexicans, of course, but who could tell the difference if you stuck them in a lineup? In Brazil, they mumbled Portuguese instead of Spanish, like their neighbors from the Rio Grande to Tierra del Fuego, but a spic was a spic in Pratt's book, even if they took advice from Aryans when state security was on the line and grew the coca leaves that helped keep freedom fighters solvent in the States.

Pratt would never trust a wetback when the chips were down, but Erdmann valued their association to a point, and it was impolite to argue with the host.

So, he would sit and listen to the greasers, hear what Erdmann had to say about the trouble they were in . . . and pray that none among them thought it was Pratt's fault.

Which would be a logical assumption, when he mulled it over. Granted, they were always killing someone in the wetback countries—revolutions and assassinations, narcodealers fighting tooth and nail for territory, bandits living in the hills—but this was different. The recent mayhem wasn't visibly political—except, perhaps the raid directed at Rivera—and the targets weren't lowly runners in the drug game.

Someone seemed intent on cleaning house, and they were starting with the wealthy allies of his host.

Much like Los Angeles, in fact.

Pratt had missed his best chance to kill the bastard who was stalking him back at Marina del Rey, and he had run for cover in La Paz, hoping that distance would serve him where brute force had failed. It seemed unlikely that the goddamned guy had followed him from Southern California, but it wasn't beyond the realm of possibility. Pratt had tried to cover his tracks, but there were ways . . .

He heard Erdmann coming and turned to find the old man entering the drawing room. It was a stupid name for anybody's den, no drawings in the place at all, but that was old-world thinking for you. Nothing wrong with that, unless you got bogged down in the decadent soft life and lost your focus on the fight for Aryan supremacy.

There was no fear of that, where Erdmann was concerned. The man was a hard-nosed second-generation Nazi, with his father's seething hatred for the Jewish parasites and better personal resources for waging covert war against the enemy.

"Our guests are waiting," Erdmann said.

"Okay. I'm coming."

"You do not approve of my associations, Justin?"

"Who said that?"

"I see it in your eyes."

"I wish we had a chance to work with Aryans, that's all."

"In time. These people have their uses at the moment. And it is their country, after all."

The old man led the way outside to where two men lounged on the wrought-iron chairs. Pratt stood and nodded through the introductions. Gomez was on his right, Rivera on the left. The colonel had a fat cigar protruding from his mouth, a pale scar like an SS lightning bolt across one cheek. Gomez wore a suit that had to have cost at least a thousand dollars, diamonds flashing on both hands. The two of them stared holes through Justin Pratt and nodded after Erdmann introduced him as a colleague from the States.

It was the closest Pratt had ever come to the source of the drugs he had peddled through intermediaries to the blacks in L.A. Now that he saw them, Pratt's original preconceptions about the drug trade were confirmed. Cocaine was a tool and a prime source of income, but the men at the heart of the business were garbage, the scum of the earth.

When they had served their purpose to the movement, they would have to be eliminated. Like the Jews and mud people. Like anyone else who stood in Pratt's way.

First things, first.

He found a chair, uncomfortable iron beneath his ass. At least the broad umbrella kept the sun out of his eyes, but it was still damned hot outside.

At least the bastard who had chased him from Los Angeles—or *maybe* chased him—couldn't reach him here. The old man's rancho was an island of security where Pratt could put his feet up, listen while his host hashed over problems with the wetbacks.

He could learn a thing or two from Erdmann, if he listened closely. Someday, maybe someday soon, the old man would be gone.

Nobody lived forever, even when their blood was pure.

THE SCHMIDT & BENDER telescopic sight put Bolan's targets in his lap. He tracked across the patio from left to right, pivoting the Walther on its bipod.

First in line, Bernardo Gomez, slouched in his custom-tailored suit, dark hair shiny with oil and slicked back from his meaty face. The dealer talked with his hands, the fingers heavy with rings, gold on his wrist and around his neck. His shoes were alligator, polished to a mirror shine.

The wages of sin.

Hector Rivera was out of uniform and wearing a conservative suit in charcoal gray, puffing clouds of bluish smoke from a six-inch cigar. The zigzag scar on his cheek resembled a brand...perhaps the mark of Zorro. Bolan wondered briefly if it was a combat wound or something less heroic, like a souvenir from some brothel knife fight. The eyes betrayed no visible emotion; they reminded the warrior of a shark's eyes, flat and black.

Tracking.

Hans Erdmann had iron-gray hair, cut short enough to show his scalp. It was a boot-camp buzz, and Erdmann had the military bearing to go with it, making Bolan wonder whether he had ever worn a uniform. Gallardo's background sketch on Erdmann told him that the man had never gone back home to Germany, but with his father's history, Erdmann would have been indoctrinated with the Waffen SS code of discipline from birth. His oval face was deeply tanned, in striking contrast to his pale blue eyes. The mouth was a narrow slash, almost lipless, beneath the blade of his nose.

Moving on.

The final face in line was Justin Pratt's. He was a youthful twenty-seven, and the bastard who had wired Janice Flynn to an explosive charge and left her to die at Marina del Rey, hoping that Bolan would go up in the same blast. Instead he had watched his troops die, bailing out of L.A. one jump ahead of his own sudden death. Now, here he was, and the tropics didn't appear to agree with him.

Four other men were visible from Bolan's hiding place, all soldiers, dressed in lightweight khaki, pacing off the middle ground with automatic weapons on display. Young men, Germanic types: the new generation. They seemed to notice nothing in particular, but Bolan guessed that they would miss nothing of substance.

They would have to die, before he moved on to more important game.

He didn't know the men he was about to kill, but Bolan knew their type. At Nuremburg, in 1947, their ancestors had tried to save themselves from prison or the gallows with a tired refrain: Only following orders. They had believed every word of it as they tried to pass the buck upstairs, to men already dead or doomed. No inkling of remorse for all the havoc they had wrought, the misery they had inflicted on mankind in their pursuit of "racial purity."

You didn't change a mind like that. There was no remedial education facility for the morally bankrupt, no effective aversion therapy for pathological bigots. They never learned from mistakes, because no mistakes were acknowledged. Defeats were always blamed on scapegoats, traitors, aliens. Brutality was justified—or, if the public heat grew too intense, specific incidents were written off as myth and propaganda, perpetuated by the "Jews' media."

Barring divine intervention, there was only one cue for that kind of hate, and Bolan was holding the curative instrument in his hands.

Proximity and timing were the keys to a successful strike. The nearest of the guards would pose the greatest threat to Bolan once he opened fire, and all of them would have to go before he could effect a safe retreat.

But for the crucial first shot, if he timed it properly...

He had one chance before all hell broke loose and it became a matter of survival, one free shot to make his point, and anything that happened after that was gravy.

Slowly, cautiously, he brought the cross hairs of his Schmidt & Bender telescopic sight to rest on Justin Pratt. His index finger curled around the Walther's trigger, taking up the slack. He took a deep breath, released part of it and held the rest.

Show time.

COLONEL HECTOR RIVERA hadn't attained his present rank by being reasonable. He could follow orders when he had to, any military man acquired that talent early on, but for the past eleven years he had more often issued orders than received them. Rising through the ranks on nerve and cunning, he had grasped the reins of state security, using the apparatus of torture and execution to purge his own enemies, along with the state's. Endemic rebellions notwithstanding, he had never been seriously challenged or threatened...until now.

"My private residence," Rivera told the others, careful to enunciate and make the most of his heavily accented English. "My home, gentlemen. Attacked in broad daylight, vandalized and desecrated. Several of my men were murdered. Explanations are required. Someone is accountable and must be punished."

"I understand, Colonel," Erdmann said. "We share your sense of urgency in that regard. Each of us is affected. We all stand to lose if the matter is not resolved."

"My situation is unique," Rivera told the German, stiffening his spine a fraction as he spoke to emphasize his military status. "If the chief of state security is not himself secure, what else remains? It takes so little in these times to shatter public confidence. If I should be replaced—" or killed, Rivera thought, and kept it to himself "—your business would be seriously jeopardized."

In fact, Rivera knew, the inconvenience would be strictly temporary. Corruption was pervasive in La Paz, and there would be no difficulty finding someone to replace him, much as he had risen to replace his predecessor, now imprisoned by the Yankee *federales* in America. The colonel understood the concept of expendability too well. No man was strictly necessary, much less indispensable.

Rivera saw a vision of his own mortality, and he didn't enjoy the view.

"My friend," Erdmann said, "we are all together in this time of trouble. A united front might be our only hope."

"Against what enemy?" Rivera asked.

The German frowned and glanced to his left toward Justin Pratt. "There is a chance," he said, almost reluctantly, "that my associate may shed some light on this."

Rivera watched the young man squirm, all eyes upon him now. What secret did he keep locked up inside himself that could have followed him so far and jeopardized the colonel, everything that he had worked for from his youth? He waited, listening, prepared to question anything and everything. Above all, he had to save himself.

"I don't know where to start, exactly," Pratt began. "You know we move some of your product in Los Angeles. We used to, anyway. Last week we started running into problems."

Pratt hesitated as he tried to pull his thoughts together. Watching him, Rivera had no sympathy. He didn't care for Americans as a rule, and he actively detested anyone who placed his own interests in jeopardy. It would be such an easy thing to make this young man disappear...but first, the colonel had to hear him out.

"Continue, Justin," Erdmann prodded him.

"Okay. The first thing was—"

Rivera had his eyes fixed on the young American when Pratt exploded. The colonel could think of no other descriptive term, although, in fact, the young man's face was actually collapsing, buckling in upon itself like a papier-mâché sculpture before the real explosion occurred, the whole back of Pratt's skull disintegrating in a cloud of gray-and-crimson mist.

The young man's body, almost headless, vaulted backward, taking the wrought-iron chair with it in a graceless sprawl. He lay there for a heartbeat, feet up in the air, before his muscles lost their final vestige of coordination and he seemed to melt.

The echo of a rifle shot came to Rivera then, the sight and sound combined to send him diving from his chair in search of cover, anything at all to save himself.

And he was terrified that it might be too late.

BOLAN VERIFIED THE HIT on Justin Pratt before he swung the Walther to his left and framed the nearest sentry in his sights. The young blonde had been facing toward the house when the Executioner fired, but he was moving now, swiveling toward the tree line, his eyes and weapon homing on the echo of the first report. He wouldn't spot the source immediately, not without a second shot to guide him, and by then . . .

The Walther WA-2000 lurched against his shoulder, no muzzle lift to speak of with the fluted barrel and the stock in perfect alignment. Downrange, the .300 Winchester Magnum round bored in beneath his target's chin, 220 grains of copper-jacketed death traveling at more than 2,400 feet per second. It was neater than a chain saw, but the end result was very similar, the body stumbling through an awkward two-step while the head flopped over to one side, nearly ripped free of its mooring.

Bolan caught the second Nazi in a fighting crouch, his submachine gun pivoting toward the warrior's hiding place. He stroked the Walther's trigger lightly as the sentry pressed his own, and bright flame stuttered from the muzzle of the SMG. Fierce hornets swarmed in the air above Bolan's head, as his weapon's Magnum round ripped through the gunner's chest. Explosive impact rocked the shooter on his haunches, bowled him over in a crumpled heap, his last burst wasted as he fell.

Number three was scuttling sideways, firing from the hip with a folding-stock assault rifle, breaking toward the cover of the bricked-in barbecue pit. Bolan hit him on the run, a clean shot through the lungs and heart, lifting the sentry off his feet and dropping him flat on his face. A tremor rippled through the corpse and swiftly passed away.

And that left one.

The gunner almost had it made, a fast break toward the house, but the Executioner had no intention of letting him slip away. The Walther cracked again and punched a tidy hole between his shoulder blades, exploding from his chest in a fist-size exit wound. The soldier was dead on his feet, but momentum carried him forward another three yards before dropping him facedown on the patio.

One round remained, and the warrior fired across the patio, a flat trajectory from the tree line to a set of sliding glass doors, rewarded with a tinkling crash as the bullet made its way inside the house. He ditched the empty magazine, reloading swiftly, and brought his eye back to the scope, tracking across the veranda.

Pratt was down and out, the tattered remnants of his head trailing off into a spreading blood slick on the flagstones. Hans Erdmann lay behind a capsized wrought-iron table, one foot protruding into Bolan's line of sight, and he was making no move to bail out. On his right, next in line, Bernardo Gomez lay curled into a fetal ball behind a chair, shaking so badly that his tremors were visible through the Schmidt & Bender telescopic sight. Beyond him, all the way to Bolan's left, Colonel Hector Rivera was the only man in motion, creeping on his belly toward the protective bulk of the brick barbecue.

Bolan led his crawling target by a foot or so and squeezed the Walther's trigger, spraying chips of stone and copper in the colonel's face. It could have been a blinding shot, but the warrior wasn't counting on his luck in that regard. One more round to keep the colonel scared and stationary, then he swung back toward the right.

Toward Gomez.

As with Rivera, Bolan could have killed the cocaine dealer where he lay. The fact that he didn't was based on strategy,

rather than pity. He intended to roll their networks up before he left Bolivia, and cutting off the heads right now
would only make his task more difficult, the secondary targets more elusive.

For the moment, Justin Pratt aside, the Executioner was
merely rattling their cage.

But that didn't mean they would walk away unscathed.

The upturned chair gave Gomez little cover, barely more
than head and shoulders shielded from his adversary's line
of fire. With seconds left before he had to break off contact and retreat, Bolan lined up his shot, fixing the cross
hairs of his telescopic sight on the dealer's left foot, snug in
its shiny alligator shoe.

Eight hundred yards, approximately, and he got it right
the first time, holding steady with the Walther as his target
splattered, blood and tattered leather flying. Gomez started
thrashing, heedless of the danger in his sudden pain, but
Bolan didn't take advantage of the opportunity to score another hit.

He turned back to Erdmann. One of the Nazi's hands had
crept into view like a beige spider, edging around the lip of
the wrought-iron table. Bolan went for it, taking a precious
second to line up the shot, squeezing the Walther's hair
trigger so softly his mind was barely conscious of the
movement. Downrange, the hand whipped back and out of
sight as if Erdmann had yanked it to safety, forewarned of
the shot, but a scarlet smudge against the flagstones gave the
lie to that illusion.

Time to go.

The Executioner fired the last two rounds in his magazine through the tall glass doors, reloading as he scrambled
to his feet and started back through the trees. It was a long
walk to the boundary of Erdmann's property, where he had
stashed his vehicle along an unpaved access road, and there
was still a chance he might be intercepted on the way. There
would be radios inside the house, perhaps a band of roving
sentries somewhere on the property, prepared to cut him off.

He had no choice. The car was waiting, other targets calling to him, and his ranking adversaries needed time to lick their wounds. Next time they met, there would be no hesitation, no unilateral flag of truce.

The Executioner was on a roll.

And he was rolling over any enemy unfortunate enough to cross his path.

6

The mountain forest of the Cordillera Oriental bears no real resemblance to the jungle of northeastern Bolivia, which sprawls across the border with Brazil. The lowland forest is a steamy, sodden place where mud squelches underfoot and fungus grows on everything, including unprotected human flesh. Upland, by contrast, there was better runoff, cooler temperatures. The jungle moss and fungus were replaced to some degree by lacy ferns, and biting insects were less prevalent.

The Cordillera Oriental had been home to various guerrilla bands since World War II, most of them left-wing revolutionary factions, but the mountain forest also sheltered mercenary bandits and, from time to time, provided staging grounds for far-right death squads organized in service to the ruling government and trained by neo-Nazi elements. Those days were gone, according to the new regime...

Hans Erdmann's destination lay fifty miles east of La Paz, at an elevation of 19,000 feet. The two-acre compound was cleared of trees and camouflaged in the standard fashion of rural drug labs, but no cocaine was processed here. Instead the camp was used for paramilitary training, third- and fourth-generation warriors of the master race keeping themselves fit and preparing for the inevitable day of conflict.

Hans Erdmann was a familiar face in these surroundings, well-known among the young men in their jungle uniforms, but he had never run for the mountain camp in such haste, fearing for his life. It was unthinkable, but it had happened all the same, his own home violated by intruders, the blood of his guests spilled on Erdmann's own turf.

Erdmann's left hand was cocooned in a thick gauze bandage, numbed with local anesthetics that would soon wear off and leave him to decide if he would bear the pain and try to keep himself clearheaded or resort to pills. Two fingers were gone, replaced by mutilated nubs of tissue closed with stitches, plus a hairline fracture of the wrist.

At that, he had been lucky. One of his surviving bodyguards had been quick with the tourniquet, quicker still on the drive to a suburban hospital where Erdmann was treated in the emergency room, his wound cleaned and sutured, a blood transfusion pronounced unnecessary. Erdmann had refused the doctor's urgent suggestion that he check himself in for overnight observation, returning to his limousine with bodyguards in tow two hours after he arrived.

It was no time for Erdmann to be lying in a hospital bed, pinned down and vulnerable to his enemies. He needed sanctuary, someplace he could hide while still maintaining contact with his network, marshaling his forces for the battle already under way.

And who, exactly, was the present enemy?

He remembered Adolf Eichmann, a personal friend of his father's, kidnapped from Buenos Aires by Israeli agents in 1960. Fifteen years later, Riga commandant Herbert Cukors had been lured from his São Paulo home by Jewish "avengers," beaten to death and left in the trunk of a Volkswagen abandoned in Montevideo, Uruguay. Klaus Barbie, likewise, had been the target of covert attacks while he dwelt in Bolivia.

The difference, Erdmann told himself, was that those heroes of the Reich had served the fatherland in World War II, while he was just a youth. Regrettably Erdmann had played no part in the Führer's Final Solution, and thus no charges had been filed against him for so-called war crimes. To be sure, the Jews who knew of his existence wished him dead, but he was viewed as a fanatic descended from madmen, relatively harmless in his self-imposed exile.

The drugs were something else, but he had taken pains to forge alliances with men of power in Bolivia, who could defend their interests with a minimum exposure of Erdmann's political contacts. Still, the business was chaotic—all the more so in neighboring Colombia and farther north, in the United States—with bombings and assassinations commonplace. It was conceivable that some competitor might try for Gomez or Rivera, risking Erdmann's life and wrath in the process.

Still...

He couldn't forget Justin Pratt, the troubles that had driven him from California, seeking comfort with Erdmann in Bolivia. There had been no time for Pratt to tell Erdmann's guests of his trouble, linking the violence in Los Angeles to recent mayhem in La Paz, before a rifle bullet ripped his head apart.

That first shot spoke volumes to Erdmann. The sniper, whoever he was, had bypassed Gomez and Rivera, even Erdmann, to pick out the stranger in their midst. Was it coincidence, beginning with the far man on the left? Erdmann scowled at the forest landscape rolling past his bulletproof window, dismissing the notion out of hand.

Young Pratt had brought his lethal problems with him to La Paz, and they had spread like a disease to threaten everyone he touched. The central question now, in Erdmann's mind, was why the sniper had restrained himself, when he could just as easily have killed Rivera, Gomez and their host.

"Five minutes," the driver said, briefly distracting Erdmann's thoughts from the carnage at his home. He was looking forward to the peace and quiet of the camp, although he knew it couldn't last.

There was a war in progress in La Paz, and Erdmann meant to back the winning side.

Tonight, tomorrow at the latest, his own Aryan warriors would be going on the attack.

IT HAD BEEN no great chore to track Hans Erdmann from his rancho to the nearest private hospital, where he and his

VIP guests were treated for their various injuries. Rivera got off easy, minor bruises, with some small cuts on his face and hands from flying chips of stone. Hans Erdmann's hand required more work, but he was discharged hours after his arrival at the hospital. Bernardo Gomez would be leaving in a wheelchair when they checked him out, hobbling on crutches if he tried to walk at home.

The dealer didn't have enough time left to convalesce with any kind of grace, but he would have a few more hours, perhaps a day or two.

Hans Erdmann, first.

The Nazi link was Bolan's prime consideration here, with its apparent links to Middle Eastern terrorism indicated by the sketchy evidence from Jordan and Iraq. Bolan knew that German military types and rocket scientists had coached the Arabs in their early wars with Israel, and aging Nazis were still welcome if, by some bizarre chance, they should find themselves in Tripoli, Amman or Baghdad.

Nazis first, drugs second.

Bolan had dealt with Latin American drug lords in the past, on more than one occasion. He knew their mind-set, the kind of arrogance that came with operating almost as a warlord in your own private fiefdom. Only the strong survived, and strength was measured in guns, explosives and muscle.

Jungle law.

The warrior had staked out the suburban hospital while Erdmann and company were inside, getting their wounds patched up. A public telephone across the street allowed him to watch the emergency exit and Erdmann's limousine while he placed a call to Ernie Gallardo, raising the DEA man on his first try.

The rest, as someone said, was history.

Gallardo didn't hesitate when Bolan asked him where Erdmann might run and hide while he licked his wounds, regrouping for the battle ahead. There was a compound in the mountains east of town, where members of the military death squads had practiced marksmanship and other things under a previous administration, marching to the tune of

"Cocaine Minister" Luis Arce. Today, the camp was a combination training and recreational facility for members of Erdmann's Fourth-Reich-in-waiting, honing their combat skills while allowing them to disport themselves outrageously from time to time, free of the civilized strictures in La Paz.

From Erdmann's point of view, it was the perfect place to hide. In Bolan's view, however, it could also be a perfect place to isolate his enemies and pin them down, cut off from reinforcements.

Perfect, right, unless it blew up in his face.

He had the camp's location from Gallardo, which allowed him to maintain some distance from the Nazi's limousine. He could have gone ahead to lie in wait, but there was still a chance that Erdmann would select a different hiding place. If that should happen, Bolan didn't want to find himself camped in the jungle, watching half a dozen Nazis practice goose-step marching, while his quarry slipped away unseen.

Eliminating Justin Pratt had lifted Bolan's spirit slightly, a blood debt repaid in kind, but the battle was far from over. As so often happened in the hellgrounds, one trail merged into another, leading the hunter in new, perhaps unexpected directions. Sometimes, there was a dragon waiting at the far end of the trail, perhaps a nest of vipers.

Bolan had been down that trail before, in all its permutations, and he knew the dangers involved. Dueling with dragons was always risky business, whatever the terrain, and Bolivia was unfamiliar ground to Bolan. Still, he was learning fast, and at the bottom line there was relatively little difference between his present setting and the Southeast Asian hellgrounds where he learned his martial trade so long ago.

Times change, along with adversaries, but the stakes were always life and death. It mattered little if his enemies were speaking English, Spanish, Arabic or Swahili... in their black hearts, where it mattered, they were all the same.

All predators, in search of easy prey.

The limo was a mile ahead of him, just visible on wide curves in the mountain road. The driver might be watching his rearview mirror, but it would be difficult to spot any tails on this kind of terrain. If Bolan hung back and navigated on his information from Gallardo, he should be all right.

At least until he left the car and started for the Nazi camp.

From there, all bets were off.

And all Bolan stood to lose, if he failed, was his life.

THE LIMOUSINE WAS on its way at last. For Arnold Brunner, it was a relief to know Hans Erdmann would be with them in a few more moments. When the driver radioed ahead from two miles out, it meant that they were safe and running clear.

Or were they?

Brunner was the mountain camp's commander, and he took nothing for granted in terms of security. The present Bolivian regime was friendly to his fellow countrymen—though not as friendly as in bygone days—but he remained alert to any hint of danger from within or from outside. The Jews were one thing, always sniffing after ''war criminals'' with their hit teams and kidnap squads, but they weren't the only peril in the modern world. There were Communist rebels in the mountains—*perestroika* notwithstanding—and even the American DEA was troublesome from time to time.

The commander was unclear on precisely what had happened in La Paz, but he knew that Erdmann was wounded. That, in itself, was a shock. The very thought of gunmen slipping past the man's security, striking at the very heart of the New Reich—it was stunning, beyond mere surprise. For the first time in years, Brunner had been forced to consider the Aryan movement without Hans Erdmann at the helm...and that, in turn, led him to reconsider his own role, vis-à-vis a possible promotion.

Not that Brunner wished to profit from the plight of his superiors. And yet...

The news from La Paz had placed Brunner's outpost on immediate alert, the sentries doubled, weapons issued to the troops in bivouac. He felt a new excitement in the camp, so different from days when practice exercises occupied their time.

And that was natural.

When Arnold Brunner killed his first man for the movement, he had been a strapping youth of nineteen years. The target was a Jewish merchant in La Paz, known to moonlight with the Israeli intelligence apparatus, feeding information on the New Reich back to Tel Aviv. It had been Brunner's pleasure to approach the old man as he walked home after work one Thursday night, inquiring after street directions, swinging wildly with the hammer when his target's head was turned. The human skull made such a satisfying sound when it was crushed, a miniuniverse of secrets bursting free.

There had been seven others since the Jew, some of them natives, one American, but Brunner always harked back to the first time whenever he felt like walking with his memories. Somehow, it bound him to the old days, fighting in the streets around Berlin in his grandfather's time, the glories of *Kristallnacht* and herding human cattle onto eastbound trains.

The good old days would come again, but that meant work, and dealing with your adversaries as they came.

Like now.

Erdmann would be safe with Arnold Brunner at the camp. It was a pledge that Brunner meant to honor with his very life.

Or with his death, if it should come to that.

Brunner's commitment to the New Reich was absolute, a blood oath he would carry with him to his grave, whenever fate decreed his life should end. While life remained, he meant to serve the cause with every ounce of strength at his disposal, in any capacity his superiors might require.

If, at some future date, he should be called to lead the movement, well, that would be fine with Brunner, too. He sometimes saw himself in full-dress uniform, leading a procession of the faithful through La Paz—or was it Hamburg, where his grandfather had come from?

The time would come, Brunner believed, when Aryan warriors would regain their honor and the territories they had lost in the betrayal that had claimed Hitler's war against the Jews. The kangaroo court at Nuremburg hadn't extinguished Hitler's righteous flame, as evidenced by recent world events. With Russian communism's demise, soldiers of the master race were on the march, striking at the enemy wherever opportunities arose.

He hoped that there would be an opportunity today.

Hans Erdmann was a hero to the young men in his service. Any one of them would gladly die to guarantee his safety, and Arnold Brunner was no exception to the rule. There was a possibility he might advance in rank with Erdmann's death, but in his mind the cause was more important than his own advancement. It would never have occurred to him to undermine Erdmann or his other leaders for personal gain. Beyond the obvious betrayal of men he admired, it would have been unpardonable treason to his race.

A warning shot rang out from the perimeter, and Brunner moved to meet the car. Whatever he could do to make the compound ready had been done. The rest came down to courage, pride and grim determination.

Arnold Brunner smiled as the limousine rolled into view.

He was ready to shine on behalf of the Reich.

BERNARDO GOMEZ SHIFTED in his wheelchair, cursing his confinement and the pain that radiated from his bandaged foot. It could have been a great deal worse, he realized, but understanding wouldn't dam the rage that percolated through his veins like acid. His overriding fury almost canceled out the pain and initial fear, even the drugs he had been given at the hospital.

He had been forced to crawl, and some of those who saw him grovel like a peasant on the ground were still alive to tell the tale. It helped that two of them, the German and Rivera, had been scrambling to save their own lives at the moment, but that still left his enemies.

Who were they? Where could they be found and made to answer for the violation of Gomez's dignity?

The act demanded vengeance, and frustration was a part of the towering rage that consumed Gomez now. Revenge was the law of survival in his business, where the first show of weakness was often a man's last. In twenty years' time, he had buried a thousand competitors, traitors, reformers and renegades bent on destroying his empire. Violent death was an occupational hazard in the drug trade, and Gomez had come up the hard way, fighting tooth and nail for his early success, battling from then on to hold the ground he had won and explore new horizons.

It wasn't the first time Gomez had been wounded, nor the worst, but somehow this occasion sparked more anger in his soul. In past encounters, he had known his adversaries and had witnessed their destruction, joining in the pleasure of eradicating those who wished him harm.

This time, though, he had nothing to work with, nowhere to begin. The young American had died before he had a chance to tell his story, and Hans Erdmann was unwilling to continue at the hospital, before he scurried out of town. They would have other opportunities to speak, but in the meantime Gomez felt exposed, almost emasculated by his shame.

He had returned to his penthouse in downtown La Paz, avoiding the rural estate where he suddenly felt vulnerable in spite of the high walls and roving security guards. There had been riflemen at Erdmann's home, as well, and they were now stretched out in body bags, awaiting disposition at the morgue. Downtown, at least, if someone came for him, they would be forced to park their car outside the highrise building, pass his spotters in the teeming lobby, board an elevator and ascend to reach his suite of rooms where fifteen soldiers waited, armed for war.

The picture windows of the penthouse were bulletproof glass, specially tinted to prevent anyone outside from seeing in, day or night. Gomez trusted the contractor, but he had drawn the heavy draperies as added insurance, guarding against the threat of some theoretical, state-of-the-art surveillance device that might not even exist. He felt safe for the moment, but the sense of security only increased his frustration and anger.

Better to be out there, hunting his opponents on the street, than holed up in his plush cave like a trembling coward. How long would it be before his long list of competitors got wind of the attack on Gomez, realized that he was cringing in the penthouse fortress rather than attempting to avenge his loss?

Of course, he had his spies and soldiers on the street, but they were getting nowhere with their questions, even when they threatened pain or death. The normal well of covert information in La Paz ran dry where this particular explosion was concerned. No news about the raid against Gomez's drug lab in the mountains, or the strangers who had killed his men near Guaqui and—apparently—rescued the DEA informer from their clutches.

That had seemed to be a different problem altogether, but Bernardo Gomez had his doubts today, with his foot bundled in gauze and his movements severely restricted by fear. Politics and cocaine were inextricably linked in Bolivia, and Gomez wondered if the Nazis—these German outsiders and their American cronies—might not be the primary targets of his unknown assailant.

And if so, then what? Was there any way for Gomez to divorce himself from the Nazis without alienating Colonel Rivera and making himself look like a coward? If his competition thought Gomez was running, they would set upon him like a pack of jackals. Rather than fight them all at once and risk losing everything he had, Gomez preferred to search out his immediate assailant, grind the man to pulp beneath his one good heel.

If he stood fast, Rivera and Erdmann would have to support him. There was safety in numbers, and their fortunes were linked through the northbound traffic in *la merca*. As the largest dealer in La Paz, Gomez was a vital asset to the cartel. His death or incapacitation would demand a sweeping realignment, disrupt the flow of cash and merchandise, perhaps destabilize the whole black-market economy.

Gomez should have felt better, but he didn't. Sitting in his wheelchair, smoking a cigar and fuming in his isolation, he was both afraid and angry. For the sake of his own self-respect, for survival itself, he needed to find and destroy the man who had wounded and embarrassed him. Without a swift and favorable resolution of this matter, Gomez would seem less than a man, in his own eyes and in the eyes of his potential competitors.

It would require a more aggressive approach, more pressure on the street to shake the necessary information loose. If his soldiers couldn't do the job, he would replace them with other, more capable men. Bolivia had no shortage of mercenary killers, and if worse came to worst, he could call on his friends in Colombia for reinforcements.

Time to start from scratch and turn the city upside down, if need be.

Bernardo Gomez was still alive, and he meant to stay that way, without surrendering his empire to a nameless, faceless enemy. Whoever tried to seize his property would have to do so over his dead body.

And the dealer wouldn't go alone.

BOLAN LEFT HIS CAR a mile north of the target site, concealed well back from the one-lane blacktop on a deeply rutted forest track. He stripped down to his underwear and put on camouflage fatigues with military webbing, rummaging in the trunk for his choice of weapons. With his side arms snug in place and bandoliers across his chest, he hefted the M-16/M-203 combination, chambering a live round in both the rifle and the 40 mm grenade launcher.

His destination lay due south, and Bolan set off through the forest at a steady, ground-eating pace. He watched for snakes and sentries, booby traps and fallen branches, making fair time over unfamiliar ground. There was no particular hurry this time, since his enemy had gone to ground. Hans Erdmann clearly meant to stay awhile and let the storm blow over in La Paz.

In any other circumstances, Bolan thought it might have been a decent plan, but Erdmann had reckoned without the Executioner.

And that would be his fatal mistake.

The altitude would be hard on runners, but Bolan took his time. On the retreat, if the warrior's raid came off without a major hitch, there would be no necessity for speed, since no one would be chasing him.

A hundred yards into the forest, he picked up a game trail running in the same general direction as his target. Bolan followed it with caution, frequently referring to his compass as a guide. The trail was deeply etched by running hooves, but the undergrowth crowded close on either side, brushing at his shoulders, sometimes slapping in his face. He brushed a clinging spiderweb aside at one point, watched the gray arachnid scuttle out of sight behind a tree trunk. Overhead, birds flitted through the branches, calling back and forth in shrill, excited voices, sounding the alarm.

He felt at home beneath the canopy of forest, traveling alone and bearing arms against an enemy who had him both outnumbered and outgunned. It brought back memories of Vietnam and other jungle settings, rural and urban, where he had placed his life on the line against other predators. He smelled the vegetation, listened to the life sounds all around him and remembered other battlefields.

Another three hundred yards, and the trail was intersected by a mountain stream, continuing across the other side. The stream was narrow enough for Bolan to clear it in a single stride without getting his feet wet, pausing to listen before he proceeded on his way.

The forest had accepted him, to some extent, though insects ceased their trilling as he passed. It is a fallacy that any man or animal can move with total silence through a virgin forest. The trick, in Bolan's experience, was not so much avoiding any sound as it was accommodating one's self to the natural rhythm of the setting, merging with the background noise and becoming a part of the scene.

He smelled the camp before he heard it, picked up sounds from the inhabitants before he had their base in sight. The men he came to kill had taken time with their facility, the camouflage to cover them from aerial reconnaissance, but they still had to eat, and the aroma of stew on the fire reached Bolan from two hundred yards out. Closer still, he picked up muted voices and the sound of a vehicle moving along some invisible track to his right.

Time to slow down, put out the psychic feelers for perimeter guards and mantraps as he closed the gap to his target. He was almost there, and he couldn't afford a slipup this close to the firing line.

The first guard Bolan spotted was a young man in his twenties, chewing gum with his mouth open, crouched with his head and shoulders protruding from a clump of ferns. The warrior watched him for a full minute, noting that the sentry seldom scanned to left or right, appearing bored and listless on the job. When the Executioner moved next time, it was with extra caution, drifting to his left—the sentry's right—and easing his Ka-bar fighting knife from its inverted sheath on his combat harness, the anodized blade immune to telltale glints of sunlight.

Stalking.

Every battle started somewhere, and the sentry's nest would be as good a place as any for the Executioner to start his sweep against the enemy.

7

Ernie Gallardo had thought long and hard about leaving La Paz. He decided against it, in essence, because flight smacked of failure and he hated the thought of turning tail with his job incomplete. Granted, he was blown, his cover shot to hell, but Mike Belasko was a wild card, adding new dimensions to the game, and Gallardo thought he could help.

Part of it was the machismo thing that haunted so many Latin men from the cradle to the grave, demanding a certain posture around the clock, now and then pushing the envelope with ridiculous risks.

Like now.

He knew the snatch had been no accident, his rescue more a miracle than anything he had a right to expect. The contract that had brought a hit team to his door would still be in effect, pursued with greater energy since his original captors bit the big one, but Gallardo still had a few tricks up his sleeve.

Or hoped he did, at any rate.

If he miscalculated, he was dead.

He decided to start with his street people, the low- and mid-level contacts who had served him so well in the past. Some of them were useless now, but Gallardo still had leverage over a handful. He knew where a few of the bodies were buried, who had scammed whom in a number of cases where dissemination of that information could result in punishment both swift and sure.

It was a gamble, but Gallardo felt up to the challenge.

Besides, he owed the bastards something for the attempt on his life. If he couldn't pursue the case to its conclusion, see them extradited to the States for trial, perhaps he could help Balasko mete out some rough justice of his own.

And it might be more satisfying, at that.

Always provided that he lived to see the end result.

He started with Ornelas the hijacker, a gap-toothed, grinning cutthroat whose one "redeeming" characteristic was a macabre sense of humor. His given name was Ismael, but a coterie of close friends called him Smiley, after the yellow grimace that climaxed each of his jokes...and some of his murders.

Ornelas owed Gallardo a favor, based upon a tip from the DEA agent that had enabled Smiley to take down forty keys of pure cocaine en route from Gomez, on the Rio Beni to the Colombian border. The owners of the shipment were a pair of brothers named Beniquez from the neighborhood of Riberatta, and they had been urgently pursuing the source of their trouble. At need, Gallardo could always drop a quarter and put Ornelas on the spot, but he preferred to milk the grinning thug for information, if he had the chance.

There was a possibility Ornelas might decide to sell him out, of course, but Gallardo thought he could control the situation if he kept his wits about him. Ornelas would think twice about dealing with a suspected Fed, but he would also remember their previous transaction, perhaps hoping for more of the same.

And if he tried to pull the rug out from under Gallardo, the man would be ready for him.

He had pulled the trigger twice on lethal adversaries in his years with DEA, and while he derived no satisfaction from killing, neither was he burdened by any overriding sense of guilt. Violent death was a regular part of the drug trade, and if Gallardo found his own life hanging in the balance, he intended to come out on top.

One brush with death was all it took to set his nerves on edge and make him ready to respond in kind. The Glock 17 autoloader in his shoulder holster was backed up by a 12-

gauge shotgun, its stock and barrel sawed off, which he kept beneath the front seat of his compact car.

All set.

And when he finished with Ornelas, there were other fish to fry, more sources to be tapped for information on the current whereabouts of Mike Belasko's major targets, their response to the attacks sustained so far.

Someone, somewhere, would have the answers he required.

ALL THINGS CONSIDERED, Colonel Hector Rivera believed he had been lucky in the strike at Erdmann's home. He'd received a few small cuts from flying stone chips on his face, but he was otherwise unscathed. None of his men had died, this time, and all the major damage was sustained on Erdmann's property.

But somehow, none of that improved the colonel's mood.

His own estate had been among the early targets, there was no forgetting that, and he couldn't pretend the raid on Erdmann's home was unrelated to the other violence he and his associates had suffered in the past twelve hours. Someone owed Rivera a blood debt, and he meant to collect payment in full.

Retribution was the colonel's specialty, a major part of counterterrorism and the maintenance of order in a state where far too many of the peasant class were illiterate Indians one step removed from the jungle. Brute force was the only language they understood, and Rivera had risen through the ranks with state intelligence on the strength of that understanding. It set him apart from other military men who could take peasants or leave them, depending on the conduct of the individual. When Rivera saw a peasant, he was looking at a problem in the making, a potential enemy to be observed, interrogated, stripped of liberty and life itself at the convenience of the state.

Not that Rivera suspected a peasant of plotting his latest misfortune. He had dealt with native revolutionaries in the past, and they were typically disorganized, their raids as often lethal to their own as to the chosen targets. In the end, some member of the rebel band would always crack—for profit or to save himself from pain—and so the others would be run to earth, interrogated for the pleasure of it, finally placed against a wall.

This time, the raids had been precise, efficient, well-coordinated. The survivors at his own estate had glimpsed one man, too large to be a native Indian, although the warrior's skill with military hardware might have skewed their memories.

On balance, though, Rivera thought his enemies were foreigners. He gave no serious consideration to the thought that one man was responsible for all their troubles.

And still, the critical questions remained: Who were they? What had brought them to La Paz? And where could they be found?

Rivera's men were on the street, had been since the initial incidents, reminding covert sources of their first responsibility—and the assorted penalties attached to failure.

After all this time there was still no response, but he was hopeful. Rivera's men had never failed him yet, perhaps since they had witnessed the expressions of his rage firsthand and understood that failure meant the same as death.

Rivera had a special stake in running down their enemies. Aside from preservation of his rank and reputation, the colonel owed his growing fortune to the pact he had formed with Gomez and Erdmann, using his office to safeguard the cultivation, manufacture and export of cocaine to the United States. Without that income, his political prestige around La Paz was nothing but a sad stroke to the ego, placing Rivera's life in occasional jeopardy without corresponding rewards.

His bank account in the Bahamas had a healthy balance, but it wasn't fat enough to see Rivera through his golden years in the style to which he had become accustomed. In order to save his life-style—indeed, his very life itself—he had to get results.

And soon.

The intercom on Rivera's desk buzzed softly, a muted sound that brought his eyes back into focus. Reaching for the telephone, he lifted the receiver to his ear and spoke one syllable into the mouthpiece.

"Yes?"

Rivera's private secretary said, "Ybarra on the line, sir."

"Very well." A click was immediately followed by the whisper of an open line. "Rivera speaking."

"Colonel." Antonio Ybarra's voice was sandpaper-rough, a childhood injury compounded by too many cheap cigars. "We have a lead."

"I'm listening."

And as Ybarra spoke, the colonel found that he remembered how to smile.

BARBARA PRICE TOOK the message from La Paz and fed it into the Stony Man computer, with an eyes-only fax to Hal Brognola in Washington. Jack Grimaldi was on the job, but his information was sparse, and it left Price hungry for more.

It seemed that Bolan was making progress, weighing in with heavy blows against the enemy, but reports always ran behind breaking events. Even now, she knew that the Executioner had embarked upon another raid, pursuing Erdmann's Nazi clique. It could be hours yet, before she found out the results, and in the meantime there was nothing she could do but wait.

As always.

Akira Tokaido breezed into the War Room, a personal cassette player clipped to his belt, the earphones clamped to his head. Despite the foam-rubber earpieces, she was treated to a muted blast of heavy metal—Poison? Megadeth?—and wondered how the young computer whiz managed to get through the day without a screaming migraine headache.

Tokaido nodded and flashed her a smile as he took his seat at the console. "How's it going?" he inquired, his right hand drifting down to mute the music as she answered.

"I suppose I ought to be encouraged."

"But you're not?"

"It's the waiting," Price answered. "By the time we get the word from Zurich or La Paz, our guys are on to some-

thing else, new risks. I don't like starting off three steps behind the pack.''

"Occupational hazard," the young man replied, forcing
a smile. "I'd rather be here than at the front lines."

"I wonder, sometimes."

"Oh?"

She was pegged for rear-echelon work as a mission controller, but that didn't dictate automatic satisfaction with her
stationary role at Stony Man Farm. She had no real desire
to test her mettle on the firing line with Bolan or the men of
Phoenix Force, and yet . . .

She knew Bolan's history, his background in association
with the government, dating back to the day when he had
"died" in Manhattan and orchestrated his own resurrec-
tion as Colonel John Phoenix. An act of treason had severed that link with the Feds, at the same time condemning
Aaron Kurtzman to a wheelchair and claiming the life of
Price's predecessor, April Rose.

Price knew the woman's story, as well—the embattled
love she shared with Mack Bolan to her dying day; the times
she had accompanied him on raids against the common enemy and risked her life along with his. At times, she found
herself making comparisons, matching herself against April
and coming up short in her own eyes, wondering if Mack
ever felt the same.

Enough!

She knew the limits of their personal relationship before
it started. There were no strings attached . . . except, perhaps, for heartstrings.

And those were so easily broken.

She couldn't replace April Rose, had no desire to try, but
neither could she pretend to have no feelings for the man
who changed her life. Sometimes, perhaps inevitably, Price
thought she had to be letting Bolan down by staying safe
behind the lines while he put himself in harm's way. What
must he think of her, each time she sent him off to risk his
life?

Except it wasn't like that, she knew. The man she loved,
without ever having spoken the word in his presence, had

been risking life and limb for years before they met. Without her, he would do the same. This way, at least, she had a chance to share some tiny portion of his time between the battles, when he came back to the Farm to rest or catch his next assignment.

Time.

It seemed to be so fleeting in the restful, loving moments, there and gone before she had a chance to savor every precious nuance. But the hunting, killing times dragged on and on, at least for those who stood by in support. It would be different in the trenches, she imagined, but would she ever know?

Tokaido was running his fingers over the computer keyboard, humming as he decoded the final lines of a report that had spewed out of a printer. Price rose and left him to it, passing through the War Room's coded-access door en route to the mess hall. A cup of coffee wouldn't solve her problems, but it couldn't hurt.

Killing time.

Right now, it was the only game in town.

ESTEBAN MORALES WAS a small-time dealer on the fringes of the narco traffic in La Paz. He handled shipments of cocaine from the locals who were satisfied to supplement their normal farming income with an acre or two of coca, gambling that the narcotics police would be too busy chasing larger prey to waste their time on what the gringos would call a mom-and-pop operation.

In his line of work, Morales met many strange characters, some of them killers, but he had never been duped by a police informer until recently. It was a first for Morales, being taken in—and by a gringo at that, the bastard worming his way into Esteban's confidence, wooing him with minor transactions at first, wriggling into his world like a parasite and taking hold.

It came as a shock when Morales learned that his new amigo was a plant, and an American federal agent in the bargain. By the time he learned of his mistake, the gringo

had been snatched and slated for disposal. No one linked
Morales to the gringo, which was fine.

Until the slippery bastard rose from the dead and came
back to La Paz.

Not that he had ever really died, of course. Someone had
blown it, let him slip away somehow, and now he was back
on the street, giving the hunters another shot. It was crazy,
but that was the gringo's problem . . . until he tried to involve Esteban Morales.

And that was a critical mistake.

The gringos had many "wise" sayings: misery loves
company; don't take any wooden nickels; the squeaky wheel
gets the grease.

Once burned, twice shy.

Morales had survived a near miss the first time, through
sheer dumb luck, and he was taking no chances the second
time around. He played innocent when the gringo agent
called that afternoon, demanding a private talk, hinting at
exposure of Esteban's operation to the police—or worse, his
underworld competitors—if Morales didn't comply.

It was perfect. A chance to be rid of the Yankee and in-
gratiate himself with men of power, all at once. Such opportunities rarely presented themselves, and Morales was
ready to seize the moment.

This time, there was no room for error.

He started with a phone call to Antonio Ybarra, widely
known around La Paz as a lieutenant of Bernardo Gomez.
And Gomez, in turn, was known to be seeking the Yankee
informer, to finish the job he had started the previous night.

Ybarra had seemed glad to hear from Esteban Morales.
Well he might, with the gift Morales was trying to drop in
his lap. If Ybarra bought his plan and passed it on to Bernardo Gomez, Esteban could write his own ticket. Beginning, perhaps, with a lucrative place in the Gomez
syndicate.

He would have to start near the bottom, of course . . . or,
would he?

Esteban's contribution would allow Gomez to recoup his
sullied honor, no small thing in a society founded on the

principles of machismo. Such a gift was priceless, when you thought about it, and Gomez would recognize that his benefactor wasn't a paid member of the organization, acting out of duty. Esteban Morales was an independent, acting from enlightened self-interest. A successful businessman like Bernardo Gomez could appreciate that and express his gratitude in concrete terms.

Or so he thought, at any rate, until the callback from Ybarra. There had been a "minor" change of plans, it seemed. Morales was no longer expected to finger the Yankee for Ybarra's men. Instead he would keep the appointment as planned, make certain there was no confusion at the crucial moment.

Details.

Morales was worried, but he reckoned he could handle the assignment. When he thought about it, he decided that a little something extra just might do the trick. If he provided more than simple information, actually played a role in the gringo's capture, he would prove himself that much more valuable to Gomez and company.

It was perfect.

If he could only stop his hands from shaking now, the rest of it would be a simple matter.

Child's play.

And with any luck at all, he might just survive to enjoy his reward.

GALLARDO ALWAYS showed up early for a meet when there was money on the table or his life was riding on the line. Tonight was a wide-open gamble, and he was taking no chances.

The drive-by looked good, for a start, scoping out the line of storefronts and cars against the curb, pedestrians idling along, some taking their time and window-shopping, others bent on urgent errands, pushing through the crowd. He passed the tavern once, spotted the Morales-mobile in the parking lot on one side and drove on around the block.

Coming back, he had the 12-gauge on the seat beside him, hidden from prying eyes beneath an open newspaper. The

Glock was wedged between his right thigh and the vinyl-covered cushion of the driver's seat, where he could reach it easily at need.

All set.

He signaled for the turn-in to the parking lot and waited for straggling passersby to clear the way, pulling in at a crawl with one hand on the steering wheel, the other resting midway between the pistol and the shotgun.

He was ready to rock.

There was an empty space next to Morales's car, the driver's side, nose to tail, and Gallardo eased in close enough for them to talk without leaving their respective vehicles. Morales played it cool, his head back against the seat, his eyes closed like he was dozing in the muggy heat. He didn't bat an eye as the DEA agent set his parking brake and left the engine ticking over.

"Hey, Esteban."

Nothing.

The first small worm of doubt was wriggling in his gut already, and Gallardo shifted his car into reverse. A glance at his rearview mirror showed no immediate danger, but he flicked the newspaper onto the floor all the same, uncovering the sawed-off shotgun.

"Yo, Morales!"

Leaning out his window, Gallardo rapped his knuckles on Morales's car, with no response. He craned his upper body through the opening to prod the man's shoulder with an index finger, cursing as the lifeless body toppled slowly to the right and out of view.

The scuffling sound behind him, on the passenger's side of his own vehicle, was Gallardo's only warning of death on the hoof. He whipped his head around, the shotgun coming up almost before he registered the presence of a stranger standing there, a shiny pistol in his hand.

The shotgun blast was deafening, a point-blank charge of buckshot slamming square into the gunner's chest and punching him backward, his limp body rebounding from a nearby car.

Gallardo didn't know where the first shot would come from, but he knew it was coming, and he ducked below the line of sight as a bullet drilled through his back window and took out half the windshield in a flying cloud of pebbled safety glass. He stood on the accelerator, heard a startled cry behind him that was followed by the solid thump of impact with a human body. A heartbeat later, and his wheels jolted over something that felt like a speed bump but wasn't—not unless they taught the speed bumps in La Paz to scream.

The car was taking hits from two sides now, at least three guns unloading on him, bullets puncturing the bodywork and blowing out the glass that remained. His high-speed reverse came to a jolting halt as Gallardo's car collided with another vehicle. He shifted gears in a near-prone position, praying that his bumper wouldn't hang him up and that the compact's engine wouldn't stall.

He risked a glance across the dashboard, felt a bullet whisper past his cheek. Then he had the car in motion, bulling forward. There was no way he could make the street without another look to find the exit, watch for traffic, and he came up with the automatic pistol in his hand.

In front of him, a shooter with a submachine gun stood his ground, already firing from the hip. Gallardo pegged two rapid shots in his direction and stood on the accelerator, giving Mr. X the choice. His target waited for the final instant, hurled himself aside too late for total safety, cursing as the compact's fender caught his trailing foot and whipped him through an awkward somersault.

Who were they? Gallardo had no time to think it through, but it was clear that someone had surprised Morales. Or, perhaps, the low-level dealer had been planning a surprise of his own, when Gomez, Rivera, et al changed the rules.

Either way, it was Gallardo's second brush with death in twenty-four hours, and that was one too many for any sane man.

Time to go.

He blundered into the traffic with a screech of tortured rubber, sideswiped a taxi and rebounded into near collision with a pickup truck. Behind him, there was scattered firing for another moment, quickly silenced as he put a moving wall of vehicles between himself and his assailants.

Safe.

No, that would be too much to hope for. He was still a moving target, would be while he lingered anywhere within the borders of Bolivia, much less downtown La Paz.

But he wasn't prepared to leave.

Not yet.

The man who had him marked for death had made Gallardo angry now, and anger canceled out his fear.

Almost.

The fear would make him cautious, while his anger kept him in the game.

And if he played his cards right, he might just come out the other side alive.

8

As such things go, the sentries had been easy. Mack Bolan had taken out three of them to start with, working with the Ka-bar in near silence, leaving the bodies where they died. He guessed there were at least two others, but he had the north and west perimeters to himself, now. Lookouts on the east and south weren't about to interfere with the Executioner's plan, and by the time they started looking for him, he would be inside the camp.

Or dead.

Whichever way it played, the time for plotting strategy was gone.

He came in from the northwest corner of the camp, a gliding shadow in the forest, closing the gap with his enemies. The aroma from the cooking fire was strong now, making his mouth water, but he concentrated on the task at hand.

The camp was laid out roughly on a north-south axis, with a one-lane dirt track granting access at the southwest corner. Several vehicles were parked at that end of the compound, under camo netting, and he recognized Hans Erdmann's black sedan, now marked with dust and caked-on mud. He reckoned that the car had to be equipped with four-wheel drive, or Erdmann would have been compelled to walk the last four miles.

The other vehicles in camp were military types, four army-surplus jeeps and a half-ton truck with OD canvas covering the back. Except for Erdmann's car, the vehicles were backed into unmarked spaces, ready for a rapid getaway.

He started counting structures in the camp. Two Quonset huts sat at this end, nearly forty feet in length and painted in a camouflage design, undoubtedly the barracks. Erdmann's mess hall was an open hut with primus stoves, and long folding tables covered with a tarp on wooden tent poles. The generator hut was prefab metal, painted green, with heavy cables snaking out the back. Three private bungalows were spotted toward the south end of the camp, in close conjunction to the motor pool. The base command post looked like plywood, with a corrugated metal roof, and Bolan knew it had to have been treated with preservatives to keep jungle rot from setting in.

He counted fifteen Nazis in the open, none of them immediately recognized. Hans Erdmann and his entourage would have the bungalows, and they would probably be resting from their morning's ordeal, backed up by the brisk drive from La Paz. The troopers he could see were in military-style fatigues, more jungle-fighting togs than standard Nazi gear, and all except the three-man kitchen crew were packing weapons.

The camp would also need a night shift, call it eight or nine men, minimum, who would be catching up on sleep inside the Quonset huts.

No less than thirty, then. Perhaps another ten on top of that. He thought the camp would be too small for more than forty men to occupy for any length of time. The latrines would be maxed out at that, and there was no pervasive stench to indicate that they were being overused.

The architects had been relying on concealment, rather than defense, and they hadn't done anything of substance when it came to clearing fields of fire. Bolan came within twenty feet of the first hut, creeping through the undergrowth on hands and knees, unnoticed by his enemies. The M-16/M-203 nosed out in front of him, the barrel tracking like a lethal antenna, locking on to first one Nazi, then another.

Easy targets, right, until he dropped the first one and the others started to scramble for cover, started firing back.

It would be anybody's game from that point on, and Bolan had to make his first move count.

He could have waited for the sun to set, but that was hours away, and in the meantime, someone might go looking for the sentries he had silenced. Bolan's one advantage in the present situation was surprise, and he couldn't afford to give it up.

The warrior shifted his position and settled in a fighting crouch, his left index finger curled around the M-203 launcher's trigger. He swiveled toward the CP bungalow, acquired his target and squeezed off. Before the HE round exploded, he was on his feet and sprinting toward the nearby hut, reloading on the run.

ARNOLD BRUNNER HAD BEGUN to let himself relax. The first excitement he had felt upon receiving Hans Erdmann's call to action was fading with time, replaced by the inevitable feeling that most—or all—of his security precautions were in vain.

To be sure, someone had tried to murder Erdmann in La Paz, but it seemed beyond the realm of plausibility that the assailants could have trailed him here, much less that they would dare to assault the camp. It did no harm to post the guards, of course.

Just in case.

He checked his wristwatch and confirmed that it was still an hour and a half until the troops were called to eat their evening meal. The stew was Brunner's favorite, next to Wiener schnitzel, but he would just have to wait with the rest.

Meanwhile, it was time to check his sentry posts, make sure that everyone was on the job, alert and doing his respective duty. It was all a part of leadership, to let himself be seen and to crack the whip where necessary.

It was seldom called for, with the present lot of troopers, but Brunner took nothing for granted. Command was a vocation, a calling, and the true officer ignored the attendant duties at his peril.

And, if the truth be told, he enjoyed the privileges of rank immensely.

Brunner buckled on his pistol belt, settling the holster comfortably on his right hip and adjusting the Sam Browne strap across his chest. He didn't stop to check the creases in his trousers, knowing they were perfect. Outside, the day was cooling down, a symptom of the altitude, but it would be full dark before the sentries needed jackets to warm themselves. Meanwhile—

He was off the porch and three paces into the compound proper when the command post exploded behind him. The shock wave struck Brunner like a giant fist between the shoulder blades, propelling him forward twenty feet, the toes of his boots barely skimming the ground. He rolled going into the fall, saved himself from a belly flop and came up shaking his head like a punch-drunk boxer.

Flames were boiling out of the ruined command post, its metal roof airborne on a column of smoke and fire. The walls were buckled outward, window frames devoid of glass, the one door lying almost at his feet. Brunner's ears were ringing, numb from the concussion, but he could still hear the crackle of hungry flames—and a new sound, harsh, insistent, hammering at his nerves from somewhere behind him.

Automatic weapons.

Brunner scrambled to his hands and knees, then came erect, groping for the Walther P-38 in its holster. All around him, his soldiers were running this way and that, armed or scrambling for the nearest weapon, ready to defend the camp against all comers. It was a disorganized reaction, to be sure, but what could he expect under the circumstances?

He opened his mouth to begin shouting orders, then snapped it shut again, aware that it was fatal folly to command from ignorance. He didn't know their enemy's location, strength in numbers, or objective. Taking the latter for granted—destruction of Hans Erdmann and the camp itself—Brunner was still without the crucial data needed to direct his troops effectively.

The pistol's weight felt reassuring in his fist, but from the sound of firing on the camp's perimeter, it wouldn't be enough. His assault rifle was lost in the blazing rubble of the CP bungalow forever beyond his reach, and he cast about for an alternate source of hardware. Running on instinct, he doubled back toward his quarters, the bungalow adjacent to Erdmann's, where he kept an Ingram submachine gun, ammunition and grenades.

One of Erdmann's personal guards was just emerging from the next-door bungalow as Brunner reached his own. The gunman barked a question at him—something in the vein of who, how many?—but the camp commander waved him off, pushed through the entrance to his quarters, homing on the military hardware in his sleeping room. He kept the Ingram MAC-10 loaded with a 32-round magazine, a live round in the chamber, with the safety on. Spare magazines went in his trouser pockets, and he clipped fragmentation grenades to his belt on either side of the buckle.

Charging back outside, he was in time to see a powerful explosion rock the western Quonset hut, where members of the compound's night shift would have been asleep short moments earlier. He wondered whether any of them had escaped—a dozen lost, if not—and then he heard a shout from Erdmann, on his flank.

He spun to face the older man, startled by the expression of fear on Erdmann's face. It seemed so alien, entirely out of place, that Brunner was shaken to his core. For just an instant, he caught a glimpse of weakness in the man he had grown up revering as a father figure and more. If Erdmann crumbled...

"You must stop them, Arnold!" he shouted. "Kill them for the Reich!"

"Yes, sir!"

He was off and running then, shouting to his soldiers, rallying a half dozen around him as he ran toward the northwest perimeter of the camp. Most of the firing seemed to be concentrated in that quarter, and he had to find out if his men were firing at shadows or a flesh-and-blood enemy.

Brunner's brownshirts formed a flying wedge behind him, weapons at the ready. They had covered thirty yards or so when he beheld a tiny object looping toward him from the general direction of his left front. It registered at the subconscious level, his doom telegraphed in a heartbeat, but Brunner had no chance to react effectively before the grenade touched down. A warning shout was stillborn on his lips, the last split second of his concentration channeled into self-preservation as he tried to swerve away, colliding with the trooper on his right.

The detonation was apocalyptic, all-consuming. Brunner was airborne, a cartwheeling rag doll, tumbling head over heels toward the unyielding earth.

He saw that impact coming and realized there wasn't even time to scream.

THE HE ROUND HE AIMED at the command post had been dead on target, dropping through a window on the northern wall and detonating inside with a sound like muted thunder. Bolan didn't see the bungalow erupt in smoke and flames, his mind already focused on the Quonset hut ahead of him, where gunmen might be waiting for him, ready to destroy him in a heartbeat.

He had the M-203 launcher primed and ready with another round by the time he reached the hut, flattening against the metal wall and scuttling toward the door that faced the center of the compound. In front of him, his adversaries were distracted by the demolition of the CP bungalow, all heads turned in that direction for the moment, but he knew that the initial shock would buy him only seconds.

If he played his cards right, it was all the time that he would need.

He reached the front door of the hut, shouldered through and found himself confronted with two rows of standard military bunks, staggered to accommodate a total of twenty or so. Roughly half of them were occupied, the sleepers struggling away with thunder in their ears, some of them groping blindly for weapons while others thought first of their boots and trousers.

Bolan gave them no time to brush the cobwebs away and react more coherently. He fired his second HE round toward the right-hand wall of the hut, holding down the assault rifle's trigger as he swept the room with a long burst from right to left. Bodies jerked in their blankets, twitching to the impact of 5.56 mm tumblers ripping flesh and fabric, startled voices raised in cries of pain and just as quickly silenced.

Backing out, he palmed a grenade from his web belt and yanked the pin, lobbing it behind him toward the smoky interior of the hut. The shock wave and shrapnel should take care of any survivors, and the warrior hardened his heart to their pain, remembering the creed they lived and died by, steeped in the blood of innocent scapegoats and "inferior races."

Back in sunlight, Bolan found a number of the Nazi gunmen racing toward him now, attracted by the gunfire and explosions on their flank. He met the nearest of them with a short burst from the M-16 and watched two soldiers go down in a tangled heap, a third man breaking for cover too late. The stream of bullets overtook him, rolled him up and left him stretched out on his back, sightless eyes focused on some point far beyond the scattered clouds above.

Bolan reloaded, feeding his rifle a fresh magazine, turning at the sound of orders shouted in German. A party of seven or eight Nazis was sprinting toward the shattered Quonset hut, still apparently unmindful of the warrior's precise location, and he meant to keep it that way. The leader was an older man, armed with a compact machine pistol, and his soldiers were young Aryan types packing assault rifles.

The Executioner dropped into a fighting crouch and let the M-203 launcher rip, an HE round looping toward his mobile targets at a range of roughly thirty yards. The leader saw it coming, tried to veer off course, but he collided with one of his gunners and lost it a heartbeat later. The blast pitched him head over heels through a cloud of smoke and dust. Two other men went down with the blast, their four companions staggering, shaking their heads and trying to get a fix on the source of their torment.

The warrior took them down with short bursts from the rifle, dropping each man in turn, working around the rough half circle from left to right. Other gunmen were finding the range now, bullets whispering around Bolan's ears and snapping at his heels. He started to run for the nearest cover, sliding in behind the generator shed directly opposite the mess tent.

In another moment they would have him pinned, and Bolan still had work to do. There had been just a glimpse of Erdmann in the distance, gaping from the open doorway of a bungalow before he slipped from view, the door slammed shut behind him. If he missed the old man, the warrior knew that he would have to count the mission as a failure. There were no two ways about it. He was here for Erdmann, and he had to make the effort, whatever it cost.

Five seconds to reload the launcher, and he was as ready as he ever would be. Bullets rattled briefly on the aluminum walls of the generator hut, someone shouting at the gunners to mind their fire and avoid destroying the equipment inside.

Bolan took advantage of the momentary lull and came out firing from the hip, Grim Death incarnate as he dropped two soldiers in their tracks and sent a third man sprawling with his left arm nearly severed, dangling by a scrap of tissue.

No strategy to speak of, now. The rest was down and dirty, throwing everything he had at any target he could see, reversing their numerical advantage with sheer ferocity. It might not work, but it was Bolan's only hole card in the present situation. If it failed him, he was dead.

And if he pulled it off, he still had Erdmann's private bodyguards to deal with at the other end.

No sweat.

From where he stood, the whole thing seemed as easy as falling into an open grave.

THE LATE ARNOLD BRUNNER hadn't been mistaken in his assessment of Hans Erdmann's fear. In fact, the old man was closer to panic, trying not to let it show, feeling the tremors in his hands as he clutched the Uzi submachine gun close against his chest.

Some Aryan warriors cherished a foolish prejudice against Israeli weapons, failing to appreciate one of the things Jews did well. Erdmann didn't share their feelings; if anything, he found sweet irony in the notion of using Jewish-made firearms against the Zionists and their stooges.

At the moment, however, fine points of irony and poetic justice were the furthest things from Erdmann's mind. His thoughts were focused on survival, and he huddled in a corner of the bungalow, peering through a window as the compound went to hell around him.

He had glimpsed one of the enemy, a tall man dressed in military style, his hands and face covered with camouflage paint. There had to be more, from the evidence before his eyes, but Erdmann couldn't pick them out to save his life.

And, he decided, it was coming down to precisely that point.

He had seen Brunner die seconds after they spoke—a loss, to be sure, but nothing compared to the harm Erdmann's death would do to the movement. Without Bormann and Mengele these days, it was no exaggeration to call Hans Erdmann the patriarch of the Fourth Reich in South America. He had worked hard for the unofficial title, proved himself in a thousand different ways through the long years of struggle, and his personal assessment owed little or nothing to ego.

Erdmann's five bodyguards were with him in the bungalow, one sharing the room as a matter of course, the others having rushed next door to protect him at the first sounds of combat. All of them were armed with automatic weapons, each an expert marksman with human kills to his credit. Erdmann had chosen the best for his personal entourage, and now he found himself wondering if they were good enough.

Too late for new auditions, in any case. Erdmann calculated that he had minutes left—perhaps only seconds—in
which to save himself from the nameless enemy.

It said something for their skill and determination that his
foes had followed him this far, tracked him to this remote
compound and somehow infiltrated the camp itself. So
much for the forest sentries Brunner had spoken of. They
would have died first thing, and that increased the body
count in favor of his enemies.

How many dead so far?

Erdmann didn't have the time or interest to concern himself with statistics. Every soldier in his army had a job to do,
and each one knew the risks involved. It was an honor to die
for the fatherland, although he didn't carry that philosophy to the suicidal extremes of the Arabs. Still, which soldiers were more revered at the end of a major conflict, than
those who laid down their lives in defense of the cause?

Erdmann had a whole new crop of martyrs today, and no
time yet in which to appreciate their sacrifice. If he wasn't
to join them in the next few moments, he would have to get
away. And that meant getting to his car, at least one man to
guard him and another to manage the vehicle in their per-
ilous escape.

It would be a close thing, even so, but Erdmann thought
they might pull it off.

As if they had a chance.

There was a window in the rear, providing ventilation for
his bedroom. It was small, but large enough for Erdmann
to negotiate when he was motivated, as now, by the prospect of imminent death.

"Kurt, Otto, come with me," he snapped. "The rest of
you stay here and slow them down."

There were no arguments, no accusatory glances from the
soldiers chosen to remain behind. They knew their business, and they were possessed of boundless self-confidence.
If they were able to stop his enemies, so much the better;
Erdmann and his soldiers would be reunited later in La Paz.
If they failed, well, such men were always expendable in
defense of the higher cause.

Erdmann led the way into his bedroom, crossing directly to a smallish window and throwing it open. He waved Otto through ahead of him—better to have a gun on the ground when he made his move—and followed awkwardly, favoring his wounded hand while the Uzi slapped at his hip, hanging from a strap around his neck.

Outside, it seemed a short run to the car, Kurt bringing up the rear, but it was open ground all the way. Danger there, if they weren't swift and lucky, and Erdmann knew he would slow down the young men. But it was their job to protect him, after all, and not the other way around. They did as they were told, appreciative of the opportunity to serve the Reich.

The sounds of gunfire were closer now, ringing like a death knell in Erdmann's ears, and he felt his legs trembling. For a moment, he was terrified they would not carry him, and then Otto hissed the command.

"Time to go!"

They were off and running in a heartbeat, charging toward the motor pool as if the demons of hell were hot on their heels.

THREE GUNNERS OPENED UP on Bolan from the center bungalow, their muzzle-flashes barely visible in filtered sunlight, bullets whispering around him, gouging divots in the earth at his feet as he ran. Three men at least, and maybe more inside with Erdmann, covering the grand old man of Bolivian Nazism in his moment of crisis.

Bolan let the M-203 launcher answer for him, lobbing a high-explosive round into the bungalow's front door and taking it down with a smoky crash. The windows blew out simultaneously, the concussion slamming glass and splintered frames from their mountings, spewing shards across the scruffy turf.

Two of the gunners came back a heartbeat later, firing wide of the mark as they tried to recover their bearings. Bolan had no way of knowing whether the third man was dead or alive, much less how many others remained inside. He took advantage of their momentary disorientation, hosing the shattered windows with precision bursts, reloading the M-203 as he closed the killing gap.

At twenty yards, he put the next HE can through the window on his left, saw a human silhouette duck back and downward from the line of fire, and then a second blast ripped through the bungalow. One of the plywood walls buckled this time, streaming flames behind it, and he glimpsed a blackened figure dancing in the middle of the fire.

Bolan plucked a hand grenade from his combat harness, jerked the safety pin and pitched it through the other window, finishing whoever might be left alive in the front-room inferno. He was contemplating entry angles to the side and rear when peripheral movement captured his attention, three men breaking from behind the bungalows and springing for the nearby motor pool.

He didn't recognize the young men running point and tail guard, but the senior citizen between them was Hans Erdmann, laboring to keep pace with his escorts. They were better than halfway to the vehicles, running for all they were worth, and Bolan made a quick check of his flank, recoiling from the vision of a Nazi picket line advancing, firing from the hip.

Priorities. If he was dead, he stood no chance of halting Erdmann's getaway. And if the old man wriggled from the trap while Bolan was pinned down...

He went to the ground behind the one undamaged bungalow, reloading the grenade launcher and assault rifle with swift, practiced movements. He had the shooters spotted in his mind, aware that they could shift positions radically while he was out of sight, but there was nothing else to go on.

Now or never.

Bolan came around the corner digging with his knees and elbows, sighting from a prone position, hearing bullets swarm a yard above his head. He fired the launcher first, toward center field, and swiveled hard to his right before the HE round exploded in the middle of the hostile skirmish line. Flash and thunder blossomed in the corner of his eye, as Bolan stroked the rifle's trigger, short bursts rippling from the weapon, dropping first one uniform and then another.

Two on Bolan's left almost got lucky, sighting on his muzzle-flashes in the shadows, but they also had the terminal jitters, wishing they were anywhere else at the moment.

Too late.

He dropped the Nazis thrashing in a stew of dust and blood, dismissed them from his thoughts in the assurance that the two of them had seconds left to live. No other opposition was visible, and Bolan rose, reloading, turning toward the motor pool.

Erdmann's dusty black sedan was rolling, backing out, the driver doubtless cursing his attempt to save time nosing in. Still, they were moving, and for all he knew the black Mercedes was a tank. He might have lost his chance already.

The Executioner moved out to meet them, pacing off the open ground, planting himself between the covered motor pool and the narrow dirt track of the access road. It was an all-or-nothing gamble, and he braced himself for one roll of the dice that would decide the present game.

Behind the tinted windshield, Erdmann's driver had him spotted, bearing down on the accelerator, still in four-wheel drive and spewing plumes of dust to prove it.

Bolan brought the rifle to his shoulder, calculating odds and angles. If the Mercedes was armored, he could waste his one best shot trying to pierce the grille or hood. If the car was equipped with run-flat tires, the M-16's whole magazine would still not be enough to stop the car from rolling past him, over him, to get away.

That left the driver, theoretically secure behind the screen of extrathick glass, and while Bolan might not reach him with the 5.56 mm tumblers, he still had the launcher. That might not be enough for a clean kill, but it was worth a shot.

He took that shot at twenty yards, the HE can dead on-target, detonating virtually in the driver's face. It didn't penetrate the windshield, even so, but it was close enough, the blast and shrapnel blinding Erdmann's wheelman, leaving the windscreen opaque with thousands of interwoven cracks.

Instinctively the driver veered off course, still accelerating, the vehicle going over in a slow barrel roll. The car didn't have enough momentum for a true, destructive crash, but it got the job done, a three-quarters roll that left it lying on the driver's side, the undercarriage facing toward Bolan.

A last round from the M-203 launcher did the trick, ignition sparking from the fuel line, bright flames running the length of the undercarriage in seconds flat. The gas tank was armored, forcing the blast upward and inward when it came, gutting the vehicle's interior in a firestorm that was no respecter of persons.

Bolan scanned the compound, seeking other targets, finding none. His job was finished for the moment, and he turned away, returning to the forest and skirting the compound, working his way back to the game trail that would take him back to his car.

Another round in the Executioner's favor, but the match point was still up for grabs. He would have to keep the heat on, press his enemies until they reached the breaking point and lost it, going down in flames.

9

The Zurich airport is actually located in suburban Kloten, seven miles north of the central city. It is the headquarters for Swissair, the Swiss national airline, and one of the top-ten busiest airports in Europe. Terminal A receives passengers arriving from Germany, and it was here that Yakov Katzenelenbogen gathered his troops, with two extra faces in addition to the usual four.

They had employed a charter flight to beat German airport security, but even then a helpful word from GSG-9 had been required to get their hardware on board. No one inspected the incoming baggage at Zurich, but Katz knew they would have to leave their weapons behind when they left the country, lacking official Swiss contacts to help with the exit.

In any case, that was a problem for later. Katz didn't know which—if any—of them would be fit to travel when the smoke cleared, much less where they would be going. It was possible that they could wrap their mission here, but he wasn't about to celebrate a mental victory before the fight was even under way.

Meanwhile, there were details to negotiate and trails to follow, final strategy to be arranged. He hoped the new and larger team could hold itself together in the crunch and function well on unfamiliar ground.

Rudolf Wetzel seemed a trifle uneasy away from his home turf, but Uri Dan took the change of scene in stride, more accustomed to stalking his country's enemies on a global scale. Katz sent Manning and McCarter off to finalize arrangements for their rental cars. They were booked into the Chesa Rustica hotel, on Limmatquai, in the central city.

Four rooms for the seven of them, to avoid comment and speculation, with Katz lodging alone.

Not that any of them planned on spending much time in their rooms.

There was a battle to be fought in Zurich, possibly the last lap of their trek from Jordan to the Alps.

Intelligence from Stony Man had placed their German rabbits at the Hotel Schweizerhof, on Bahnhofstrasse, near the main railroad station. Their Arab contacts, traveling on diplomatic passports, were lodged at the five-star Baur au Lac, on Talstrasse, fronting Lake Zurich. They were two travelers from Jordan, on the face of it, and Katz ignored the names of their passports, assuming that any merchants of terror would be wise enough to cover their tracks on paper.

The hotels were a starting point, and nothing more. Katz didn't suppose for a moment that his chosen targets would conduct their clandestine business in such public surroundings. None of them were safe at home today. They couldn't guarantee security in the most lavish of hotels, fabled Swiss neutrality notwithstanding. Anyone could bug a hotel room or tap the telephones, plant fiber-optic cameras in the heating registers or furnishings.

They would be branching out, in search of someplace more discreet, which meant that Katz and his commandos had to watch all four, plus any lackeys in their entourage, until the final meet had been arranged.

How long?

There would be urgency, with the events from Germany still fresh in mind, new problems to solve, enemies to be identified and speedily eradicated. They were starting out from scratch, presumably without a solid clue to work from, and that was a point in Katzenelenbogen's favor.

Manning and McCarter came back with the car keys, led the way to the parking lot where the rental companies kept their vehicles in numbered slots. They had a pair of Volvo four-door sedans, one navy blue, one gray. They parceled out the hardware and chose their seats, four traveling in one car, three in the other. Courtesy maps from the rental desk

NO RISK, NO OBLIGATION TO BUY ... NOW OR EVER!

CASINO JUBILEE
"Scratch'n Match" Game

Here's how to play:

1. Peel off label from front cover. Place it in space provided at right. With a coin, carefully scratch off the silver box. Then check the claim chart to see what we have for you—ALL YOURS! ALL FREE!

2. Send back this card and you'll get hot-off-the-press Gold Eagle books, never before published. These books have a total cover price of $16.98. But THEY ARE TOTALLY FREE; even the shipping will be at our expense!

3. There's no catch. You're under no obligation to buy anything! We charge nothing—ZERO—for your first shipment. And you don't have to make any minimum number of purchases—not even one!

4. The fact is thousands of readers enjoy receiving books by mail from the Gold Eagle Reader Service. They like the convenience of home delivery . . . they like getting the best new novels before they're available in bookstores . . . and they love our discount prices!

5. We hope that after receiving your free books you'll want to remain a subscriber. But the choice is yours—to continue or cancel, any time at all! So why not take us up on our invitation, with no risk of any kind. You'll be glad you did!

FREE SURPRISE MYSTERY GIFT COULD BE YOURS FREE -- PLAY CASINO JUBILEE!

CASINO JUBILEE
"Scratch'n Match" Game

SCRATCH HERE

PLACE LABEL HERE

?

CHECK CLAIM CHART BELOW FOR YOUR FREE GIFTS!

YES! I have placed my label from the front cover in the space provided above and scratched off the silver box. Please send me all the gifts for which I qualify. I understand that I am under no obligation to purchase any books, as explained on the back and on the opposite page.

164 CIM AQMV (U-M-B-07/94)

Name _____

Address _____ Apt. _____

City _____ State _____ Zip _____

CASINO JUBILEE CLAIM CHART

🍒🍒 🍒🍒 🍒🍒		WORTH 4 FREE BOOKS, PLUS FREE MYSTERY BONUS GIFT	
🍒🍒 🔔 🍒🍒		WORTH 3 FREE BOOKS	
🔔 🔔 🍒🍒		WORTH 2 FREE BOOKS	CLAIM N° 1528

Offer limited to one per household and not valid to present subscribers.
All orders subject to approval.

THE GOLD EAGLE READER SERVICE: HERE'S HOW IT WORKS

Accepting free books places you under no obligation to buy anything. You may keep the books and gift and return the shipping statement marked "cancel". If you do not cancel, about a month later we will send you four additional novels and bill you just $14.80*—that's a saving of 12% off the cover price of all four books! And there's no extra charge for shipping! You may cancel at any time, but if you choose to continue, then every other month we'll send you four more books, which you may either purchase at the discount price. . .or return at our expense and cancel your subscription.

*Terms and prices subject to change without notice. Sales tax applicable in N.Y.

BUSINESS REPLY MAIL

FIRST CLASS MAIL   PERMIT NO. 717   BUFFALO, NY

POSTAGE WILL BE PAID BY ADDRESSEE

GOLD EAGLE READER SERVICE
3010 WALDEN AVE
PO BOX 1867
BUFFALO NY 14240-9952

NO POSTAGE
NECESSARY
IF MAILED
IN THE
UNITED STATES

showed them how to find the Chesa Rustica, along with every other point of interest in a ten-mile radius.

"We check in, drop the bags," Katz told them, standing in the parking lot, "and then we get to work. They have a lead already, and we're playing catch-up. Anything we get from this point on, we'll have to work for."

And so it began.

TARIM SUDAIR FELT NOTHING but contempt for the Western democracies, overrun as they were with sex, crime and general decadence. It was a testimony to the Jewish influence, he supposed, a corruption of the moral fabric that had once produced Crusaders, a Napoleon, an Alexander the Great. None of them compared to Arab warriors, in the last analysis, but they were still a far cry from the simpering eunuchs who postured as "strongmen" today.

It would be a pleasure for Sudair to see their pustulent societies swept away, perhaps plagued by the same kind of internecine warfare that had torn Yugoslavia apart in the wake of Soviet Russia's disintegration. Let every major European city from London to Warsaw and Budapest be savaged like Beirut, with bodies rotting in the street, white bodies, sacrificed on the altar of an Islamic jihad.

First, though, Sudair had to repair his own connections and defenses, protect his own flanks. Little or nothing had gone according to plan in the past two weeks, and now their German outposts lay in ruins, everything Sudair had worked for, over months and years, destroyed by total strangers in the space of days. He felt the rage pent up inside him, but Sudair valued self-discipline over all other personal traits. A man without self-discipline was nothing, prey to every whim and foible as he wandered down the aimless tracks of life.

The Germans possessed discipline—some of them, at any rate—but he hadn't been impressed with their performance in recent days. Where was the stereotypical clockwork efficiency, the blood of ice and nerves of steel? Today's "Aryan" warriors talked a good battle, but Sudair couldn't picture any of them standing fast in the snow before

Stalingrad's gates. It remained to be seen whether they possessed the necessary strength of will to save themselves, but
if they failed—and that was still a possibility—Sudair didn't
intend to go down with the ship.

The Zurich meeting was designed to help him find out
how much of their European plan could still be salvaged. He
had written off the Aryan Resistance Movement in America, scanning late intelligence reports with a scowl of dis-
gust on his face, reading of mass arrests, indictments that
would put the so-called soldiers of the master race away for
years to come.

The South American connection still had promise, but he
was aware of troubles brewing there, as well. He didn't
know the full extent of violence in Bolivia, but his allies
there were better organized, more deeply entrenched than
Justin Pratt's toy soldiers in the States. If, as Sudair feared,
the mayhem around La Paz was an extension of the slaughter in Los Angeles, Hans Erdmann and his drug-dealing
cronies would hold the line. They had years of experience in
killing off their competition, making bodies disappear
without a trace. To be sure, they weren't on a par with Islamic warriors of the holy quest, but they would do in what
the Americans called a crunch.

Arranging details of the meeting had required some
thought. Sudair didn't trust the most expensive of Western
hotels, with their snooping maids and house detectives, so
many places to hide a miniature camera or listening device.
Even with his personal security entourage, he couldn't be
sure that his suite had been properly swept for taps and
bugs.

No, they would have to meet somewhere else, in a place
of Sudair's choosing, arranged in advance but without
enough warning for his enemies to mount a major counter-
intelligence operation. Zurich proper was hopeless, but he
had arranged for the lease of a villa at Bremgarten, several
kilometers south, overlooking the Reuss River. Rolling,
wooded grounds behind an eight-foot wall of stone would
provide plenty of concealment for his security agents,

countless obstacles to defeat eavesdropping with long-range directional microphones.

On balance, Tarim Sudair would have preferred to hold the conference in his own country, even in Iraq, but the Germans couldn't afford that kind of exposure at the moment.

Zurich would do in the crunch, he was sure of it. His enemies were busy tearing up the landscape in Berlin, and they would never miss two men among the hundreds of pathetic would-be Hitlers readily available for slaughter.

They were coming out of a dark tunnel, and Sudair had seen his first glimpse of the light.

To him, it looked like a righteous, cleansing flame.

RUDOLF WETZEL was waiting when Gerhard Kasche emerged from the Hotel Schweizerhof, turning north on Bahnhofstrasse toward the central railroad station. Kasche didn't hail a taxi, preferring to cover the three blocks on foot. He took no special precautions, only once checking his trail by the clumsy maneuver of stopping short of a store's display window, casting furtive glances back in the direction from which he had come.

Wetzel made no effort to conceal himself or look too casual, the classic errors perpetrated by surveillance amateurs. He continued walking north in an assertive manner, even met Kasche's gaze for a moment, letting his eyes slide away with a show of total indifference. The two of them had never met, and there was no good reason for the Nazi to suspect one man among the dozens of pedestrians who clogged the Bahnhofstrasse sidewalk.

Simple.

Wetzel actually led Kasche for half a block, but the Nazi soon caught up in his urgency to be about his business. There were no more checks from that point on, a straight run to the depot, where he made his way inside. Wetzel followed at a discreet distance, mingling with the general ebb and flow of travelers and well-wishers, losing himself in the crowd. He tracked Kasche from a distance, following more with his eyes than his feet, moving only when it seemed that the National Vanguard's leader was about to drop from sight.

In such fashion they traversed the great room of the station, making their way into Shopville, a pedestrian concourse of widely varied retail shops situated in the central square, watched over by a statue of Swiss statesman Alfred Escher.

Kasche seemed to dawdle here without direction, first window-shopping, then ducking inside this or that boutique to briefly examine a piece of merchandise. He purchased nothing, passed no conversation worthy of the name with any sales clerk.

Wetzel sensed that Kasche was waiting for a contact, which, in turn, meant Wetzel had to wait, as well.

No choice.

For all of Wetzel's alertness, the Arab seemed to come from nowhere. One moment, Kasche was standing alone at the entrance of a shop that specialized in high-priced climbing gear; the next, he had a shadow, short and swarthy, with a thick mustache and dark hair slicked back from a ferret face. It was the sort of countenance one saw on wanted posters, advertising a reward for information on the whereabouts of Arab terrorists in Europe.

He could have missed the whole exchange by blinking, bending to tie his shoelaces, almost anything at all. The Arab muttered something from the corner of his mouth, pretending all the while to scrutinize a bright display of climber's axes. Six or seven words, no more, and Wetzel cursed his inability to read the bastard's lips.

His business done, the Arab moved away without a backward glance, almost brushing shoulders with Wetzel as he passed. The GSG-9 agent felt a sudden urge to trail the stranger, but Kasche was his assignment, and he couldn't leave the job half-done. A message had been passed, but Kasche didn't pursue the Arab, seeming to take no interest whatsoever in the path of his departure.

Very well.

Wetzel stuck to his assignment and shadowed Kasche along the central aisle of Shopville, falling in behind him as the Nazi doubled back and left the station. He walked south on Bahnhofstrasse, back to his hotel.

Upstairs, the message would be shared with Josef Buhler, but they had no ears inside the suite. Whatever passed between the ranking Nazis would remain unknown to Wetzel and his friends, at least until their targets made another move.

And it was coming, Wetzel knew. Kasche and Buhler wouldn't tarry long in Zurich, no more than a day or two, at most. They would be missed in Germany before much longer—by police, in Kasche's case, and by his followers in Buhler's. As well, it wouldn't be easy for the Arabs to remain at large in such a city, covering their tracks.

He found a public telephone outside the Hotel Schweizerhof and dialed the number of Katzenelenbogen's room at the Chesa Rustica. Wetzel's report was terse and succinct, devoid of irrelevant details and idle speculation. His instructions were explicit.

Watch and wait.

He only hoped he wouldn't have to wait too long.

JOSEF BUHLER HAD his shoes off, stockinged feet propped up on a stylish coffee table, when Gerhard Kasche returned to their suite at the Hotel Schweizerhof. The National Vanguard leader seemed breathless, his face flushed, as if he had run all the way back from the railroad station.

"What is it?" Buhler asked, afraid that someone had pursued Kasche, blown their cover at the very start, before they ever set eyes on their contacts.

"I was met on schedule," Kasche informed him, moving toward the minibar to pour himself some schnapps. "An Arab, no one special."

"Were you seen?"

Kasche made a sour face around his liquor glass. "The place was full of tourists," he replied. "No one appeared to notice us."

"You were alert?"

"Of course." The Vanguard leader seemed to be insulted, but it didn't keep him from the schnapps. "I know my business, Josef."

"Very well. What of the meeting?"

"A villa near Bremgarten, south of the city. I have the directions. They expect us at nightfall, no later than nine o'clock."

"Transportation?" Buhler asked.

"We take the hired car," Kasche replied. "They have security in hand, I'm told."

"I hope so, Gerhard."

"Have no fear. I will drive. The rest is all arranged. We are safe here, I think. Have no fear," he repeated.

And that was the problem, Buhler realized. He *was* afraid. The last few days at home in Germany had been a nightmare. Buhler was a man of politics, albeit in extremis. His war against the Jews and foreign trash was fought with words, but lately Buhler had been forced to deal with a rather different reality, blood and bullets in the streets of his native Berlin, driving Buhler from his home and family.

The wife and children were secure, at least. Before he left Berlin, Buhler had made arrangements for them to evacuate the city. He believed they were beyond the reach of his unknown enemies, and Buhler hoped the same was true for himself.

If not...

The cause had always been an abstract thing to Buhler, something he could fight for at the ballot box and public rallies, never quite believing that the day of fire and judgment would arrive. If and when the party came to power, a problematic question in itself, he somehow thought the Jews and other worthless races would be wise enough to move away. Before the storm, this time, with history to urge them on. He didn't visualize another Holocaust, although, in abstract terms, he was accustomed to discussing sacrifices for the movement.

Now, it seemed he might become one, and the prospect chilled him to the bone.

The meeting with their Arab allies might provide some reassurance, though he wasn't sure precisely how. He was embarrassed, for a start, by the violence he had left behind him in Berlin. It spoke ill of his personal ability to control situations—even his own troops—when unknown enemies were running wild in the streets, assaulting his comrades at random.

The Arabs admired strong men who dealt from positions of power...and what would they think of him now? Buhler anticipated a certain loss of respect, perhaps camouflaged behind extraordinary courtesy as the camel jockeys were wont to do. He would have to persuade the Arabs of his ability to put things right, salvage anything possible from the ruins he had left in Germany.

It would be difficult, but not impossible. His background as a politician would be useful here, the knack he had developed for telling different constituents what they wanted to hear, stroking their egos and playing to their innermost fears. To be sure, it was easier in the fatherland, where he shared a common background with his followers, but almost anyone could be persuaded or seduced with proper effort.

Buhler already shared a common cause with the Arabs, and that was a point in his favor. Likewise, it would be expensive, perhaps impossible, for them to recruit new European allies at this stage of the game.

He would strive to remain optimistic, in spite of the odds, and see what would come of the game.

The German only hoped it wasn't already too late.

URI DAN PICKED UP his target as he left the Baur au Lac hotel on Talstrasse, fronting the lake. The Israeli agent had procured a taxi for the day, leaving the two rented cars to his comrades, and the driver seemed relaxed, undismayed by a situation that smacked of Hollywood. They had been waiting for the best part of an hour when the Arab showed himself, tipped the Baur au Lac's valet and climbed behind the steering wheel of a Hertz sedan.

He recognized the driver from his periodic study of terrorist mug shots at Mossad headquarters in Tel Aviv. Shiraz Najaf was an Iraqi government official attached in theory to the national defense apparatus, in reality assigned as a liaison officer with terrorists abroad. Dan had read the Arab's file; he was aware of links with the PLO and various terrorist cliques throughout Europe and Asia. Shiraz Najaf had been linked to covert arms shipments and the financing of terrorist actions from Spain to Sri Lanka. Uri Dan wasn't especially surprised to see him here, prepared to deal with German neo-Nazis as comrades in arms.

The common thread was an abiding hatred for Israel and her allies, chiefly Britain and America.

"Follow that car."

The taxi driver complied without question or complaint, falling in behind the sedan and rolling south, leaving Zurich behind them and rolling toward Bremgarten. The idyllic rural setting might have lulled Dan into something like complacency, but he had seen too much in years of battling Arab terrorists to let a peaceful landscape distract him from the job at hand.

Ahead of them, the sedan showed brake lights, slowing for a right-hand turn into a driveway flanked by ivy-draped stone columns. The vehicle was out of sight by the time Dan's taxi reached the driveway. Leaning forward in the back seat, he tapped the driver on his shoulder.

"What is this?" he asked.

"All villas here," the cabbie said. "Some of them summer homes for businessmen from Zurich and Lucerne, the rest available for rent to visitors. We follow him inside?"

"Not this time. I need to find a telephone."

"There is an inn not far from here," the driver told him, pointing toward the next curve in the road.

"Let's go," the man from Tel Aviv replied. "I haven't got much time."

KATZENELENBOGEN TOOK the call in his suite at the Chesa Rustica, memorizing the directions Uri Dan provided. Thirty seconds saw it done, and he replaced the telephone receiver in its cradle, turning back toward Calvin James and Rafael Encizo. As the most conspicuous members of Phoenix Force, they had remained at the hotel with Katz, while the others fanned out to shadow their targets around Zurich.

"That was Uri," he informed them. "He's at Bremgarten, a few klicks south of town. One of the Arabs pulled into a villa off the highway, probably a rental. Uri thinks he's found the meeting place."

"And you?" James asked.

"We'll have to wait and see."

"It suits me if they take the meeting out of town. Cut down on rubberneckers in the line of fire."

"He recognized the subject," Katzenelenbogen said.

"Which one?" The question came from Encizo.

"The Iraqi. One Shiraz Najaf. According to Uri, he coordinates traffic between Baghdad and outside terrorist groups."

"Like the Vanguard, for instance?"

"You got it in one," Katz responded.

"That fits, then," James said.

"So far."

"And Buhler met an Arab at the railroad station," Encizo added.

"In passing, right. My guess would be he picked up the directions to their meeting place."

"We'll have it covered when he makes his move."

"Bremgarten?"

"It's a decent bet. Whichever way it goes, we'll be on top of them."

"How many hardmen was it?" Encizo inquired.

"Four Jordanians from the embassy," Katz replied, "plus three more off the flight from Amman. That's on top of our targets. Nine Arabs, the two from Berlin, plus their driver. A dozen, for sure."

"If they've rented a villa, I'd figure on housemen," James said, "some kind of advance team. The Germans would fit in real well, hereabouts."

"And it would keep the Vanguard delegates from feeling like the deck was stacked," Katz said.

"How many, would you think?" Encizo asked.

"No way to tell, without a recon on the site," James answered. "We could get a rude surprise."

"That cuts both ways," the Cuban stated.

"We don't have any choice," Katz told them.

"No choice at all," James agreed.

"Looks like we'll have to kick some ass," the Cuban warrior beamed.

"And try to keep from getting ours kicked, in the process," Katz put in.

"I'd like to have a look around that villa," James said. "Check out the grounds, count heads, whatever."

"That's a problem," Katzenelenbogen replied. "There's only one way in and out, apparently. If it turns out to be the meeting site, I'd look for sentries posted all around the grounds."

"I had a little something else in mind."

"Such as?"

"We're killing time here, Rafael and me. Suppose we make like tourists for a while and see what we can see?"

"I'm listening."

"They've got these helicopter flights each hour on the hour," James told him. "See the mountains, see the lake, whatever."

"See the villa?" Katz suggested, smiling.

"If you tip the pilot something on the side, I wouldn't be surprised."

"We're talking wooded grounds."

James shrugged. "It's worth a shot, at least. Poor visibility beats flying blind, you know?"

"No argument," Katz said. "What kind of reservations do you need?"

"Fact is, they're made." James flashed a winning smile. "We leave inside the next five minutes, we should just about get there on time."

"Go plan," Katz told his men.

10

Colonel Hector Rivera was suspicious of the German facing him across his desk. He was a younger man than Erdmann, certainly, but with the same flint in his eyes, a frown that seemed to be the Nazis' favorite expression. Dannecker was next in line, with Erdmann gone, but he would take some getting used to... if they had the time.

"I tried to tell Hans he was safer in La Paz," Rivera said, "but he insisted on retreating to the mountains. There was nothing I could do to help him in the circumstances. If his own men failed..."

"What's done is done," Dannecker stated. "I'm interested in what happens next."

A cool customer, Rivera thought to himself. Ice-cold, in fact. If Dannecker felt any grief for his departed comrade and commander, he managed to hide it well. Rivera supposed it would violate the tenets of the so-called master race to weep or show emotion in the face of violent death. Behind the slate-gray eyes, Dannecker's mind was ticking over like a precision timepiece.

"We are making every effort to discover those responsible," Rivera said. "So far, unfortunately, there is little to assist us."

"Little?"

"Nothing."

"The young American believed his enemies had followed him from the United States," Dannecker said. "Have you pursued that possibility?"

It galled Rivera, sitting in his office while a civilian demanded explanations of his official actions. A civilian and a foreigner, at that. It mattered not to him that Dannecker was born in Bolivia; he would always be a German, by his own definition, and Rivera secretly resented his presumption in attempting to meddle in questions of state security. Still, it would be counterproductive for Rivera to spark a debate at this point in time, making powerful new enemies for himself in the process.

"What should I pursue?" Rivera asked, keeping his voice as calm as possible. "The young man never had a chance to tell me any details of his plight. Señor Erdmann could have enlightened me, perhaps, but he was busy leaving town, and now..." Rivera spread his open hands, a helpless gesture, waiting for Dannecker to comment.

"You have the capability of learning who has come into the country in the past few days."

"Of course, if they arrived on scheduled airlines. Over three days' time, two thousand seven hundred Americans and Western Europeans flew into La Paz. It will require some time to check them all, confirm their travel documents and stated destinations. In the meantime, if our adversaries found another way across the border, I can only speculate as to their whereabouts."

"That sounds like a confession of inadequacy, Colonel."

Rivera stiffened, biting off the first retort that came to mind. He could have reached across the desk and throttled Dannecker, or punched a button on his intercom and summoned soldiers with their clubs and pistols to administer a beating—but at what cost to himself?

It was a fact of life that German immigrants held a substantial share of power in Bolivia. Investments dating from the 1930s had grown over time, with interest compounded in the form of cunning political donations and practical contributions to the state: schooling military officers and leaders of the secret police, arranging foreign loans and capital investments, sage advice on technical solutions to the Indian problem—it all added up. Throw in the millions earned from their association with the major narcodealers, and you had a power base to reckon with.

And the last thing Rivera needed at the moment was a new war in the making with his allies.

"I would welcome your suggestions for improvement," the colonel said stiffly.

"Your informers are reportedly omniscient," Dannecker replied. "They must know something."

"One of them reported contact with an agent of the Yankee DEA," Rivera said. "A trap was set. Unfortunately something went awry. My contact lost his life. The target managed to escape."

"Another failure, then."

"We have the agent's name and his description," Rivera said. "We are searching for him even now."

"With what result?"

"So far—"

"He has eluded you," the German said, sneering.

"It is impossible for my men to be everywhere at once."

"Perhaps we need more men," Dannecker suggested.

"Pardon?"

"I feel the need for reinforcements, Colonel. I assume you would have no objection if I called in certain special friends?"

"From Germany?"

Dannecker smiled vaguely, rising from his chair with a kind of serpentine grace. "I will keep you informed of any developments."

"A wise decision."

"We aim to please," the Nazi told him as he left the room.

And something told Rivera that the hours ahead would hold small cause for comfort, much less pleasure.

Rivera thought he would be lucky if he managed to survive.

ERNIE GALLARDO was waiting when Bolan pulled into the restaurant parking lot. He stepped out of the space between a semitrailer and a garbage bin. He wore a floppy trench coat in spite of the evening's lingering warmth, and the muzzle of a riot shotgun poked out from under the coat as he slid into the passenger's seat of Bolan's car.

"I was afraid you wouldn't make it," Gallardo said.

"Here I am."

"The bastards nearly had me, man. I had some feelers out, you know? Street people, this and that. My contact set me up, or someone squeezed him, I don't know. He bought it, either way. I had to ditch my car and bag another one. They're breathing down my neck."

"Who's 'they'?"

"The shooters looked Hispanic," Gallardo said. "We could check a couple of them at the local morgue."

"You ought to think about a change of scene," the Executioner replied.

"And let you have all the fun? No thanks."

"We're rid of Erdmann, anyway."

"You found him, then."

"His mountain place, just like you said."

"That must have been some rumble."

"It was touch and go," Bolan replied, "but I nailed it down."

"He was the one you wanted, right?" Gallardo sounded edgy now. "Does this mean you're finished?"

Bolan shook his head. "Not even close. Erdmann was a part of it, but he's replaceable. Unless I miss my guess, they'll have somebody standing in his place before the day is out. I want his contacts, too—Rivera, Gomez, right on down the line."

"You're biting off a lot," Gallardo said.

"You mean we are."

"Oh, yeah?"

"Unless you're hanging in around La Paz to watch it from the sidelines."

"The hell with that," the man from DEA replied. "Just tell me when and where."

"I want to keep them guessing," Bolan said. "If they're off balance, we come out ahead."

"Sounds like you've got a plan."

"I'm getting there."

In fact, the first steps of his plan were already complete, two of his primary targets laid to rest. It wasn't over yet, by any means, but he had come this far without a hitch. He still had far to go, with many possibilities for failure, but the general course was clear.

He had identified his enemies and rattled them enough to send them scurrying for cover. Justin Pratt and Erdmann were dead, Bernardo Gomez wounded and hiding in fear of his life. Hector Rivera had his agents working the streets of La Paz, but they had already lost Gallardo twice, and that would be enough to shake the colonel's confidence.

Perhaps, with any luck, enough to breed mistakes.

The victory wasn't assured, by any means, but Bolan had a fair start on the game. If he could keep his adversaries reeling, perhaps even turn them against one another, he would be points ahead.

A close game, any way you played it, but he had a fighting chance. No more than that, perhaps, but it was something.

IT WAS A STROKE OF LUCK, Karl Dannecker thought, that one of the sentries at Erdmann's camp had survived. Otherwise, it might have been days before Dannecker found out that Erdmann was dead, Arnold Brunner and the others with him. It was bad enough losing his mentor by violence, that loss compounded by the ignorance of so-called allies, without having the grim news delayed.

And yet, Dannecker decided, the news wasn't all bad. Granted, they had lost too many men without a clue to the identity of their assailants, but Dannecker still had a chance to profit from the experience. He stood in Erdmann's place today, his elevation arranged months earlier, when the Bolivian führer still thought he might live forever.

Times change.

It was a new game now, and Dannecker was confident that he could win it. But he also knew that confidence wasn't enough. It would require intelligence and strength, the latter quality involving more than one man's private fortitude. The recent mayhem, climaxed by the deadly raid on Erdmann's mountain hideaway, had cost the movement dearly in terms of manpower. They weren't ruined yet, by any means, but a few more such episodes would leave Dannecker to hold the fort with a handful of elderly men whose last great military effort lay a half century behind them.

What Karl Dannecker needed most at the moment were reinforcements he could trust, men who were loyal to the cause and skilled at their craft, ready to obey his orders without questions or hesitation. Soldiers of the Reich.

And he knew where to find them.

The transatlantic calls took fifteen minutes of his time. He tried Berlin first, Kasche's private number, and was told of Gerhard's sudden trip to Zurich. No one in Berlin could process his request without Kasche's approval, and so he had placed his second call to the Hotel Schweizerhof, in Zurich. Josef Buhler answered the phone, and they exchanged vague pleasantries before Kasche came on the line.

"Good day, Karl. How did you find me here?"

"I got the number from Berlin. We need to talk."

"I'm here on urgent business. There have been . . . difficulties in Berlin."

"And here, as well," Dannecker replied. "Hans is dead, Gerhard."

There was a moment of stunned silence, Kasche collecting his wits before he spoke again. "How can this be?" he asked at last.

"The same way that it happened to our comrades in America, and to your own men in Berlin. Our enemies are everywhere."

"So it would seem. The Jews?"

Instead of answering, Dannecker said, "I need your help."

"In what respect?" There was a cautious note in Kasche's voice.

"With reinforcements, Gerhard."

"Ah." Another moment's hesitation. "We were under attack as of yesterday, Karl. How can I spare—"

"If we fail here," Dannecker said, "everything comes down to you. Your loss, Gerhard. No more link to the old guard, no more merchandise from La Paz. Your American investments are already going or gone. How much can you afford to lose?''

Kasche thought about it for a moment, postponing the inevitable, clearly hooked. Dannecker heard the musical clink of ice cubes and pictured Gerhard sipping whiskey, trying to calm his nerves.

"I can spare fifteen men."

"I need twenty, at least."

"Karl—"

"At least." There was steel in his voice, the satisfaction of dealing from strength. Berlin might be the fatherland, but today German patriots were hamstrung by Jew-sponsored laws, heavily dependent on support from their kinsmen abroad.

"Twenty, then. I will speak to Berlin. With luck, they can leave—"

"Tonight," Dannecker finished for him. "I need them here by noon at the latest."

"I'll see what I can do."

"I know you will. Thank you, Gerhard."

He broke the connection before Kasche had the chance to speak again, raise some new objection and talk himself out of providing the troops.

No fear of that.

Dannecker knew how much the National Vanguard depended on its link to the German old guard for legitimacy in the realm of racial politics. Without that bond to the holy Third Reich, the spiritual root of their movement, Kasche's skinheads were no more than street toughs playing Nazi in their spare time. Dannecker had the power to shift support to some other faction—the Spear of Destiny, for instance, or the Aryan Sons of Valhalla—and he could cut off the flow of cocaine that enabled Kasche to arm his troops with the latest in black-market military hardware.

All unnecessary, now.

Kasche would provide the troops he needed, and Dannecker would take it from there. He had been waiting for a chance to prove himself, and now he had it. Even starting at a disadvantage, he would still prevail.

It was his destiny.

THE SINALOA Trucking Company occupied a corner lot on Calle Estrada, in the northeast quadrant of La Paz. In theory, the company was owned by a consortium of local investors, its drivers employed hauling produce from outlying farms and moving residential furniture. In fact, Bernardo Gomez owned the firm in its entirety; the only produce carried by the Sinaloa Trucking fleet was coca base en route to covert labs, or finished product bound for market.

Bolan made the drive-by with Gallardo riding shotgun, counted eight trucks in the parking lot and saw lights burning in a room behind the office proper.

"Night crew," Gallardo announced. "They work all hours hauling flake, you know?"

"They're going out of business."

Gallardo grinned. "I'll drink to that."

They parked downrange and walked back to the corner lot. The gate was chained and padlocked, short work for bolt cutters, and they made their way inside. It was thirty yards to the office past dark, silent trucks, Bolan scanning for lookouts and packing an Uzi, while Gallardo brought up the rear with his 12-gauge shotgun.

He had no idea how many men were waiting for them in the office, but it made no difference now. They were committed, no turning back. One man or a dozen, Bolan meant to follow through.

He took the concrete steps three at a time, his rubber-soled shoes muffling the sound of his progress. The knob turned at his touch, their targets confident enough to think that they were safe behind the chain-link fence with loops of razor wire on top.

It was a common error and a fatal one.

They followed voices down a short, dark corridor that connected with a storage room. Four men were seated at a folding table, playing cards, while number five was off to

Bolan's right, a short guy pouring coffee into a ceramic mug.

The night crew.

Bolan had them covered with his Uzi when he spoke. "Knock, knock."

They could have suffered whiplash, five heads swiveling to face him in a heartbeat, their eyes wide with shock, several mouths hanging open. Taken absolutely by surprise, they needed something like a second and a half to snap the spell—and then, all hell broke loose.

The four men at the table scattered, leaping off in different directions like explosive shrapnel, the guy with the coffee dropping to a crouch and fumbling underneath the loose tail of his shirt. The Executioner saw guns in holsters, shotguns and an automatic rifle propped against the wall, and knew that he could lose it here, unless he kept his wits about him.

He started on his right, with Mr. Coffee and the nickel-plated automatic in his hand. The guy was shaky on his feet, but he was first to reach his hardware, while the others were still scrambling for their guns or seeking cover. Even scared to death, the guy was lining up his shot, the autoloader rising in a two-handed grip.

Bolan stroked the Uzi's trigger, drilled three rounds into the gunner's chest and slammed him back against the counter, toppling the coffeepot to shatter at his feet. Gallardo's shotgun roared behind him, answered by a bleat of pain, the thump of deadweight landing on the floor.

The Executioner tracked on, still firing from the hip, and he caught number two in midair, pudgy arms outstretched to reach an AK-47 standing in the corner, hopelessly beyond the gunner's reach. A stream of parabellum manglers stitched the warrior's target from the armpit to the hip and punched him through an awkward barrel roll. He wound up on his back in the middle of the floor, immobile.

Gallardo fired again, and Bolan saw his target vaulted backward by the impact of a short-range buckshot charge. The gunner touched down on his shoulders, wobbled through a clumsy somersault and collapsed on his face.

That left one, the shooter on his knees, a snub-nosed revolver sprouting from his fist. His first shot burned past Bolan's ear, six inches off the mark, and there would never be a second. The Executioner's Uzi stuttered, spitting half a dozen rounds from fifteen feet, exploding crimson from the target's chest. Gallardo's final shotgun blast came in a heartbeat later, snuffing out whatever spark of life remained.

"Okay, let's get the trucks," Bolan said, backing toward the door as he prepared to leave the dead behind. He dropped a couple of incendiary sticks in the office as they were leaving, both men clear and moving toward the trucks before they popped and sizzled.

The plastique charges were fist-size, each with a radio-remote detonator implanted before they left the car. Four in all, and he placed them on alternate vehicles, wedged against the fuel tanks.

Finished.

They were halfway to their car, the office burning brightly from within, when Bolan paused and keyed the transmitter clipped to his belt. Downrange, the Sinaloa trucks went off like giant firecrackers, ruptured fuel tanks spewing tongues of flame. All eight of the vehicles were ablaze in seconds flat.

"I'd say they're out of business," Gallardo quipped.

"So far, so good," the Executioner replied, and struck off toward the waiting car.

THE CALL TO MUELLER, in Berlin, was difficult for Gerhard Kasche, but he had no choice. Dannecker had made it plain that noncooperation would have painful consequences for the Vanguard and himself. It galled him, taking orders from a man he barely knew eight thousand miles away, but he couldn't afford a rift with any of his allies at the moment, not when unknown enemies were breathing down his neck.

It was true, regrettably, that many German patriots—most, in fact—still associated the heart and soul of the Aryan movement with aging survivors of the Third Reich.

The association was natural enough, a symbolic link to *Der Führer* and the other men who gave the movement life, but those who did their part in World War II were old men now, some of them senile, barely able to control their bowels and bladders. All the great and notorious figures were dead, in any case, leaving a hodgepodge of camp guards and mid-level officers to represent the cause. As most of these were still in exile, facing prosecution in the fatherland, they necessarily communicated with the faithful from a distance. Hans Erdmann had controlled those channels of communication, and that power now devolved upon Karl Dannecker.

And there were, as Dannecker so aptly pointed out, considerations beyond the political. Wartime investments in South America were still a major source of income for latter-day Aryan activists, nearly rivaling the profits from sale of Bolivian cocaine in reunified Germany. Domestic appetite for the drug was growing, deliberately fostered by Vanguard dealers among the immigrant trash and radical, left-leaning youth. Aside from needed revenue, the cocaine was a useful weapon for debilitating and disorienting their potential enemies. When the time came to strike...

But all that was in jeopardy today. Not only was the Vanguard under serious attack, but mayhem had been wrought on their associates abroad. Now, there was Dannecker, demanding reinforcements in La Paz, threatening to sever communications and the traffic in cocaine unless Kasche complied with his demands.

So be it.

Twenty men wasn't so much to ask. When Mueller tried to argue, Kasche overrode his objections, resisting the impulse to shout. He made himself understood on the second try, and Mueller agreed to arrange a special charter flight. The German National Party had its own jet on stand-by in Frankfurt, but the weapons would be problematical.

No matter. Dannecker was short of men, not guns. If he couldn't afford to arm the reinforcements Kasche sent him, it would be his problem, not Berlin's.

He ordered Mueller to select the best men they could spare, all proven warriors, faithful to the cause. Some would have killed before, and all of them were trained with modern weapons, capable of anything.

It would be good for Kasche, he realized, to have his own men rescue Dannecker. In one stroke, Kasche would reestablish the primary role of Berlin as the heart of the Aryan movement. So it had been in the beginning, so it ever would be. Kasche would see to that, if he was fortunate enough to live.

11

The German social club was situated half a mile from downtown La Paz, on Avenida Bolívar. In normal times, adherents of the Fourth Reich gathered there to drink beer by the liter, sing marching songs from World War II, and rant against the Jewish influence abroad. The walls were hung with posters dating from the 1930s, Aryan youth immaculate in their striking uniforms and spit-shined jackboots, carrying the swastika banner against their subhuman enemies. Nazi battle flags were on open display, beside framed black-and-whites of Hitler, Göring, Himmler and the boys.

Of course, this night wasn't a normal evening for the Nazis in La Paz. Their social outings had been canceled by the recent spate of violence, but they needed somewhere they could meet and plot their moves in something like security.

Bolan had watched thirteen men enter the club, arriving in twos and threes. They didn't wear their uniforms, but they would all be packing hardware underneath their coats. How many more inside? He had no way of estimating, but it hardly mattered. He was banking on surprise to gain an edge, raw nerve to see them through.

Five minutes passed, with no more new arrivals. Gallardo shifted in his seat. "How long?" he asked.

"Right now. Front or back?"

"I'll go in through the kitchen, maybe fix myself a snack."

"Two minutes."

Gallardo hit the asphalt running, with the 12-gauge cocked and locked. Bolan counted sixty seconds in his head before he left the vehicle, crossing the darkened parking lot with long strides, the Uzi tucked beneath one arm, an OD satchel of explosives slung across his shoulder.

Ready.

Ninety seconds put him on the threshold. He had observed the others knocking, and he followed their example now, gripping the Uzi tightly in his right hand as he waited for an answer.

Would the Nazis be expecting anybody else? If not, would the inevitable lookout answer with a bullet through the door?

Another moment, and the door inched open, showing Bolan half a face. He took a short step forward, jammed his Uzi through the opening, its muzzle sinking into doughy flesh. The jarring impact drove his adversary backward, rocking on his heels, and Bolan followed through. The gunner had one hand clapped to his eye, the other fumbling for a pistol tucked between his belt and a protruding gut.

The Uzi stuttered, three quick rounds at point-blank range, and Bolan's target melted like a sagging straw man, crimson spouting from the fresh holes in his shirt. A tremor rippled through his body and was gone.

So much for the surprise.

In front of him, tall double doors obscured the main room of the social club, but they wouldn't be soundproof. Bolan hit the swing doors running, plunging headlong into a shoulder roll that carried him across the polished hardwood floor. He came up in a crouch, the Uzi tracking, sharp eyes taking in the layout of the room—the long bar on his left, round tables staggered between the entrance and a small stage at the far end of the room. Perhaps a quarter of the tables were occupied—say fifteen, twenty men—and one man on the stage, caught with his mouth open, stalled in the midst of his harangue.

The frozen moment seemed to stretch interminably, then the nearest opposition members started scrambling for their hardware, groping under shirts and jackets, two men breaking off in the direction of the bar.

The warrior held down the Uzi's trigger and swung the subgun from right to left, bright cartridge cases pattering around him on the floor. He swept the nearest tables, watching men go down with curses and startled cries of pain. He gave up counting, caught one of the runners near the bar and rolled him up, slamming him headfirst into the brass foot rail.

The Uzi's slide locked open on an empty chamber, and Bolan reached for a backup magazine. He dropped the empty, and had a fresh mag in his hand when Gallardo burst in from the kitchen, squeezing off a charge of buckshot at the tall man on the stage. His target vaulted backward, head over heels, as the DEA agent spun to face the room at large, pumping another round into the shotgun's firing chamber.

Gallardo's appearance gave Bolan the breather he needed. He reloaded the Uzi and palmed a frag grenade from his satchel. Rolling to his left, he freed the safety pin and pitched his bomb toward the bar, saw it bounce once before it dropped out of sight. He came up firing, dropped two Nazis from their straight-backed chairs, then dived prone again as the grenade went off behind the bar. Long shelves of liquor bottles shattered, shards of glass and smoking shrapnel peppering the room.

Half the Nazis were down now, the others caught in a cross fire and scrambling for any cover they could find. Upturned tables and chairs offered little sanctuary, with the Uzi hacking at them from one side, Gallardo's 12-gauge blasting from the other. Six men left, then three, then none.

The ringing silence took Mack Bolan by surprise. He knew that it was over, but the adrenaline rush of combat still sang in his veins, and he reloaded the Uzi automatically—just in case.

"All clear?" Gallardo called out from the general direction of the stage.

"Looks like." Bolan rose to his feet, surveying the battleground.

"I'd say it's time to go."

"Suits me."

He dropped a handful of incendiary sticks behind him, laying down a trail as they retreated to the exit. By the time they reached the street, the social club was burning brightly from within.

"They won't be holding any fascist sing-alongs in that joint for a while," Gallardo commented.

And that was something, anyway. The Nazis who were still alive and kicking would be forced to learn a different tune.

AARON KURTZMAN TOOK the call from Langley, Virginia, at 10:05 p.m., Eastern Standard Time. The caller was a midlevel functionary in Clandestine Operations at CIA headquarters, assigned to the European theater of operations. His message, in turn, was relayed from a contact in Berlin, an infiltrator in the National Vanguard and its political arm, the German National Party.

The word was brief, concise and chilling.

Twenty members of the Vanguard had embarked from Berlin aboard a private aircraft registered to the German National Party, bound for La Paz. The trip, including a refueling stop at Miami International, would put the soldiers in Bolivia sometime between 11:00 a.m. and noon the next day. Customs might conceivably delay the troops in Florida, but Kurtzman had no reason to believe they would be packing any contraband to warrant an arrest.

There would be ample hardware waiting for them in La Paz, and stalling them with red tape in Miami would only postpone the inevitable. Anything could happen in the space of fourteen hours, and Kurtzman deemed their mission would be better served by warning Striker in advance. He could be waiting for the new arrivals when they landed, if he wasn't fortunate enough to have his business wrapped by then.

And there appeared to be small chance of that.

The late word from La Paz had Striker well on track, but he still had far to go. Two of his primary targets were still at large, with troops at their disposal, and Hans Erdmann's passing had left a new warlord in charge of the Bolivian

Reich. Importing gunners from Germany was a new wrinkle, and Kurtzman wasn't sure how it would tip the balance of their deadly game.

If Striker lost it in La Paz...

Kurtzman filed that thought away before it had a chance to put down roots. The hotel number in La Paz would put him through to Jack Grimaldi, chafing at his leash and taking messages for Striker when he clearly would have relished joining in the battle. So far, Striker hadn't needed wings, but when he did, Grimaldi would be standing by to give the job his all.

He got an outside line and tapped out a dozen digits, waiting while the international connection hummed and crackled in his ear. He got a busy signal on the first three tries, and got through to a desk clerk on the fourth attempt. He asked for room 427, and the operator pulled it off without a further hitch.

Grimaldi picked up with the first ring still in progress, making Kurtzman wonder if he had been sitting on the telephone. "Hello?"

"It's Shenandoah, Fly-boy."

"What's the word?"

Kurtzman laid it out in cryptic terms, with reference to freight delivery of twenty pieces and the estimated time of arrival in La Paz. Grimaldi wouldn't write the message down, but he wouldn't forget it, either. When he got in touch with the Executioner, somewhere down the line, he would deliver the decoded bulletin and let the big guy plot his strategy.

Simplicity itself... except that Striker would be carrying the ball from there. Whatever his reaction to the news of reinforcements coming from Berlin, it had to be distracting, and Kurtzman knew the smallest level of distraction was enough to get a combat soldier killed.

And, then again, the warning just might save his life.

That was the plan, in any case, but only God knew how it would work out. At least the hellfire warrior wasn't flying solo on his South American campaign. Grimaldi could support him, if it came to that, and he also had the DEA agent, whose superiors were going apeshit over his defection to a more aggressive style of play.

New rules.

Kurtzman only hoped they would be adequate to win the game.

IT WOULD HAVE BEEN an understatement to report that Colonel Hector Rivera was angry when he heard the news. Blind screaming fury was closer to the truth, but he controlled the feeling with an effort, as he slammed the telephone receiver back into its cradle and pounded his fist on the desktop until his hand felt tender and bruised.

Enough.

He was confronted with a situation that he couldn't change. The only option still remaining was control, to some extent—an effort to manipulate events, wherever possible, to his advantage.

It wouldn't be easy, but Rivera paused and lighted a fat cigar to calm himself, enjoying the aroma of the fragrant smoke. The facts: Karl Dannecker had stepped into the void produced by Erdmann's death. The move had obviously been arranged, though Erdmann hadn't bothered to consult Rivera on his choice of a successor. German arrogance again, but if Rivera tried to strip the man of his authority, he would immediately lose a crucial group of allies at the very moment when he needed them the most.

The latest word: a group of twenty killers was presently en route from Germany. The number was hardly imposing, but Rivera thought he should have been consulted first, as the Bolivian officer in charge of state security. It was a galling breach of protocol, but there was still an outside chance that it could work to his advantage.

There were deadly enemies abroad, their names and number still unknown. It mattered little to Rivera how they were uncovered, or by whom, as long as it was done in timely fashion. If the new arrivals could contribute something to the common defense, more power to them. There were ways of taking public credit for their actions after the fact, utilizing the standard publicity machine. German mercenaries wouldn't be anxious to advertise their tactics, and that was all to the good . . . assuming they had any success to start with.

Twenty men made no substantive difference in a city the size of La Paz, unless one of them managed to pull a trigger at precisely the right moment, giving Rivera and his allies their first clear handle on a situation that was rapidly deteriorating. If events continued on their present course, it might soon be too late.

Unthinkable.

Forty-eight hours earlier, Colonel Rivera would never have imagined himself in this position, forced to defend his clandestine empire—his very life itself—against strangers who wished him dead. He was accustomed to dealing with enemies, and ruthlessly, but the old tactics hardly applied to the present conflict, where his enemies were fleeting shadows, striking at will and melting away, so far untouchable.

Part of Rivera's fury derived from frustration. Two days and counting, with no word of substance from his numerous informers on the street and in the countryside. He had absolved the standard suspects—drug competitors of Gomez's, Israeli avengers, left-wing radicals, Rivera's personal enemies from past administrations. None of them were seemingly involved in the recurrent violence of the past two days.

And that left . . . who?

His agents had been working overtime, Rivera hounding them unmercifully, but he had nothing yet to show for all their effort. His only consolation at the moment derived from the fact that his enemies showed no sign of letting up on their attacks. They were continuing to press the issue, and experience taught Rivera that haste bred mistakes. Inevitably one or another of his enemies would stumble, leave some trace of his identity behind.

The colonel only hoped the break wouldn't arrive too late to save himself and all that he had worked for through the years.

The intercom buzzed on his desk, Rivera's secretary announcing Karl Dannecker's arrival in the outer office. The colonel took another drag on his cigar, acknowledged the news and asked his secretary to have the German wait a moment.

Dannecker.

Rivera knew him, in passing, from occasions when the man had accompanied Erdmann to various meetings. Dannecker kept his mouth shut at those conferences, seemed to merge with the scenery, snapping to attention when Erdmann asked for a cup of coffee, a cigarette, clarification of some minor point in their conversation.

Most of what Rivera knew about Karl Dannecker was hearsay, verified by personal investigation in La Paz and outlying districts. Researching his business associates was standard procedure for the colonel, and the results were often startling. In Dannecker's case, his agents reported that the man had begun his service to the Bolivian Reich as an assassin, logging at least a half-dozen murders to his credit. In later years, he had graduated to a role as Hans Erdmann's right-hand man, elevated from the rank of street soldier to a command-level officer in the Nazi apparatus.

And now, with Erdmann's death, he stood at the helm of that clique, capable of wielding the power Erdmann had formerly possessed. For Colonel Rivera, the critical question remained: how much of that power was still in effect, and how much had been lost to their mutual enemies in the past two days?

He respected Karl Dannecker in the same way one respected a venomous reptile, understanding its potential for destructive violence, but even the most lethal viper could be outwitted, defanged and dismembered.

Rivera hadn't reached that point with the German, as yet—might never reach it—but he meant to reserve all his options. The colonel already had Dannecker under surveillance, the better to find him at a moment's notice if remedial action was necessary, but he hoped they could work something out. His association with Erdmann had been profitable, even enjoyable on occasion, and he would give Dannecker a fair chance, all other circumstances permitting. But he meant to deal with the German from strength, prevent La Paz from becoming Dannecker's personal hunting preserve.

Rivera checked the wall clock, deciding he had kept his new associate waiting long enough. He stretched out a hand to the intercom, keyed the transmitter button and addressed the outer office in his best, most diplomatic tone.

"Please send Herr Dannecker in," he said, and settled back to wait.

JACK GRIMALDI CAUGHT himself pacing again and stopped with an effort of will. He checked his watch again and found two minutes had elapsed since the last time, going on fifteen since Kurtzman's call from Stony Man. Grimaldi cursed, wishing there was some way he could get in touch with Bolan, anything at all that he could do beyond just sitting still and waiting for the ax to fall.

Granted, it could have been worse news, but the last thing Bolan needed at the moment was a fresh infusion of enemy troops from abroad. Bolan and his hastily recruited sidekick from the DEA were outnumbered as it was, waging war against near-hopeless odds.

What else was new? How many times had Grimaldi been witness to the big man turning things around and ramming desperate odds down an enemy's throat? Still, each campaign was a separate problem, fraught with unique problems, and the play could blow up in Bolan's face at any turn.

If and when that happened, Grimaldi wanted his piece of the action, standing fast at Bolan's side instead of warming a bench on the sidelines. The feisty pilot had never been comfortable in passive supporting roles, away from the heart of the action. Bolan would be needing him before the game played itself out, and Grimaldi meant to be there for him when the moment came.

But first he had to pass the word.

Grimaldi had been waiting for the telephone, but it still managed to startle him, jangling at his elbow and bringing the pilot half out of his chair. He hoisted the receiver as the second ring began, and answered with the number of his room.

"Four twenty-seven."

"How's it hanging, Wings?"

Grimaldi felt himself unwinding at the sound of that familiar voice. "It's hanging tough. I got a message from the ranch."

"That so? What's happening?"

"The opposition has a team of salesmen coming in from Germany. An even twenty, so I'm told. Unless they get held up in traffic, they should hit La Paz around 11:25 tomorrow morning."

"That's an interesting development." If Bolan was concerned, it didn't come through in his voice. "Somebody ought to meet them at the airport, maybe say hello."

"Sounds good," Grimaldi said. "I'll be there."

"Not so fast. I need you hanging in for contact with the ranch."

"It's getting old." There was an edge of irritation in Grimaldi's voice. "I hate this sitting on my ass and watching life go by."

"Life's not the problem, guy."

"If I wanted guarantees, I could have gone to work for the Salvation Army."

"Not this time," the Executioner repeated, standing firm.

Grimaldi knew there was no point in arguing with Bolan once the big guy made up his mind. The pilot could always throw over the traces and turn up for the party uninvited, but it would be a breach of Bolan's trust, an abrogation of his own responsibility.

"I hear you."

"I'll be checking in again before the party," Bolan said. "Keep your ear to the ground and let me know what you hear."

"Right. Will do."

"The time's coming."

"I hope so."

"Count on it."

The line went dead, a dial tone humming in Grimaldi's ear before he cradled the receiver.

12

Staking out the airport on the outskirts of La Paz was feasible but risky. Bolan took Gallardo with him for a drive-around, scouting the perimeter and strolling once around the terminal to eyeball the security arrangements. Uniformed police were on the prowl, but there was nothing of the military presence felt in Germany and other countries where terrorism had struck home with a vengeance. Gallardo confirmed that thieves and smugglers were the airport's chief concern, with heavy emphasis on cargo pilferage and small-fry drug runners who tried to circumvent customs without paying the usual bribes.

He needed range for what he had in mind, but it was good to know that he wouldn't be faced with any sort of paramilitary backlash in the crucial moments following his strike. Police inside the terminal would be confused at first, disoriented by events, and by the time they got their act together, Bolan and his companion should be gone.

With any luck.

He started looking for the stand, a long view of the major east-west runway that would still leave Bolan well within effective striking range. He needed altitude to beat the ten-foot-high retaining wall surrounding the airport on three sides, but Bolan had to stay within a thousand yards or so of his selected target zone.

The warrior found the perfect setup in an elevated stand of trees five hundred yards from the retaining wall, another 450 yards from there, give or take, to the midpoint of the central runway.

It was perfect for the Walther WA-2000.

Gallardo had the wheel, with Bolan riding shotgun. After circling the stand once, the DEA agent braked long enough for Bolan to go EVA, lifting the sniper's rifle from the floorboard in its OD duffel bag.

"I can't pin down the time," Bolan said, "but you won't have any problem knowing when it happens. Hang in close enough to get back here before the uniforms roll out."

"You've got it, Chief."

Bolan was in among the trees before Gallardo disappeared in the compact, heading back toward the public parking lot. The warrior moved through the ferns and tall grass on foot, pausing to kneel here and there, double-checking his field of fire. When he had it down pat, he lowered the duffel bag, knelt beside it and removed the Walther WA-2000 from its padded nest.

A heavier piece would have been reassuring, but Bolan was banking on the Walther's flat trajectory and superior rate of fire to make up the difference. If he played his cards right, there would be no need for an elephant gun with armor-piercing ammunition to drive his point home.

He sat in the weeds behind the Walther, checked his watch and scanned the airport before him with a pair of compact field glasses.

His target was a Canadair Challenger, converted from the original LearStar 600 with addition of the "T"-tail design. With twenty-eight passengers on board, the twenty-one-foot plane was capable of cruising at 561 miles per hour, at an altitude of 36,000 feet.

Bolan's target this morning was traveling light.

The Walther held six rounds, and it would either be enough or it wouldn't. Coordination over distance was a problem when it came to rapid fire, but he had earned his reputation with "impossible" shots at longer ranges than this. In Vietnam and afterward, Bolan's specialty had been sniping missions, and he left the Asian hellgrounds with 97 registered kills to validate his label as the Executioner.

How many since that time?

He had given up keeping score when the war came home with a vengeance, understanding that it was no longer a numbers game, but rather a war of hearts and minds. The names and faces merged sometimes, but they were all available for recall if he felt the need.

Not now.

The ETA on Bolan's target was still five minutes off, with no guarantee of a timely arrival. It was fifty-fifty that there would have been some delay in Miami, through no fault of Kurtzman and the Stony Man team. Mechanical problems, delay in refueling, or hassles with immigration could all slow the hit team's progress by minutes or hours. As a private flight, the Berlin special wouldn't even show up on the terminal arrivals screen.

A gamble.

Every moment that he sat behind the gun and waited for his target to arrive increased the odds of Bolan's being spotted by a passerby, reported to police inside the terminal. He had concealed himself with all deliberate care, but anytime you left yourself a clear shot at the world outside the stand, there was a possibility of being seen.

The risk would be increased a hundredfold once Bolan started shooting, but he knew that going in. The time required to execute his plan was minimal, and if he hit his mark, the focus of attention would be some 950 yards downrange.

A funeral pyre, to help his adversaries read the writing on the wall.

IF PATIENCE WAS the virtue of the saints, Karl Dannecker suspected he would never qualify. He hated waiting, even though he managed to disguise his irritation, the restless feeling that urged him to rise from his seat and pace the airport concourse. Dannecker needed to set an example for his troops, make them understand that adversity wasn't necessarily disaster. They could rebound from early losses, even the loss of a valued leader, without falling apart, but they had to keep their wits about them and respond aggressively.

His call for reinforcements from Berlin was part of that response. Twenty men wasn't a great number, but their arrival would still be a shot in the arm for his men in La Paz, who had been battered for the past two days, with raids continuing throughout the night.

Dannecker had lost track of the dead, with new reports still rolling in, but he suspected that at least one-quarter of his fighting force was lost. He didn't know what sort of loss Rivera or the narcodealer, Gomez, had sustained, nor did he care, as long as they were able to assist him in the coming battle.

The Berlin contingent would be coming in unarmed, eliminating any hitch with customs at the airport. Dannecker had weapons waiting for them, vehicles with drivers born and raised around La Paz, men who would be able to locate their targets on command.

He hoped that it would be enough.

Dannecker was sick and tired of taking lumps in an uneven battle. It wasn't the Aryan way to sit still and take a beating without some effective response. He preferred the blitzkrieg approach, rolling over opposition with superior force. Thus far, unfortunately, there had been no opportunity for striking back. Until the enemy was singled out, located and identified, retaliation was impossible.

And that, Dannecker knew, was the source of the frustration that urged him to pace the floor, burning off nervous energy that would otherwise gnaw at his vitals like acid. Control and discipline were everything, beyond the strict Hitlerian philosophy, a central part of Dannecker's personality. His men expected no less, and leadership was crucial at the present time.

The flight was running late, five minutes by Dannecker's watch, but that was no surprise in La Paz. The great majority of flights were late, departures as well as arrivals. It was part of the mañana atmosphere so prevalent in Latin America, the very antithesis of German efficiency, but Dannecker had learned to adjust over time. It grated on his nerves when he couldn't demand immediate results from native colleagues.

Perhaps, in the final analysis, their shared misfortune of the past two days would be a blessing in disguise. It could be helpful if Gomez and Rivera were shaken up a bit—even replaced by different, younger men who would be more responsive to Dannecker's lead.

Hans Erdmann had fallen into the rut of dealing with his native associates almost as equals, maintaining his distance on ethnic grounds while relying on Gomez and Rivera for much of his commercial success. That symbiotic relationship would exist until such time as the Fourth Reich was able to seize control of Bolivia at large. That day was still a distant dream, pushed back still further by their recent humiliation at the hands of strangers.

Dannecker meant to change all that, beginning the moment his reinforcements touched down on the runway outside. He was launching an offensive independent of the others, and to hell with Rivera if the colonel dared to object. State security had done nothing to help him so far, nothing to justify the years of bribes and favors that lay behind them. It was useless, having government officials on the payroll, if they couldn't do their jobs.

Two of Dannecker's bodyguards stood at the broad picture window, watching the skyline. One of them turned now, facing his master, and spoke two words.

"The plane."

Dannecker rose from his seat deliberately, slowly, moving to join his men at the window. It crossed his mind that he was terribly exposed to sniper fire—a new paranoia he was only just acquiring—but Dannecker stood his ground, refusing to cringe and hide like a spineless coward.

He would lead by example, demand the respect of his subordinates and all the lesser men around him. As for his enemies, the day would come—and soon—when it would be their turn to run and hide.

He watched the Canadair Challenger, still small in the distance, circling into its approach. Dannecker imagined the young men on board, restless from their long flight, hungry for action, none of them fluent in Spanish. They were his to arm and do with as he pleased.

If Colonel Rivera complained ...

Dannecker shrugged away the train of thought. He would deal with that problem if and when it arose. In the meantime, there was cause for optimism, a gift from the fatherland descending in its final approach to the runway.

The tide of battle was about to turn, and it was running his way.

STAKED OUT in the airport parking lot, Ernie Gallardo felt like the proverbial sitting duck. Each time a pedestrian passed him, moving to or from the terminal, Gallardo imagined eyes scanning his face, the car he occupied, imagining the worst. Would someone report him for loitering, send police from the terminal to question him or make him leave?

He took a deep breath, trying to relax. For all intents and purposes, he would resemble someone waiting for a party to arrive or leave. Granted, most welcoming committees gathered inside the terminal, but Bolivians enjoyed their privacy. If Gallardo remained where he was, did nothing further to attract attention, he would almost certainly be left alone.

Part of his uneasiness, Gallardo realized, lay in the fact that he couldn't see the runway from where he sat. Neither, for that matter, could he glimpse Mike Belasko's position. Time was slipping away, the German flight already late, and the DEA agent felt as if he were stuck on the outside, looking in ... with nothing to see.

He wondered if his first clue would be engine noise or gunfire. Planes were taking off and landing all the time, with only moments in between, and he had no realistic hope of telling one flight from another.

That left it to the sound of rifle fire, and by the time he heard those echoes, it would all be coming down around Gallardo's ears. He would barely have time to start the car, roll back to Belasko's sniper nest and pick the guy up before security tightened the noose.

Were there procedures in place to seal off the airport in cases of emergency? More to the point, how long would it take police in the terminal to link garbled reports of gunfire with the chaos that followed?

Every second would count in their race to escape, each obstacle a potential disaster. Reinforcements from outside the airport would take time, even with a general alarm, but if Gallardo got hung up anywhere between the parking lot and Belasko's stand, the two of them were roasted. They would have one chance to get away.

The sawed-off 12-gauge pump was underneath his seat, the Glock 17 semiautomatic in its shoulder holster. Gallardo hoped they wouldn't have to shoot their way out of the airport, but he was ready for anything at the moment.

It was crazy, when he thought about it. Three days earlier, he had been cruising along in the midst of his biggest case ever, looking forward to the day when his reports would produce indictments, his courtroom testimony send top-flight Bolivian dealers away for the rest of their lives. A late-night raid on his apartment had left Gallardo close to death, and Belasko had saved his bacon at the last possible moment. But the shocks hadn't stopped there.

Overnight, as if at the flip of a switch, he was transformed from a run-of-the-mill federal agent into a raving vigilante. How many men had he killed in the past twelve hours? When had he last touched base with his DEA control at the embassy in La Paz? How likely was it that he would survive to see another day?

Incredibly, in spite of everything, Gallardo felt good. For the first time in months, perhaps years, he was running on instinct, without the shackles and blinders required when you followed "the Book." Rules and regulations had gone out the window, and if that spelled the end of his DEA career, so be it. Unmarried and childless, Gallardo was ready to make the sacrifice, risk jail if that was what it took to finish the job at hand.

Except, he knew, it wouldn't be a jail cell waiting for him if he dropped the ball. Colonel Rivera might be head of state security, but he and his comrades were playing a different game, with personal wealth and survival riding on the line. Rivera wasn't interested in bringing anyone to court. In fact, unless Gallardo missed his guess, state security agents had probably been involved in the two attempts on his life—if not as triggermen, at least in the planning stages.

No.

It was war to the knife, and the knife to the hilt. Gallardo had always gone into the field with the knowledge that this time, this mission, might end in his death, but mortality had never seemed so absolutely real before this mission. Last week, if anyone had asked Gallardo where he planned to be a year from now, he could have come up with a ready answer, rough career plans, something. As it was, he couldn't see tomorrow, much less next week, next year.

If he was moving toward his death, so be it. There were worse things in the world, Gallardo thought, than laying down your life for something you believed in, standing like a man and swallowing your medicine, regardless of the taste.

It came off sounding like a load of macho crap, but it was still the gospel truth. Sometimes, a man *did* have to do what he had to do, no circumventions or excuses to lighten the load.

Who was it who said "Death always came with the territory"? Richard Ramirez? No matter. Even a sick bastard like the Night Stalker got one right from time to time.

In fact, Gallardo had begun to suspect, death *was* the territory.

And he was learning how to make himself at home.

BOLAN SAW the Canadair Challenger coming, first in his field glasses, then through the Schmidt & Bender telescopic sight attached to his sniper rifle. He barely heard the twin Avco Lycoming turbofan engines, distance and the sound of his own pulse in his ears combining to muffle the sound.

They were still well beyond effective range for the .300 Winchester Magnum cartridge, but the gap was closing with each second that passed. The Challenger was painted brilliant white, with blue stripes running down each side. A private jet, no corporate logo.

Fine.

He knew the players, had them spotted coming in. He didn't need a special name tag to identify his target.

Bolan lay stretched out behind the Walther, stock against his cheek and shoulder, staring through the eyepiece of the scope. He saw the aircraft's landing gear locked into place, wheels braced for touchdown at the nose and under each wing. No crew members were visible behind the windscreen's glare, but the warrior didn't plan on going for the pilots.

It wouldn't be necessary.

Physics was the key—momentum, gravity and traction.

He saw the plane touch down on the runway, waiting, while the Challenger rolled toward him on a steady course, decelerating by the moment.

He would never have a better chance.

His finger tightened on the rifle's trigger, taking up the slack. The rifle lurched against his shoulder once, twice, cartridge cases spinning off to the right. He saw the plane nose over, trailing sparks instead of dust now, tortured metal screaming as he shifted to his left and squeezed off three more rounds in rapid-fire.

The right wing sagged and buckled, snapped on impact with the runway, oily flames exploding from the ruptured fuel tank. He saw the Challenger begin to drift broadside, going over in a lazy barrel roll, the left wing rising like a huge shark's dorsal fin. For several heartbeats it was upright, jutting from a cloud of smoke and flame, before it toppled over and smashed to the ground. The second fuel tank burst immediately, feeding the fire, disgorging bright streamers of fire.

Bolan didn't need the scope now, or the glasses. He was packing up the rifle when the blazing aircraft broke in two behind the wing mounts, scattering seats, bits of wreckage and tiny stick figures along the burning runway.

Hell on earth.

He felt no pity for the fascist gunmen, couldn't hear their screams and wouldn't have responded if he did. "Aryan" warriors bled and died like anybody else. They took their chances when they stepped off into battle, showed no mercy for their chosen enemies, and they would get none from the Executioner.

Sirens were wailing out on the runway, red-and-yellow emergency vehicles racing toward the jumbled wreckage of the aircraft. Bolan could imagine the panic in the control tower, breathless instructions shouted into microphones, while commercial flights stacked up in a holding pattern overhead.

An ambulance joined the stampede, but Bolan didn't like their chances of finding survivors in the wreckage. Anything was possible, of course, and it would make no difference in the long run if a handful of the Germans managed to survive.

Bolan had already made his point, driving it home with a vengeance.

No one was safe from his wrath in La Paz and environs. There was no place for his enemies to hide away.

Scorched earth.

A car raced toward him, and Bolan stepped farther back, out of sight, until he recognized the compact with Gallardo at the wheel. He emerged from cover, jogging around the car and stowing his duffel bag before he slid into the shotgun seat and slammed the door behind him.

"Jesus Lord," Gallardo said, "you sure don't mess around."

"If you're going to do something," Bolan replied, "do it like you mean it."

"Right. We're out of here."

"Sounds like a plan."

Bolan leaned back in his seat, willing himself to relax. It was down to the firemen and paramedics now, sorting through smoke and rubble, searching for a spark of life. He left them to it, thinking past the airport toward his next objective, scoping pressure points and planning how to rattle his opponents next time out.

Rivera? Gomez? Erdmann's replacement as head of the Reich?

There was time, yet, for Bolan to scope out the play, give the dust from his latest strike a chance to circulate and settle while he lined up his next move against the enemy.

Any way he looked at it, they were coming down to the wire.

It only remained to be seen who would survive the game.

13

Surrounded by uniforms, sick of their questions, Karl Dannecker stared at the wreckage and scowled. It had all been thought out in advance, every step of the way, but his enemies were there before him.

Waiting.

He had listened to the officers and their report of gunshots heard before the blazing crash. The sound hadn't reached Dannecker inside the terminal, but he had witnessed the result, a heart-stopping nightmare that seemed to take forever—and, in fact, took less than sixty seconds on the clock.

Disaster.

There were two survivors of the crash, one badly burned, the other with a laundry list of broken bones. The pair had been removed by ambulance, while firemen in their silver suits and airport personnel in yellow coveralls were picking through the wreckage, extricating charred remains.

With the flight crew, that meant nineteen dead, a line of sheet-draped corpses growing on the tarmac. None of them were known to Dannecker, and he didn't bemoan their loss from any personal perspective. They weren't his friends, or even his equals ... but they might have been his last, best hope of getting through the next few days alive.

Demanding replacements from Berlin was out of the question. Dannecker already looked like an incompetent fool, and there would be enough explaining to do as it was, without issuing new ultimatums. In less than a minute, he had lost his advantage, realized that he was no longer dealing from strength.

How had the bastards found out his surprise? Rivera knew about the reinforcements, as did Kasche and Buhler in Berlin. Dannecker thought it was safe to rule out treachery by his own lieutenants in La Paz, but any or all of the others were possible candidates. It wouldn't have required a conscious betrayal, at that: a loose word in the wrong quarter would be enough, making its tortuous way to the wrong set of ears.

Nazi philosophy wasn't all goose-stepping delusions of racial superiority, by any means. The ever-present flip side was pervasive paranoia, every true believer constantly on guard against a world of lurking enemies. The Jews were only part of it, allied with all the mongrel races, leftists and "progressives," weak-kneed Christians, homosexuals and feminists—in short, the dregs of mankind. The enemy was everywhere, alert to any scrap of information that would offer an advantage in their never-ending effort to destroy the master race.

Dannecker's nostrils wrinkled at the smell of burning flesh, a subtle undertone to the pervasive odors of jet fuel, scorched rubber and melted asphalt. The aroma of death wasn't new to the Nazi—he had grown up with it, killing his first man at eighteen, sometimes riding along with Bolivian army patrols when they raided the outlying Indian villages—but this time was different.

This time, it smelled like defeat.

Time to go. The feeling of exposure had returned, though logic told him that his enemies had to have fled immediately after the shooting. Even so, the back of his neck was tingling, the short hairs bristling, as if he were being watched.

By whom?

Dannecker didn't know if the police were finished with their questions yet, but he had no more to say. If state security needed to speak with him for any reason, Colonel Rivera would know how to get in touch.

Meanwhile Karl Dannecker had other, more pressing matters on his mind. Like salvaging his new position in the Reich, for instance, and keeping himself alive.

The thought of hiding like a coward galled him, but it might be unavoidable, if he couldn't identify his enemies and track them down. Pride was one thing, but survival took priority.

In order to command the party, Dannecker would have to save himself from those who wished him dead. And that, he realized, would be no small task in itself.

THE FIRST BANK of La Paz occupied the ground floor of a downtown high rise, six blocks from the Hall of Justice. The decor was conservative, befitting an institution that served the Bolivian elite. The bank's clientele included wealthy ranchers, mine owners, captains of industry, esteemed professionals...and some of the country's most notorious drug dealers. The latter clients went unnoticed, for the most part, but their choice of banking institutions was no great surprise.

In fact, a controlling share of stock in the First Bank of La Paz was owned by Bernardo Gomez, and the bank had been used to launder his stock for years, funneling millions of untaxed dollars into numbered accounts in Switzerland and the Bahamas.

"You're sure about this deal?" Gallardo asked, as they pulled up outside the bank.

"I'm sure," the Executioner replied.

"The plane was one thing. Knocking off a syndicate bank in broad daylight is something else."

"Just keep the engine running, okay?"

"Right. I've seen the movies."

Bolan crossed the sidewalk with an easy, rolling stride. The satchel in his hand was heavy with the Uzi submachine gun and a pair of smoke grenades. He let a gray-haired businessman precede him through the glass revolving door and into the lobby of the bank. The air-conditioning shaved ten degrees off the outside temperature, instantly drying the perspiration on Bolan's forehead as he scanned the lobby, homing in on the desk reserved for new accounts.

A middle-aged accountant type was waiting to receive him, reasonably fluent in English, happy to accept a new account with frequent large deposits and no questions asked. The banker might assume that Bolan was a narco-dealer, but it wouldn't cross his mind to ask—not when an opening deposit of a quarter-million dollars was concerned.

"One thing," he said, "before we finalize this deal."

"Sir?"

"Would it be possible for me to have a peek inside the vault?"

"A peek?"

"A look around." His smile was radiant. "Security, you understand?"

The banker hesitated, glancing over Bolan's shoulder toward the rear of the bank. "Inside the vault, sir?"

"It wouldn't take a minute," Bolan assured him. "Just to put my mind at ease."

The banker thought about it for another moment, finally putting on a cautious smile and nodding. Money talked.

"If you would come with me, sir?"

"My pleasure."

Bolan took the briefcase with him, falling into step behind the banker. Twenty paces brought them to the vault, the huge door standing open, an inner door of tempered steel bars blocking the way. The warrior's escort fished a long key from his pocket, turned it in the lock and rolled the wall of bars aside.

They stepped into the vault, and Bolan scanned the ranks of safe-deposit boxes ranged on either side from floor to ceiling. A smaller room, in back, had shelves stacked high with currency and sacks of coins.

Bolan placed his briefcase on a nearby shelf and sprang the latches, smiling as the banker turned around. "I've changed my mind."

"Sir?"

"Forget about the new account. I'm making a withdrawal, instead."

The banker tried a smile for size and missed it by a fraction. "Pardon?"

Bolan let him see the Uzi. "We'll start with Bernardo Gomez, okay? He'll have a safe-deposit box, I wouldn't be surprised. If you're not sure about the number, you could look it up."

The banker did as he was told, thumbing through a box of index cards, extracting one and turning toward the wall of boxes on his left. "I need a second key," he said, fingering the fat ring in his hand.

"Make do with what you have," the Executioner instructed, stepping forward with the Uzi in his fist. "Which box?"

The banker pointed, stepping back as Bolan aimed and stitched a 4-round burst across the foot-wide metal door. The sound was almost deafening, the explosive impacts of the parabellum rounds ripping the door free, revealing the deep box inside.

Moments remained, at most, before security guards responded to the noise. He pulled the box free, dropped it on the floor, knelt beside it and opened the lid. He scattered diamond necklaces and broaches, digging deeper for a stack of deeds and stock certificates, a ledger filled with names and numbers, yet another jammed with dates and what appeared to be locations, some including points of latitude and longitude.

"Get in the back," he told the banker, stuffing everything inside his briefcase. He lifted out a smoke grenade and thumbed free the safety pin. He tossed the can in front of him, giving the cloud time to drift before he emerged from the vault in a crouch, the briefcase in one hand, his Uzi in the other.

Women screamed all around him, jostling men on their race to the exit. Bolan joined the stampede, tucking the Uzi under his jacket and wedging it tight with his elbow. The outside heat was almost a relief. At least the air was relatively clean.

He found Gallardo waiting for him at the curb, an incredulous smile on his face. "Geez," he said, beaming, "is there anything you can't do?"

"Stick around," the Executioner replied. "I'm learning as I go."

"What's next?"

The warrior drummed his fingers on the lid of the briefcase on his lap.

"We're going public," Bolan said. "It's time Bernardo got his fifteen minutes of fame, don't you think?"

IT TOOK FORTY MINUTES for news of the robbery to reach Bernardo Gomez in his penthouse fortress. No one had dared to call him at first, and once the decision was made, Gomez couldn't be reached at the usual numbers listed for home or business. One of his underlings took the message on the third attempt and passed it on, with some misgivings, to his boss.

As expected, Gomez took the news badly, raging at the messenger and smashing the first object within his reach—a piece of stolen pre-Columbian sculpture for which he had paid a small fortune six months earlier on the black market. A glass-topped coffee table was also shattered in the process, the combined destruction serving to calm Gomez for the moment.

He wasn't relieved to hear that nothing in the way of cash or jewelry had been taken by the Yankee bandit, who had still not been identified. It was the choice of loot, in fact, that most infuriated Gomez, indicating that his adversaries knew more than they should about his business.

Possibly enough to bring him down.

The deeds were bad enough, confirming ownership of various expensive properties around La Paz, controlled by handpicked front men, none of whom would be exactly thrilled to have his link with Gomez made public. Some of them were politicians, others wealthy businessmen with fortunes of their own to safeguard. Careers would be ruined if this news got out, and there was worse in store.

If the deeds were a problem, the ledgers were potential disaster. One listed payoffs to public officials in Bolivia, Peru, the Bahamas and the United States. There were hundreds of names in all, paired with dates and amounts of the bribes paid by Gomez to keep his empire running smoothly, with a minimum of interference from the law. Gomez had maintained the list for future blackmail rather than accounting purposes, but it could backfire on him now with horrendous results. An entire network would be shattered beyond repair, with no safety net in place to catch him when he fell.

The second, smaller book was a directory of sorts. It listed every drop and drug lab, storage place and distribution point, plantation and preserve that serviced Gomez and his web of allies in the cocaine trade. It would be possible, at some expense, to move the labs, and anyone could rent another warehouse, choose another stretch of swamp in which to drop the next load of merchandise from a boat or low-flying aircraft—but what was one to do about the coca farms, vast acreage controlled by Gomez and his allies? He couldn't uproot a farm and move it somewhere else, for God's sake. Granted, the La Paz authorities knew all about the ranchos, but they had been paid to close their eyes and lose their memories.

What would become of his arrangements with the government if word got back to the Americans?

Disaster.

Gomez had dispatched a team to grill the bank employees, find out anything they could about the bandit who had placed Gomez's fortune—possibly his life—in jeopardy. It seemed unlikely that interrogation would produce results, but even an improved description of the man would be a help.

God knew it would be more than what he had to work with at the moment.

Which was nothing, as it stood.

He needed something soon, before it was too late.

Too late for Gomez to escape the sinking ship.

THE STOREFRONT OFFICE of *The Liberator* operated on a shoestring budget, secondhand electric typewriters and an ancient photocopier, with government surplus desks and chairs showing rust beneath flat primer paint. The staff was young—two men sporting facial hair, three women in braids and peasant garb.

Bolan had the weekly newspaper's background courtesy of Ernie Gallardo. He knew *The Liberator* had been closed down twice under previous regimes, its editors imprisoned, one of the reporters shot and killed at home by "persons unknown," believed to be a military death squad trained by Hans Erdmann's Aryan commandos. The new atmosphere of freedom in La Paz made anything seem possible, and so the paper had resurfaced, but its staff still lived with nightly death threats, periodic bomb scares at the office, neo-fascist scribblings on the wall outside.

It was perfect.

Everyone present eyed Bolan with frank suspicion when he breezed through the door, toting the same briefcase he had filled with stolen documents at the First Bank of La Paz. The receptionist heard his request to speak with the editor, hesitating for a long moment before she keyed the intercom and summoned a man in his late twenties.

"I am Eduardo Obregon," the young man said. "And you?"

"My name's irrelevant. The one you're interested in would be Bernardo Gomez."

"Would I?"

"We should talk about this in your office, don't you think?"

The young man thought about it for a moment, then finally nodded. "Come with me."

When they faced each other across a cluttered desk, Bolan opened the briefcase on his lap. "I don't suppose you heard about a dustup at the First Bank of La Paz this afternoon?"

"There was a robbery," said Obregon. "I understand that cash and stocks were taken."

"Not exactly."

The warrior dropped the deeds on his desk in a heap, leaving Obregon to browse for a moment, watching his dark eyes go wide. At last, he said, "Are these legitimate?"

"It all depends upon your point of view," the Executioner replied. "They're stolen, but I haven't altered anything. They read the same right now as when they came out of Bernardo's safe-deposit box."

The young man had begun to smile, as if against his will. "To publish these would be extremely dangerous. It would be an admission of complicity in theft, at least."

"Not if a stranger dropped them off. You take photocopies for your files and phone the police."

"The deeds are everything?"

"The deeds, and these." He set the ledgers on the man's desk, content to know that photocopies had already been posted to the American Embassy in La Paz, in care of Gallardo's control.

Obregon frowned as he thumbed through the ledger of payoffs. "All these are bribes?" he asked.

"That, or Gomez has a hell of a Christmas list."

"And these . . . what are they? Compass points? Locations?"

"Do your legwork," Bolan suggested. "See where it takes you."

"I know this address," Obregon said, pointing midway down the second page. "A warehouse, not so far from my apartment building."

"Gee, I wonder what they're storing?"

"How much do you want for these?" the young man asked.

"I'll take a rain check on a cup of coffee."

"Pardon?"

"Forget it," Bolan told him. "This one's on the house."

"And you are . . ."

"Someone you'd be better off forgetting, if you get my drift."

"I understand."

Bolan rose to leave, the briefcase lighter now. Obregon's voice stopped him at the door.

"For myself only," the young man said, "who are you?"

"Nobody," the Executioner replied. "I'm only passing through."

14

Driving south from Zurich, Yakov Katzenelenbogen led the two-car caravan. Uri Dan rode shotgun, Rudolf Wetzel seated in the back, with heavy duffel bags of military hardware stacked around his feet. McCarter, Manning, James and Encizo occupied the second vehicle, running a discreet sixty yards behind. The drive to Bremgarten was a scenic marvel, but Katz had other matters on his mind.

The helicopter overflight of their intended target had consumed two hours, James and Encizo coming back with diagrams, a layout of the villa, its detached garage and servants' quarters. There had been no opportunity for counting sentries, with the urge for haste and the overhanging trees.

No matter. They were going in regardless, seven guns against whatever might be waiting for them at the villa. Katz was fresh out of options at the moment, intent on pressing his one small advantage for all it was worth.

Surprise.

Kasche and Buhler theoretically had no idea they had been followed from Berlin. As for the Arabs, there was no good reason to believe they were overly suspicious. Renting the villa was a normal security precaution, given the troubles Kasche and Buhler had experienced the past two weeks. They were on guard, but in the absence of an overt threat...

It had been relatively simple, trailing the Germans and Arabs from their respective hotels to the Bremgarten hideout. Everyone was present and accounted for inside the walls, intent on carrying their secret business off without a hitch.

They drove past the villa, checking out the wrought-iron gates, and caught a winding access road into the hills beyond. They climbed for two kilometers and found a place to drop the cars on a gravel turnout. Changing into camouflage fatigues, they parceled out the hardware, choosing weapons, slinging bandoliers. When they were ready, Katzenelenbogen gathered the team around him, running over the instructions one more time.

"Remember your positions when we split, all right? That's Rafael and Calvin on the north side, Gary and David on the south. I take the eastern perimeter with Rudolf and Uri. It's crucial that we all go in together. No one jumps the gun. Let's synchronize, on me."

The warriors set their watches, sounding off around the circle from left to right. Katz nodded satisfaction and adjusted the shoulder strap on his Heckler & Koch MP-5 SD-3 submachine gun, double-checking the safety by feel.

They were as ready as they ever would be.

"Let's do it," Katzenelenbogen told them, leading off along the vestige of a southbound game trail. It was slow going for the first hundred meters or so, getting the feel of the land, but then he established the pace, making up time as the trail widened out. Another kilometer, give or take, and Katz suspected they would have to leave the trail, correct their route of march, but they would make time while they could.

The meeting would be under way by now, and Katzenelenbogen didn't want to keep his adversaries waiting any longer than was absolutely necessary.

TARIM SUDAIR SURVEYED his German colleagues with a condescending air. They dressed well, kept their quasimilitary bearing, but he couldn't put their recent failings out of mind. For all their noise about the master race, they came to him with tails tucked firmly between their legs, running from a near disaster in their homeland, beaten and humiliated by an enemy whom they couldn't identify.

In other circumstances, given time to pick and choose, Sudair would gladly have abandoned them to meet their fate alone, but he had an investment to protect. The Germans also had a certain value to his cause as scapegoats, if the plan went totally awry. They were well-known for their hatred of the Jews, as likely to be blamed for the conspiracy at large as anyone.

So much the better.

"And you still have no idea," he said, "who has been giving you such problems in Berlin?"

"We're working on it," Gerhard Kasche responded.

"So much work, with no result."

The German bristled, but he held his tongue. Beside him, Josef Buhler tried to force a smile and came up short. "We still have confidence," he said, "that we will manage to identify and purge our enemies."

"Of course. And in the meantime, we have work to do."

Shiraz Najaf cleared his throat. "It is a shame about your comrades in America."

"They have their own concerns," Buhler said.

And made their own mistakes, Tarim Sudair thought to himself, but said, "It will retard our plans."

"In one locality, perhaps. As for the rest—"

"You must regain control," Najaf interjected. "Our plan calls for significant moves against Israel and her allies. We accomplish nothing while you hide in bunkers and defend yourself against these unknown enemies."

"And what of you?" Kasche snapped. "This all began with your damned convoy in the first place."

"Our convoys pay the way for much of what you call your own. Without that commerce, and the drugs you buy from South America, you would have nothing."

"Much the same was said in 1924," the Vanguard's leader answered with a sneer. "*Der Führer* still emerged in triumph."

"And his empire was destroyed, as I recall, in 1945."

"Betrayed by Jews and Communists!"

"In any case, a monument to failure."

"We have not come here to be insulted!"

"And I meant no insult, I assure you. We have new business to discuss."

"Of course," Buhler said, still the voice of reason.

"Then, shall we proceed?"

The older German was about to answer, but he never got the chance. Outside, some distance from the house, an automatic weapon stuttered, half a dozen rounds and nothing more. Najaf bolted out of his chair, followed closely by Buhler and Kasche. Sudair kept his seat a moment longer, his hands white-knuckled where he gripped the arms of his chair. He refused to panic.

"What is happening?" Kasche asked.

"A worthy question," Sudair replied. "We should endeavor to find out."

DAVID McCARTER CROUCHED in the shadow of a stately evergreen, twenty meters due east of the point where Gary Manning had gone to ground. The villa lay a quarter mile in front of them, the peaked roof barely visible from McCarter's position. No sentries were visible, but they were out there. He could feel them waiting, somewhere up ahead.

At a wave from Manning, the two men moved out together, on diverging paths. Too close together, and they would be asking for an ambush. They were meant to flank the villa on this side, cut off any retreat to the south once the real action started. The MP-5 submachine gun was slung across one shoulder, but the weapon in McCarter's hand was a Browning BDM autoloading pistol, fitted with a compact silencer. The piece was cocked and locked, the Briton's index finger curled around the trigger.

Fifty meters and counting, still no sign of any opposition on the grounds. The whole estate was silent, and McCarter might have thought it was deserted if he hadn't followed Kasche and Buhler to the very gates himself.

He nearly missed the lookout, partly hidden by a sculpted hedge. A young man was urinating in the grass, one hand engaged, the other cradling a submachine gun with the muzzle pointed toward his feet. He missed the first approach of an assailant on his blind side, finally heard McCarter coming as he was about to zip his fly.

The gunner swiveled in his tracks, a shocked expression on his face, a flash of brightly colored boxer shorts where he had failed to hoist his zipper. He had one hand clasped around the subgun's pistol grip, a warning shout on his lips when McCarter pulled the trigger.

The Browning coughed once, twice, the parabellum manglers drilling home an inch or so apart, dead-center in the young man's chest. McCarter's human target staggered backward, his cry of alarm effectively silenced, but nothing could halt the reflex action of his dying muscles as his finger clenched around the trigger of his SMG. A short burst ripped from the weapon's muzzle, churning the dead man's foot to bloody pulp, then the gun kicked free and fell silent as the sentry toppled over on his back.

And that was how they lost the critical advantage of surprise.

McCarter started sprinting toward the house, his pistol holstered, bringing up the Heckler & Koch submachine gun. Shouting erupted from the general direction of the villa now, and that meant other gunmen on the way. They couldn't know exactly what was happening, but they would be alert to trouble, spoiling for a fight.

How many? There was no way to know for certain until he met the opposition. One bright spot: if the majority of lookouts gravitated southward, it would help the others close to striking range.

Plan B.

If anything went sour, do your best and buy the team some time.

He cast a sidelong glance at Manning, found the tall Canadian keeping pace with his assault rifle at high port. The angry voices were growing closer by the heartbeat, closing fast.

Instinctively McCarter knew that it was better not to meet his adversaries on the run, with nothing in the way of cover. Veering off, he dropped behind a looming evergreen and caught a glimpse of Manning breaking to his right, sliding under cover of a low stone ledge. They made brief eye contact, Manning smiling as if he were out for a stroll in the park.

McCarter braced himself and waited for the shit to hit the fan.

CALVIN JAMES HEARD the first burst of shots in the distance, freezing in place while he waited for all holy hell to break loose. Unsilenced weapons meant a sentry firing—which, in turn, meant trouble coming off the mark. Glancing to his left, he saw Rafael Encizo huddled in the fragile cover of some ferns, attempting to prepare himself for anything that happened next.

It was time to move.

Whatever else was happening beyond the villa, on the far side of the grounds, their enemies had been distracted. James wasn't fool enough to think that every gunner on the north side of the property would leave his post—it might turn out that none of them responded to the sound of shots—but James predicted that the firefight was about to make his life much easier.

Conversely, if he let himself grow overconfident, it just might get him killed.

He moved out on his own, letting Encizo decide the matter for himself. He had already swapped the silenced Browning for the H&K assault rifle slung across his back, and he flicked off the safety lever with his thumb.

From this point on, the silencers were window dressing. All that counted was a steady hand and who shot first.

James spotted the first targets forty yards out, some two hundred yards from the house. Two gunners were attempting to decide if they should check out the unseen action or hold their ground, and curiosity was winning when the taller of them suddenly beheld a black man jogging toward them with an automatic rifle in his hands. They broke in opposite directions, a professional response, one grappling with a submachine gun while the other braced a shotgun at his hip.

The automatic weapon would be first. James fired a short burst on the run, crimson spouting across his target's chest as the 5.56 mm tumblers found their mark. Explosive impact punched the gunner off his feet, unloading half a dozen wasted rounds before he hit the grass and half rolled over on his side.

Number two got off a shotgun blast before James brought the H&K around to meet him, squeezing off another burst. The buckshot missed James by a yard, his target jerking through an awkward two-step, reeling like a hopeless drunk before he sprawled facedown on the ground.

On James's flank, Encizo opened up with his submachine gun, the stubby MP-5 K laying down a screen of cover fire. James spun in that direction, saw a sentry dancing to the sharp, staccato tune of the Cuban's SMG. The shooter went down in a heap, another charging up to take his place. James met the new arrival with a 3-round burst that pitched him over backward in a lifeless sprawl.

He broke in the direction of the villa, running hard with Encizo behind him. Someone started firing up ahead, the bullets going wide, their source invisible. He kept on going, dodging like a broken-field runner on his way to the goal line, ducking his head each time a hostile burst of fire rang out.

A hundred yards and counting, well inside the danger zone.

He wondered where the others were, how they were getting by. It all came down to this, the bloody trek from Jordan to Berlin and on to Zurich. So many deaths along the way: so many more to come.

With any luck at all, he wouldn't be among them when the smoke cleared. And if he was, well, he wouldn't be going down alone.

URI DAN WAS CLOSE ENOUGH to touch the Arab sentry when the young man sensed his presence, spun to face him with an AK-47 rising into target acquisition. Dan shot him in the face, his eyes clenched against the spray of blood a parabellum round produced at point-blank range.

He leaped across the prostrate body, sprinted twenty meters, and flattened himself against the wall of the detached garage. Around him, weapons hammered from the villa, others answering among the trees. For the moment, no one was firing at the Israeli. He took the opportunity to catch his breath, recouping from the long run that had carried him this far. The German, Wetzel, was somewhere behind him, bogged down in a duel with two Arabs, and Dan had also lost track of his one-armed countryman. As for the others, he had a general fix on where they were supposed to be, but even the best-laid plans had a way of disintegrating once the guns went off. If they were anywhere close to their targets right now, Dan figured they were points ahead.

And he had no doubt whatsoever that the worst was yet to come.

A sound of running footsteps on his flank brought Dan's head around. He half expected Wetzel, but the new arrival was an Arab gunman in his early twenties, breathless, gasping as he ran. A moment later, and he would have recognized his peril, but he didn't have that moment. It was gone.

The Uzi hammered out a 4-round burst, Dan's target stumbling over some invisible hurdle, going down on his face. The Israeli took the chance of leaving cover, scooping up the dead man's Kalashnikov assault rifle before he ducked back to the wall. A short burst fired in his direction by an unseen sniper missed him cleanly, ripping through the body of his latest kill.

He checked the AK-47's load and found twenty-one rounds in the curved magazine. His adversary had either been conservative with his ammunition, or else the young man had reloaded shortly prior to meeting Dan. In either case, the more powerful weapon would serve the Israeli well, and he could try to pick up extra magazines along the way.

Dan risked a glance around the corner, checking out the villa. There was no one moving in his line of sight, but that didn't mean he was in the clear. Blank windows might conceal a troop of gunmen, and he couldn't see the servants quarters, farther to the west.

The shout came from the general direction of the villa, someone calling out in German. Dan recognized the language well enough, but not the words. His scalp was tingling, goose bumps rising on his arms. His hands were close to cramping as they clutched the AK-47 in a death grip, and he had to make himself relax by force of will.

It stood to reason that their targets would attempt to flee while there was a chance, leaving the sentries to fight a rearguard action and buy the leaders some time in which to escape.

And that, in turn, would mean his targets had to reach their vehicles.

In the garage.

He waited, heard the shout repeated, the excited voice drawing closer.

Time to move.

He came around the corner in a crouch and met three men approaching the garage. The pointman was a stranger, early twenties, but he recognized the other two. Gerhard Kasche, of National Vanguard fame, was the second in line, with neo-Nazi politician Josef Buhler bringing up the rear. Kasche and the young man were armed, Buhler emptyhanded, concentrating on his stride. All three looked stunned as Dan stepped in front of them, his captured AK-47 leveled from the waist.

The pointman tried to save it, swinging up his weapon, but the Israeli got there first, holding down the Kalashnikov's trigger and catching the gunner with a chest level burst that spun him around, his long legs twisted into a corkscrew of flesh and bone.

The Kalashnikov swept on, the stream of 7.62 mm bullets chopping away at Gerhard Kasche, the German's body jerking like a spastic marionette, blood and mangled tissue bursting from his wounds. When he fell, it seemed as if his skeleton had turned to sand and run down to his feet.

Buhler tried to run, a high-pitched squeal escaping from his lips, but there was nowhere he could hide. The stream of bullets caught him in midstride, clipping his spine and punching him forward, arms outflung in a hopeless effort to catch himself. His face plowed up a three-foot strip of lawn before he came to rest and lay rock still.

A feeling of relief swept over Uri Dan, replaced immediately by a newfound urgency.

He still had work to do, and letting down his guard could get him killed.

He took the AK-47 with him as he moved out toward the house.

KATZ ALMOST HAD THE ARABS, coming out the front. There was a limo waiting for them, with the engine running, and one man occupied the back seat. A second man dived toward the open door, a grim expression on his face.

Two gunners on the front steps of the villa spotted Katzenelenbogen and laid down a burst of cover fire from their automatic weapons. On his left, a low stone wall provided marginal shelter, and Katz threw himself behind it, landing belly-down. Above him, jagged stone shards flew like shrapnel, bullets shattering on impact.

Katz palmed a fragmentation grenade from his web belt, yanked the pin and lobbed the bomb overhand. No aiming this time; he was using the grenade as a diversion, counting off the seconds in his mind until it blew.

The blast seemed almost muted in the open yard, eliciting a startled cry from someone near the villa. Katzenelenbogen came up firing at the gunners on the steps, one of them clutching at a bloody thigh, the other crouching with an arm raised to protect his face. They died there, riddled where they stood, and toppled down the steps together in a heap.

The limousine was moving out, picking up speed from a standing start, its passengers invisible behind the tinted windows. Katz unloaded with the MP-5 SD-3, stitching lacy spiderwebs across the windows, understanding instantly that they were bulletproof. He tried the tires, emptying the rest of the magazine before determining that they were run-flat models. Chips of paint flayed off the starboard doors before he ditched the empty magazine and scrambled for another, knowing it was useless.

Rudolf Wetzel planted himself in front of the hurtling tank, his H&K assault rifle shouldered, squeezing off 3-round bursts as the juggernaut closed to point-blank range. His bullets rattled off the grille, chipped divots in the hood and scarred the windshield—all in vain. The rifle's magazine was empty when he tried to cut and run.

Too late.

The limo plowed him under, tons of metal barely noticing a rag-doll figure crushed beneath the wheels. Katz wasted a burst on the trunk and rear window, cursing bitterly as the vehicle found traction, spitting Wetzel out behind and racing toward the gate.

A bullet whispered past his face, and Katzenelenbogen spun to face the shooter, putting all his rage into a rising burst that ripped the Arab from crotch to throat. The guy was dead before his body hit the asphalt driveway, barely twitching where he lay. Bright streams of crimson tracked across the pavement, pooling in depressions here and there.

A shout from Uri Dan brought Katzenelenbogen's head around. He saw the Israeli jogging toward him, scanning for danger on his flanks as he ran.

"What's happening?" he asked, still hoarse with rage.

"Scratch Kasche and Buhler. I found them out by the garage."

"I missed the others, damn it!" Katz was furious. "They're gone."

If Dan judged him for the statement, he concealed it well. "No reason to stay, then."

He had a point. Katz found the plastic box clipped to his web belt and pressed the lower of two buttons, holding it down. A corresponding box on Dan's belt gave out a muffled chirping sound, the same as every other member of the team would hear—the signal to withdraw.

Katz caught himself with a correction. One of them, at least, would never hear the bell that closed the round. He moved toward Wetzel's body, lying twisted in the middle of the drive. He lay facedown, sparing Katz and Dan from seeing the expression in his eyes.

"We need to take him with us," Katzenelenbogen said.
"Of course."
The stooped together, took the corpse beneath each arm
and double-timed in the direction of the trees.

15

Bernardo Gomez had decided that discretion was the better part of valor. If his German comrades could be stricken at the airport in La Paz before they even had a chance to leave their aircraft, it was clearly time to move on.

And he thanked God, whoever or whatever that might be, that he had planned ahead for such contingencies, without regard to macho pride.

The fortress outside Sucre was his fallback option, just in case the heat around La Paz became too great. In the five years since the renovations had been completed, he had never been compelled to hide there, so he used the hideout as a plush vacation home.

One benefit of power, he had learned, was feeling relatively safe when others in your line of work were forced to scurry through the shadows, hiding out like rodents, living day by day. His small competitors couldn't afford to buy the loyalty of police and soldiers, couldn't field an army on command to save them from their enemies.

But power had its limits, which was one more painful lesson of the past few days. A private army stood for nothing if your enemies were like the wind, invisible, beyond the reach of common men. All the guns in the world were no help without targets, and bribes were no use against madmen, fanatics.

It was time to hide and hope that time would do the work his soldiers, and Rivera's, were unable to accomplish. If the Germans lost their power base around La Paz, so be it. Gomez would invite Karl Dannecker to join him in seclu-

sion, keep their treaty in effect whatever the Nazi decided to
do.

The foot was better—or at least he told himself it was.
The wheelchair was a hindrance, granted, but he had his
bodyguards around him, settled in the comfort of an armored limousine and rolling south toward Sucre. Other
gunners waited for him there, some sixty men in all, with
weapons enough to arm a military regiment.

But would it be enough?

He hoped so.

Underneath the gruff exterior, Bernardo Gomez felt a
germ of fear that ate into his soul like acid, making him feel
less than half a man. The wound was one thing—anyone
could suffer injury in combat; it could even be a plus for
Gomez, if he demonstrated courage in the face of pain—but
in the past few days, the dealer had begun to picture death.
Not afterlife, because he had no faith in hell and understood that heaven, if it happened to exist, would be beyond
his reach. The deathscape in his mind was silent, pitch-black
nothingness, a void from which there could be no escape.
Each man and woman on the planet reached that destination soon enough, and Gomez felt no need to rush the journey.

Not if he could sacrifice another in his place.

Perhaps, in Sucre, he would have the chance.

Ideally, though, the war would pass him by. His own
troops, plus Rivera's and the men still serving Dannecker,
would catch a break for once and find the strangers who had
lately made Gomez's days a living hell. If not, experience
still told them that guerrilla warfare was a transitory thing.
Each day his adversaries spent around La Paz increased the
odds against their own survival, and professionals would
know that, going in. They had already spent more time and
energy pursuing him than Gomez would have, if their situations were reversed.

Unless it was a debt of honor.

In that case, only death would see the matter settled, one
side or the other annihilated in a blaze of violence. Things
like that were always happening across the border in

Colombia, and the Bolivian regime had seen its share of mayhem during recent years.

Bernardo Gomez had no wish to be the target of a vendetta, but he would be forced to play the cards as they were dealt. If luck was with him, moving south to Sucre might provide him with a whole new hand.

If not, well, when his enemies came looking for him, they would have to make their move on unfamiliar ground, against imposing odds.

It was the best Gomez could manage in the circumstances, and he only hoped that it would be enough.

IF THERE WAS ANYTHING on earth Karl Dannecker hated worse than Jews, it was a coward. He had personally executed men who failed to do their duty out of cowardice, and it repulsed him to think of himself in that category, ranked with the scum of the earth.

But he was running, all the same.

Bernardo Gomez had invited him to Sucre, following the airport massacre, and something had compelled him to accept. It wasn't fear, or so he told himself, but something else he couldn't name. Discretion was a part of it, the recognition that a savvy leader sometimes had to cut his losses and retreat before he sacrificed himself and everything he had.

And something good might come of the maneuver, after all. His enemies might lose their focus and decide La Paz held nothing more of interest for them. They might even make a mistake, grow overconfident and leave themselves open to a lightning counterattack.

What a relief it would be, going on the offensive for a change, instead of fighting one last-ditch holding action after another, seeing them fail.

Dannecker spent little time in Sucre, preferring the hustle and bustle of La Paz, but he knew the city well enough to find his way around. Gomez's fortress was a few miles east of town, a property designed for armed defense. He would be safe there, with his allies—Dannecker would never think of them as friends—and in the meantime he would have his soldiers on the street.

Those who remained.

His army was depleted, to be sure, but they weren't defeated yet. Worse routs had been reversed, transformed into resounding victories. The Communists at Stalingrad, for instance, or the Zionists in 1948. The luck that favored Jews and Slavic atheists could also work for righteous Aryans, if they were clever and determined.

And it didn't harm to make his adversaries work for their reward.

The highway from La Paz to Sucre was the best in all Bolivia, which meant that it was kept in adequate repair and seldom washed away in rainy weather. East of Potosi, it was uphill all the way, climbing into the Cordillera Central at an altitude of 18,000 feet or better. Dannecker chewed gum to keep his ears from clogging up, but it never seemed to help.

A minor inconvenience, in comparison to being shot and killed.

He thought about the past two days, his elevation to leadership of the Reich, followed almost at once by the embarrassment of the fiasco at the airport. Dannecker needed a solid victory to recoup his prestige and he needed it soon. His subordinates were loyal, taught from childhood to follow orders without question, but they were also human, with eyes to see and ears to hear. Two days in office as their leader, and he had already shown signs of weakness, climaxed by what some would call running away.

And would they be so very wrong?

It made no difference if he managed to concoct a miracle and save the day. Or, in the abstract, if his colleagues saved it for him.

Dannecker wasn't concerned about who claimed the credit, just as long as he maintained his share of the ongoing profits.

They were beyond Sucre now, and still climbing. Forty minutes brought them to the rutted access road, rising steeply toward the Gomez estate. The mountains and forest were part of his security system, but the same had been true near La Paz, at the camp where Dannecker's enemies had tracked and killed Hans Erdmann.

Trees and snakes wouldn't dissuade the hunters if they got this far, but Dannecker was hoping they might lose the trail.

This once, a lucky break would do him good.

And he was overdue.

Armed guards were waiting for them at the wrought-iron gates, one stepping forward and handling his automatic rifle like a weightless toy, bending down to peer inside the car. He muttered something to the driver, got a reply and nodded, waving toward his comrades on the gate. Dannecker watched them roll the tall barrier aside, and then he was passing through, the gate closing behind him.

He had six gunmen with him, including the driver, all armed to the teeth. Dannecker counted twenty more on the grounds before the limo reached Gomez's mansion, parking at the head of the circular driveway. The man wasn't there to greet him, but the houseman wore an impeccable thousand-dollar suit that barely showed the bulge of hardware underneath his arm.

"If you would come with me, sir?"

"Of course," Dannecker said and followed him into the dragon's lair.

JACK GRIMALDI HAD BEEN waiting for the phone call ever since their mission briefing at Stony Man. For several days he'd sat on his hands and passed messages along like someone's secretary, watching others do the grunt work, take the risks.

And when the summons came, it was delivered in the form of three short words: "I need you."

"Where and when?" Grimaldi made no effort to disguise his eagerness. He memorized the name and address of a small downtown café, confirming twenty minutes as his ETA.

"Okay, I'll see you," Bolan told him, and the line went dead.

No time to waste.

Grimaldi double-checked the Beretta autoloader in his shoulder rig, scooped up the keys that fit his rental car and left the suite. Ten minutes for the drive, five more to find a parking place. He watched for shadows as he walked back to the restaurant, found no one on his tail, and he arrived some ninety seconds early for the meet.

"You made good time."

The voice was close behind him, almost in his ear. Grimaldi turned to face Mack Bolan. "I'm motivated. Are we having supper now, or what?"

"Not quite. Gallardo's waiting in the car."

"Lead on."

They walked around the block and found the DEA agent sitting at the rental's wheel. He turned the engine over as Grimaldi got in back and Bolan took the shotgun seat. They merged with traffic, driving aimlessly while the Executioner talked.

"They're off and running," he said. "Rivera, Gomez, even Dannecker."

"That's Erdmann's number two?"

"Affirmative. Our information is that all of them have left La Paz and headed south, for Sucre."

"What's the draw?"

Gallardo answered that one, meeting the Stony Man pilot's eyes in the rearview mirror. "Gomez has a hardsite several miles outside of Sucre. It's a kind of home away from home, the place he goes to hide when things get out of hand, which doesn't happen very often, by the way."

"That's progress. Are we sure they'll all wind up together?"

"It's a chance we have to take," the Executioner replied. "If they were headed out of the country, I suspect they'd catch a flight. As far as hideouts in the neighborhood of Sucre go, Bernardo's got the only fort available."

"Sounds like you need some wings," Grimaldi said.

"My thoughts, exactly."

Grimaldi had prepared himself for this eventuality, afraid that it might never come to pass, that he would still be sidelined, playing secretary when the final curtain fell. His military contacts in the States and in La Paz had managed to supply him with an aircraft that would do the job.

It was waiting for him at a private airfield southwest of La Paz, along the highway to Viacha. Half an hour would get him there, another fifteen minutes to get airborne, roaring south toward Sucre and his enemies.

No time at all.

"Sounds like we ought to get a move on," Grimaldi said, smiling ear to ear. "I wouldn't want to come this far and miss the show."

IT RAN AGAINST THE GRAIN for Hector Rivera to flee La Paz under fire, but he seemed to have no viable options. His agents on the street had let him down, and the colonel drew an important distinction between honor and foolhardy risk.

It was better, after all, to live and fight another day.

Rivera had considered driving south to Sucre with a military escort, but he finally dismissed the notion as unnecessarily dangerous. Whoever his enemies were, they had shown an uncanny ability to spot targets and penetrate defensive perimeters, enough so that he didn't choose to risk the highway, even in an armored caravan.

The army helicopter was his second choice. Eight soldiers traveled with him, packing automatic rifles and grenades. It was a tiny force, compared to those already ravaged by his enemies in previous encounters, but Bernardo Gomez had an army at his walled estate near Sucre, ready for the worst.

Or so Rivera hoped.

It shamed him to admit that he was frightened by the past two days' events. In no prior situation had Rivera felt so helpless as he did today, in spite of his prestige, authority and rank, the troops at his disposal. It came down to nothing in the end, when he was faced with enemies who kept their wits about them, struck from hiding and refused to cower in their peasant villages.

He hoped he'd have an opportunity to discover the identities of those who had come close to shattering his life. Rivera thought there still might be a chance to save the day if he could only run his adversaries down and punish them for all that they had done. In one bold stroke, he could restore his reputation, make himself look even bolder than before. The near disaster might rebound to his advantage, but he had to save it soon, before his losses mounted any higher and his public image suffered any more.

Below him, mountain peaks were cloaked in forest, unbroken green, the highway miles to the west. Rivera had insisted on flying overland, without following the highway, to make pursuit more difficult. No aircraft had been seen to follow them, and members of his staff had checked the helicopter for homing devices, ruling out one more angle of attack.

It would be relatively simple, even so, for enemies to find out where he was. Out of necessity staff members in La Paz had been told the colonel's destination, and he had no doubt that there were leaks around the office. Still, determining his whereabouts and reaching out to strike him were entirely different things. With Gomez and his soldiers, plus Dannecker and any men he brought along, the Sucre fortress should be more or less impregnable.

More or less.

There was a time, Rivera thought, when he would have said the same thing of his own home, or the Erdmann estate. He had been proved wrong on both counts, and his usual confidence was shaken. That, in itself, was a new experience for Rivera, unique in a meteoric career marked by dramatic progress through the ranks to his present position of power. He would never be the president, of course, and he had no desire to be. It was far better, in Rivera's view, to hold down a support position, make himself indispensable in that post, reap whatever profits he could manage on the side.

Thus far, it had been one triumph after another, even with some of them closely contested and won at a price. Rivera had always triumphed over adversity, left his competition in the dust—or in a shallow grave—and he had banked a fortune in the process.

All in vain, if he was killed by total strangers at the moment of his greatest triumph. It would all have been a waste, his life a grim charade.

They rumbled over Sucre, rotors chopping at the air, his pilots homing in on the grand estate Gomez occupied a few miles east of town. Rivera knew the way by heart. He recognized the access road that branched off from the highway, climbing through the trees. A few more moments, and he saw the wall that ringed Gomez's property—no small expenditure in itself, eight feet of native stone and concrete, topped by razor wire, with inside catwalks for patrolling riflemen.

The guards were ready for him as the helicopter circled, dropping gradually to treetop level. Every man Rivera saw was carrying some kind of weapon—automatic rifles, shotguns, submachine guns, most of them with pistols on their hips or slung beneath their arms. They looked like country bandits, only better dressed. There was an air of savagery about them that designer clothes could never take away.

They were the kind of men you wanted on your side when there was killing to be done.

Rivera didn't feel at ease, not yet, but he was getting there.

The helicopter came to rest on solid ground, the rotors drooping as they lost momentum and slowed to a stop. He waited for the dust to settle, waited while an escort came to greet him from the great house. Gomez didn't come in person, but Rivera told himself that it was best to leave the slight go unremarked. Time enough for keeping score later, if all concerned were still alive.

It might still come to pass that Gomez was among the final casualties of this fiasco, and in that event, his empire would be up for grabs. Rivera saw himself as a front-runner in that eventuality, well placed to help an underling of his own selection take the helm.

But he would have to be alive to pull that off.

Rivera stepped down from the helicopter, shook hands with the houseman and let himself be led back toward the mansion with his soldiers in attendance. For the first time in the past two days, he felt a measure of security, but it was shaky. Fragile.

He couldn't escape a dark sense of foreboding, even here, inside the eight-foot walls with sentries on patrol.

Gomez's troops would have to prove themselves. And if they failed . . .

Rivera wouldn't dwell upon that prospect. It depressed him far too much, and what he needed at the moment was a lift.

He concentrated on the fortune he had earned and all that waited to be grasped, the power it could buy. It was a prize worth fighting for—worth risking all he had.

Including life itself.

BOLAN AND GALLARDO LEFT Grimaldi in La Paz and started driving south, directly from their rendezvous. The trip would give the pilot time to reach the airstrip where his warbird waited, take the ship aloft and be there waiting for them when it counted.

Doomsday numbers were falling.

Bolan heard them in his mind and knew that he was running out of time. The campaign in Bolivia had already lasted longer than most of his lightning strikes, and he had begun to feel exposed, more like a fish in a barrel than a blitzkrieg warrior on the offensive. Any prolonged exposure increased his risk, a chance he had been willing to take in this case, but there were limits, even so.

He meant to close the show in Sucre, catch his enemies inside the killing jar and slap the lid on tight. Failing that, he would have to consider cutting his losses, settling for any gains he had made and pulling out of Bolivia before he pushed his luck too far. That choice would be a bitter pill to swallow, but Bolan had lived with worse in the past.

And, in all probability, he would again. But this day they had a fighting chance.

Driving south, it was the "they" that bothered Bolan more than anything. Grimaldi was a member of the team at Stony Man, recruited from the Farm's inception, but Gallardo was a different story. In the past two days, a combination of frustration, rage and hunger for revenge had driven the man to discard the rule book, but he wasn't trained for a prolonged guerrilla war...or living with the consequences of it, if he managed to survive.

It felt like a betrayal, leading Gallardo into combat when the young Fed's preparation and his background were so different from Bolan's own. Gallardo had done well so far in their encounters with the enemy, but he wasn't a soldier. Sometime soon his sense of private outrage would inevitably start to wane, he would begin to think about the life he was discarding in pursuit of personal revenge...and he would waver, maybe at a crucial moment when the stakes were life and death.

With that in mind, he had considered leaving the agent in La Paz, but Sucre and the Gomez hardsite had the feeling of a three-man mission at the very least. Ideally Bolan would have wished for Able Team and Phoenix Force to back him up, but that wasn't an option. He would work with what he had and make the best of it.

Or the worst, from his enemy's perspective.

The odds weren't his first consideration, though they had to factor in to any estimate of potential victory. Surprise and the Grimaldi edge would make a major difference, possibly enough to see them out the other side alive and more or less unscathed.

With any luck.

It wouldn't take a miracle to crack the Sucre hardsite. Bolan was a skilled professional, with years of battlefield experience, and he had beaten killer odds before. To some extent, a warrior made his own luck in the hellgrounds, building on a combination of self-confidence and preparation, guts and strategy.

The good news: if he blew it, Bolan wouldn't have to suffer with the knowledge of his failure very long. The dealer's gunners would make sure of that.

"How long?" he asked Gallardo, trying to distract himself.

"An hour, give or take."

A lifetime, right, for some. And when the smoke cleared, Bolan wondered who would be among those chosen to survive.

He shrugged it off. No point in speculating on a future he could never read.

The warrior settled back and closed his eyes.

16

Grimaldi's warbird was a Bell AH-1T Apache helicopter, ferried into Bolivia by U.S. Army pilots with special dispensation from the Bolivian government, its mission kept carefully under wraps. Colonel Rivera's machine at state security had been specifically kept in the dark, to prevent any moves that would frustrate any last-minute maneuvers like the one in progress.

The Apache measured fifty-eight feet from nose to tail, its dual-bladed overhead rotor forty-eight feet in diameter. A single 1,970 shaft horsepower T400-402 engine with coupled power sections gave the whirlybird a maximum cruising speed of 172 miles per hour. Designed as an armed attack-and-antiarmor craft, the Apache weighed in at 8,032 pounds without lethal hardware, accommodating some three tons of munitions when it was loaded.

Grimaldi was pushing the limit tonight, prepared for anything the Gomez hardsite could offer. In the Apache's nose, a TAT turret mounted two M-28 miniguns chambered in 7.62 mm, each with a cyclic fire rate of six thousand rounds per minute. The wing-mounted armament were a mixed bag, deliberately varied to give Grimaldi some combat stretch. On the pilot's left, an ML-82 general-purpose bomb provided the Apache with massive kill capabilities, backed up by an M-20/19 rocket pod nesting nineteen 2.75-inch rockets. On his right, there were two quad launchers: one carried four Hellfire missiles, ninety-five pounds each, with a range of five thousand meters; the other packed four TOW missiles, their two-stage solid-propulsion engines covering a range of three thousand meters, guided by an FLIR-augmented Cobra TOW sight in the Apache's nose.

For safety's sake, he had engaged the chopper's built-in IRCM jamming unit, thereby frustrating military radar along with any high-tech security Gomez might have installed at his rancho. The less warning his enemies had of Grimaldi's arrival, the better it would be for all concerned.

He hoped that Bolan and Gallardo were making good time on the road. It wouldn't do for Grimaldi to arrive in advance of the ground troops, blowing their surprise advantage with an overflight that put the defenders on guard. He had synchronized his watch with Bolan's in La Paz, but there were still any number of factors beyond their control: unpredictable delays on the highway, at the airstrip, even marching through the woods to reach the target zone. Bolan was packing a walkie-talkie, tuned to the same frequency as Grimaldi's radio. They had a signal arranged, and the pilot was ready to skirt the target site for up to forty minutes until radio contact was achieved. If Bolan and Gallardo hadn't arrived by that time, he would have a choice to make.

And Grimaldi already knew what his choice would be, damn right.

Given the option of an ineffectual retreat or dumping his load on the target, it was really no choice at all. If Bolan and Gallardo failed to meet the final deadline, for whatever reason, Grimaldi would be going in with everything he had. It was better than nothing, and if some mishap delayed Bolan en route to the strike—or derailed him entirely, God forbid—at least the enemy would get a taste of grief in the bargain.

And after that, what?

He wasn't a ground soldier, never had been, never would be. If his best friend in the world was killed, there was little he could do but dump his load on Gomez and hope for the best. If nothing else, he could raise hell among the soldiers, teach them the price of picking the wrong side.

He was going for broke this time out, with or without Mack Bolan on the ground.

Scorched earth.

The only game in town.

BERNARDO GOMEZ TOOK a glass of brandy from the tray his houseman carried, settled back and waited while his two guests helped themselves. Rivera sipped his drink at once—no class—while Dannecker was more attuned to social situations, waiting with his glass in hand while Gomez scanned the small assembly, holding court.

"A toast." The dealer raised his glass. "To the destruction of our enemies."

His guests went through the motions, but it didn't take a psychic to reveal that both of them were clearly skeptical. Threats and brave talk were one thing, but they still had no clear fix on who their adversaries were, much less where to find them or how to put into effect the plan for their destruction.

They weren't seated on the patio this time. The lesson from their last collective gathering was fresh in mind, the ringing sound of rifle fire, the wound that left Gomez in his wheelchair, days away from walking with a cane. The study featured muted lighting, leather-covered furniture and a giant picture window that faced onto wooded grounds. The heavy blinds were drawn over double-thick, bullet-resistant glass—a further hedge against the threat of a determined sniper lurking on the grounds.

As if the enemy could find him here.

"Your preparations are impressive," Dannecker allowed.

"I only hope," Rivera said, "they will be good enough."

"Rest easy, Hector." He left off the colonel's rank deliberately, to take his mammoth ego down a peg. "You came here of your own free will, I think."

"And I have not decided whether I will stay." The colonel sounded petulant, but Gomez noted that he made no move to rise and leave.

"Your choice," the dealer said. "Your helicopter has been fueled for the return trip to La Paz."

Rivera frowned and drained his brandy, glancing toward the houseman for a refill. Gomez smiled at the colonel's discomfiture, shifting in his seat, enjoying the feel of solid wood and leather beneath him. Security was hard to come by these days, but Gomez felt he was getting there. Slowly but surely, the near panic of recent days was beginning to fade.

He felt safe.

"A change of scene," he said, "combined with more effective measures for security. Assuming that our enemies could find us here—a prospect I regard as slight, though not impossible—they cannot reach us with the tactics formerly employed."

"You hope," Dannecker commented.

"I guarantee. In Señor Erdmann's case, regrettably, he trusted nature to provide perimeters. Deployment of his troops was—dare I say it?—too conservative. I always strive to learn from such mistakes."

The German didn't seem to take offense. He owed his present rank to Erdmann's death, and while the two of them were friends and colleagues, personal advancement sometimes severed family ties. In one respect, Dannecker might also feel indebted to the common foe, but Gomez wasn't fool enough to think the German would hesitate when payback time arrived. He knew Dannecker's reputation, researched the background of all his business colleagues, in fact, and realized that the Nazi was a killer in his own right.

Gomez had come up the hard way in his chosen profession, eliminating anyone who challenged him or offered serious competition. Dannecker had killed a dozen men or so, but Gomez numbered his victims in the hundreds. Between the two of them, there was no contest.

"You are confident, then?" the German asked.

"Completely. When we—"

Gomez never had a chance to finish his statement. At that moment, the house was rocked by an explosion, plaster dust filtering down from the ceiling, settling on the dealer's suit and fouling his brandy. He started to rise, forgetting his wounded foot, and sat down sharply as the pain flared in his leg. Rivera dropped his glass, staining the expensive carpet as he scrambled to his feet.

The colonel had begun to shout in Spanish, fear and anger pouring from his lips.

And that was when the lights went out.

THE MARCH OVERLAND used up an hour and a half, on top of driving time between La Paz and Sucre. Bolan was acutely conscious of the passing time, each footstep bringing him closer to his target. His wristwatch was a tyrant, reminding him that Jack Grimaldi would be on the way in his Apache gunship, eating up the miles and closing fast.

An overturned bus on the southbound highway had threatened to slow them, but Gallardo had managed to negotiate the wreck in good time, driving on the shoulder of the road. It was smooth sailing from there, with no traffic to speak of until they reached Sucre, breezing through the official Bolivian capital and out the other side, winding ever higher into the mountains.

Aerial photographs helped a bit with the final leg of their journey, but the forest was thick here, blinding the camera's eye over significant areas. A mountain stream told Bolan when they were within a quarter mile of the Gomez property, and he reluctantly eased his pace, going on full alert for booby traps and early-warning security devices.

He found the trip-wire first, connected to a Claymore mine that would have shredded Bolan and Gallardo in a heartbeat once the switch was thrown. Next up, a peasant mantrap, springy saplings bent and set to whip across the trail with sharpened wooden spikes attached. He circumnavigated both obstacles, walking Gallardo through the deadly maze, and they appeared to have smooth sailing on the other side.

Until they reached the wall.

Trees and undergrowth had been cut back from the outer wall to a distance of fifteen feet, providing guards on the catwalks with an open killing ground. No sentries were immediately visible from where he stood, but they wouldn't be far away. There were no overhanging trees to help them clear the wall and coils of razor wire.

The Executioner had come prepared, forewarned by aerial photographs of the Gomez estate. The heavy satchel slung across his shoulder contained a shaped plastique charge and detonator, along with smaller charges and incendiaries. When the time came—soon, now—he was going *through* the wall.

Gallardo had been skeptical at first, until he met Grimaldi and was briefed on the Apache gunship's capabilities. They now possessed an edge of sorts, assuming that Grimaldi made it to the target site on time.

He heard the helicopter's rotors seconds later, still a distant sound, but drawing closer by the moment. On his hip, the walkie-talkie hissed with static, once, a second time—the recognition signal. Bolan keyed the set's transmitter button, answering the call without a spoken word.

No instructions were necessary at this point in the game. Grimaldi had his orders, and without specific contradiction he was programmed to proceed against his target.

Bolan seized the moment, scuttling out of cover while Gallardo watched his back and stayed alert for sentries on the catwalk. Crouching in the shadow of the wall, he placed the heavy plastique charge and set the timer, thirty seconds counting down.

It was a short run back to cover in the trees. Grimaldi skimmed overhead a heartbeat later, homing in on the dealer's mansion at the center of the property. A rifle cracked somewhere to Bolan's left, and startled voices shouted warnings, already too late. Huddled under cover of the tree line with Gallardo, Bolan counted off the doomsday numbers in his head.

Five seconds, and he heard the helicopter gunship open fire.

On four, a powerful explosion rocked the Gomez mansion.

Three seconds, and the crack of small arms echoed in the darkness.

Two.

"Hang on!"

The plastique exploded in a smoky thunderclap, its shock wave rippling through the earth where Bolan lay. The bulk of jagged shrapnel was directed inward, stones the size of footballs hurtling like buckshot in a killing radius of twenty yards.

The Executioner was up and running, even as the echo of the powerful explosion died away. Gallardo followed closely on his heels, the sawed-off 12-gauge shotgun slung across his back, an Uzi submachine gun in his hands. They reached the shattered wall and plunged through the smoking breach.

Into the killing ground.

KARL DANNECKER was on his feet before the tremors of the first explosion had subsided. Plaster dust coated his shoulders like dandruff, and framed portraits had toppled from the walls. Heavy draperies had absorbed the glass from shattered windows, and the German heard brittle fragments patter on the floor.

Their host was backing his wheelchair around in a half circle, rolling toward the study door. Dannecker brushed past him, threw the door open and lurched into the hallway as a new explosion rocked the house. Gomez's houseman met him, fresh blood streaming from a gash along his hairline.

Dannecker sidestepped the Bolivian, calling out for his own men as he ran along the corridor, following the sound of voices. Rounding a corner, he found two of his Aryan commandos facing off against three Bolivians, all with weapons cocked and leveled.

"Idiots!" he shouted, slapping down the nearest guns and stepping in between them. "There are enemies enough outside."

He dragged the skinheads after him, leaving the Bolivian gunmen to seek out their own leaders for instructions. At the first sound of attack, Dannecker had instantly rejected any thought of trusting Gomez to protect him. Traveling to Sucre had been a last-ditch effort in the first place, and the German already regretted the move.

Too late.

He had no idea how many hostile guns were waiting for him on the grounds, or how the enemy had tracked him here. It made no difference in the long run, since he had one priority, and only one.

Escape.

"The others," he demanded.

"Waiting with the car," one of his soldiers answered, speaking with an unaccustomed tremor in his voice.

"There's no time to waste," Dannecker snapped. "Let's go!"

JACK GRIMALDI HEELED the gunship over, circling back for another run at the big house, lining up his sights. He caught a group of soldiers milling on the lawn and squeezed the trigger for his miniguns, the twin streams of 20 mm armorpiercing rounds ripping through their ranks, blowing them away.

So much for infantry in the face of superior air power.

He gave the trigger another gentle squeeze for the hell of it and watched a stretch limousine detonate in the driveway, streams of burning gasoline thrown in all directions from the ruptured fuel tank. A flaming scarecrow staggered from the wreckage, capered through an awkward little jig and finally collapsed.

The helicopter made a circuit of the burning house, attracting ground fire from defending troops. Grimaldi had used two Hellfire missiles on the structure already, shattering the northwest corner of the second floor and blasting the front porch into rubble. Marble columns lay across the asphalt driveway, broken into pieces like gigantic sticks of chalk.

He swung toward the servants' quarters, lining up his sights for a low-level bombing run. He released the ML-82 general-purpose bomb a dozen yards short of his target, trusting physics to do the rest. Grimaldi was already climbing out of the run, banking hard left, when the high explosive projectile bored in through the roof, detonating inside.

The servants' quarters seemed to swell, the walls and roof ballooning from within before they shattered outward, spewing wreckage across the grounds. A bulky section of the roof shot skyward, wobbling end over end like the world's largest flapjack. Shingles and sections of shattered lumber filled the air like confetti, tumbling back to earth on a cushion of flame.

How many men inside?

Grimaldi seldom thought of taking human life in concrete terms. He understood the end result each time he dropped a bomb or squeezed a trigger, but it did no good for him to dwell on individual casualties. Instead he concentrated on targets, this building or that vehicle, and observed the results of an attack with dispassionate eyes.

It was cleaner that way, safe inside his airborne cocoon, cut off from the smell of death and the screams of the dying. It was the closest anyone would come to sanitizing the filthy business of warfare.

Grimaldi swung wide over the wooded grounds, holding the armored Apache just out of small-arms range as he circled back toward the heart of the action.

INSIDE THE WALL, Bolan broke in one direction, Gallardo in another, moving out to flank the house. The DEA agent's heart was in his mouth, the thunder of explosions from the great house serving as a homing beacon, small-arms fire the sharp, staccato background music in a symphony of death.

They had surprised the sentries on the wall, slipped past them in the aftermath of the explosion, while the helicopter drew their fire. Between the twin surprises, it had been no contest.

Easy, right.

Too easy.

Dodging through the trees, Gallardo almost stumbled on a sentry crouching in his path. The gunner gave a startled squawk and bolted to his feet, an automatic rifle swinging up to tag Gallardo. The agent nailed his target with a 3-round burst that punched the gunner backward and

bounced him off a nearby tree trunk, dead before he toppled to the grass.

Gallardo kept on going, past the twitching corpse and
toward the house. Floodlights had been mounted to illumi-
nate the grounds, but most of them were dead now. In their
place, great fires provided light to hunt by, casting giant
shadows on the lawn where gunmen scurried back and forth
in search of prey.

The sleek Apache circled overhead, its rotors chopping at
the air, unloading on the hectic scene below with rockets and
a pair of 20 mm Gatling guns. The local infantry was firing
back with everything it had, but without result. Gallardo
couldn't tell if the gunners were missing due to hasty shots,
or if the gunship's armor was deflecting well-aimed rounds.
In either case, the helicopter ranged at will above them like
an angel of destruction, raining death on the men below.

Gallardo saw his opening. He came in from the west,
running all-out toward a line of vehicles parked in the circular driveway. One car, a limo, was already in flames, its
puncture-proof tires melted down to the rims, a blackened
human figure stretched beside it on the asphalt. Gallardo
veered away from the burning hulk and pounded toward the
fourth car in line, a shiny Jeep Wagoneer. No gunmen were
close enough to intercept him, but a soldier on his right,
some fifty yards away, caught sight of him as he closed the
gap.

The rifleman's first round was hasty, high and wide.
Gallardo heard it rattle overhead, despite the other sounds
of combat vying for attention. He threw himself forward,
sliding the last few yards on his belly, coming to rest behind
the Wagoneer. A burst of rifle fire ripped into the Jeep,
punching out window glass, thumping hard against the
starboard door and fender.

It was progress, of a sort.

He worked back toward the rear end of the Jeep on hands
and knees, dropping prone as he reached the back bumper.
Craning his head for a quick look around, he saw the gunman advancing at a quick trot. Gallardo brought the Uzi
into line and sighted down the barrel, lining up his shot. He

stroked the trigger lightly, remembering not to jerk it, and watched the shooter sit down hard, his body going slack.

Gallardo chose his moment, lurching to his feet and coming out of cover, and sprinted toward the mansion.

All he had to do was make it there alive.

17

Inside the wall, Bolan moved north, circling back toward the house after he had cleared a hundred yards of wooded ground. One of the sentries on the catwalk tried to drop him, but the gunner's hands were shaking and he blew it. Bolan spun to face him and stroked an HE round out of the M-203 launcher. The sentry took flight, spinning head over heels to the ground.

The warrior reloaded his hand cannon on the move, keeping to the shadows as best he could, content to let the Apache draw fire for the moment, distracting the ground troops. Every second counted, and aside from wreaking havoc on their adversaries, one of Jack Grimaldi's primary goals was buying time.

Five hundred yards and closing fast, in front of him the Gomez mansion was in flames. Chalk that up to Grimaldi's handiwork, and more to come. There were no hostages inside the house to fret about. Aside from Bolan and Gallardo, every man on the grounds was a legitimate target, armed and dangerous, part and parcel of the viper's nest Bolan had traveled so far to destroy.

It wouldn't be a clean sweep, of course, that was too much to hope for. But the leaders were here, along with their most trusted lieutenants, and that made it worth the risk. They had taken two days of continuous pounding, watched a major portion of their liquid assets go up in flames, and there was nowhere else to run.

The buck stopped here.

Fifty yards left, and a shout came at Bolan out of the semidarkness on his left. Muzzle-flashes followed hard on the heels of a strained, angry voice, and then the bullets were swarming around him, gouging splinters from tree trunks and clipping the ferns and grass. The warrior threw himself to one side, going down behind a tree and bouncing back into a combat crouch, the M-16/M-203 combination braced across his knees.

The gunners were shouting back and forth to one another now, too anxious to be careful. He was able to distinguish three voices. Two of them were circling to his left, the loner to his right. Bolan went in that direction first, playing to their weakness. He met the solitary runner closing in and hit him with a rising burst that hacked him in a rough diagonal from right hip to left shoulder. As the shooter went down on his face, the others fired on Bolan's position. They were late with their response, and he ducked back behind the tree.

He came out firing on the other side, his M-203 launcher belching a high-explosive round from thirty feet. It burst between them, shrapnel ripping flesh and fabric, one of Bolan's targets managing a high-pitched scream before he died.

A burst of automatic fire from somewhere on Bolan's right told him that Gallardo had engaged the enemy. But there was no time or opportunity to help the man from DEA this time around.

Just now, this moment, it was each man for himself.

He had a destination fixed in mind, the faces of his targets burned indelibly into his memory. He would know the enemy when next they met.

Soon, now.

Whatever lay in store for Bolan and his adversaries, one fact still held true across the board.

The game was rolling, which meant all of them were running short of time.

THE WHEELCHAIR GAVE Bernardo Gomez trouble, as he went through the study door. He skinned his knuckles on the doorjamb, cursing at the sudden stab of pain, and shouting for his soldiers to assist him. Three of them ran forward, and a strapping pair bent down to hoist their boss from his chariot. Gomez's meaty arms snaked around their shoulders, clutching tight. The third man brought his chair out through the doorway, and they lowered the dealer back into the seat when it was clear.

"Come on, goddamn you! Hurry!"

He rolled toward the stairs with one man pushing him, the other two in front. Gomez heard the muffled sound of helicopter rotors overhead before a stream of automatic fire ripped through the shingles, sounding like the world's largest machine gun.

Gomez had one priority, and that was escape. With aircraft involved, it was clear that he had sadly underestimated the enemy force and their strategic capabilities. Embarrassment before his colleagues was one thing, but the imminent risk of death something else again. Let Rivera and the German scold him later, at their leisure. All of them would have to be alive for that to happen, and the odds of that seemed marginal, at best.

They reached the stairs, a haze of smoke and dust hanging in the air ahead of them. Six more of Gomez's men had gathered in the parlor below, two of them peering out through shattered windows while the others paced the room with automatic weapons at the ready. Sounds of battle echoed from the grounds outside—raised voices, small-arms fire and powerful explosions—with the pounding of the helicopter's engine over all.

"We must get out!" Gomez snapped. "Right now!"

This time, the young men hoisted him with chair and all, grunting as they carried him down the broad staircase. Gomez clung tight to the metal arms of his wheelchair, trembling from the strain and fear that he attempted to disguise with anger.

Not that he felt any deficit of rage. His last-ditch sanctuary had been challenged, and from all appearances, he was about to be humiliated once again. The change of scene and reinforcements stood for nothing, as his adversaries seemed to plan ahead for every move, employing military hardware to defeat the best troops he could field.

But there was still a chance for him to slip away.

If all else failed, Gomez had sufficient cash reserves to live in splendor for the rest of his appointed time on earth. Accounts in Venezuela, the Bahamas, Switzerland and Liechtenstein were fat enough to keep him like a potentate for years to come.

But first he had to make it through the night.

They reached the bottom of the staircase, and his straining soldiers set him down with grunts of relief. One of them huddled with the nearest gunner, then came back scowling to Gomez.

"The front door is blocked, sir. Rubble from the explosion."

"The back, then," Gomez ordered. "There is no time to waste. Have a car brought around."

"Yes, sir."

One of the gunners ran off to do his bidding, barking orders at the others nearby. Two men wheeled Gomez around and pushed him toward the rear of the house. The dealer's stomach was knotted with tension, hands clenched in his lap as if for prayer, but praying was the last thing on his mind.

Survival took priority, and he wasn't at all convinced of his ability to manage that. Another blast was audible outside, this one some distance from the house. He thought about the servants' quarters and detached garage. Was either one of them intact? He didn't care, as long as he could make it off the property alive.

Gomez was painfully aware of passing time, the moments slipping through his fingers like water poured into a bottomless sand pit. For all he knew they were cut off, already trapped, but he wouldn't lie down and die without attempting to escape—and in the process take as many of his adversaries with him as he could.

They hurried through the kitchen and reached a service entrance, one of the soldiers pushing through ahead of him, submachine gun at the ready. Gomez smelled the reek of gun smoke, heard the cries of frightened, wounded men, but he was unmoved by the plight of his subordinates. He had risen to his present status through total self-absorption, and that quality of egotism didn't fail him in extremis.

As if on cue, a limousine pulled into view, halting in line with the back door, its engine idling.

"Hurry!" Gomez shouted to his soldiers. "We must go!"

He tucked his arms in, just in time to save his elbows as the *pistolero* shoved him through the door. To hell with paint and woodwork.

"Never mind the chair!"

His soldiers lifted Gomez, bore him toward the car and wrestled him inside. They filed in behind him, doors slamming, the driver putting his vehicle in gear.

Safe?

Not yet, but getting there.

Bernardo Gomez slouched back in his seat and kept his fingers crossed.

KARL DANNECKER HIT the ground running, surrounded by five of his men. He had picked up an Ingram machine pistol in transit, and he carried the weapon clutched against his chest like a protective amulet, knowing full well that the gun and guards together might not be enough to save his life.

Dannecker's team had escaped from the house via sliding glass doors that fronted a flagstone patio and swimming pool. A helicopter thundered overhead, and the German and his men flattened themselves against the nearest wall until it passed by, raining death on someone away to their left.

They broke for the cars then, running around the house in semidarkness, single file, a couple of his men firing at shadows in their near panic.

It all seemed to have fallen apart in seconds flat, his hope of safety and security blown apart by the first blast that ripped through the house. Dannecker knew that nothing would ever be the same again. The whole Reich was in jeopardy, but all he could think of at the moment was self-preservation. Where was the master race without its anointed leadership? What were the troops to do without generals in command?

One of the Bolivians met them, coming around the corner, his automatic rifle jerking upward in surprise. Two of Dannecker's soldiers fired in unison, cutting the young man down in his tracks.

Forget him. What was one dead greaser in the balance, when the future of Aryan culture was at stake?

The driveway came into view, with vehicles burning brightly, drifting clouds of smoke obscuring Dannecker's view of the grounds. He picked out muzzle-flashes in the darkness, shadow figures running to and fro, but he had no idea which ones were enemies or friends.

It made no difference, now.

He wondered briefly where the rest of his bodyguards had gone, then put them out of mind as swiftly as the thought had come. They were expendable, perhaps more useful to the movement as martyrs than as mere cannon fodder.

One of his cars had exploded in flames; the other showed some damage to the body and windshield, from shrapnel or concussion, but he suspected it would serve their purpose.

First, however, they would have to reach the vehicle, get in and start the engine, navigate grounds that had become a shooting gallery.

"The keys?" he asked a gunner on his right.

"Left in the car."

A lucky break. "You first."

The skinhead didn't hesitate. He even smiled, as he broke for the driveway, knees and elbows pumping in a headlong sprint.

He almost made it.

Dannecker was never quite sure where the bullets came from, but he saw their effect. The runner seemed to stumble, lurching through a half turn to his left, jets of crimson exploding from his chest and shoulder. Gravity took over, dragging him down. Another bullet helped him get there, detonating like a giant firecracker inside the skinhead's skull.

And that left four.

"Together, next time," Dannecker commanded. Something told him that his soldiers might distract the unseen gunmen, thereby giving him a better chance to reach the limousine. If he could get there, if he found the keys in the ignition, if he managed to escape the killing ground in front of him, he would be rescued.

If.

It was a clear-cut case of nothing ventured, nothing gained.

"Come on!"

He shoved one youth in front of him, then followed, trusting that the others would be on his heels. A wild exhilaration gripped him, giving Dannecker a speed and power he would never have suspected he possessed. He overtook the pointman swiftly, passed him, gaining on the limo.

He was halfway there before the helicopter gunship circled back to catch him in the open, nosing over in a strafing run. He saw the muzzle-flashes, but the sound of gunfire never reached his ears.

Karl Dannecker never heard the 20 mm rounds before they ripped into his chest, exploding flesh and bone, a double punch shearing off his blond head at the lower jawline. He tottered two steps backward, then lost his balance, melting to the grass, his four remaining soldiers dead and gone before he hit the turf.

If anyone present marked the passing of a superman, it didn't show.

ERNIE GALLARDO FED his Uzi submachine gun a fresh magazine, then left the protective cover of the vehicle that sheltered him. The Apache helicopter had come in for a final assault on Gomez's mansion, literally bringing down the house, raising plumes of smoke that blotted out the moon and stars. Gallardo took advantage of the cover, running in a crouch around the ruins of the once great palace. It was little more than ashes, now, and the DEA agent wondered if the dealer was inside.

He heard the limo coming well before he saw it, braced himself for action, with the shotgun tucked beneath one arm, the Uzi up and aiming through the pall of smoke. The vehicle came into view, a hurtling juggernaut, and Gallardo had perhaps two seconds to decide his strategy.

For all he knew, the limo might be armored, but he had to play the hand as it was dealt. He held down the Uzi's trigger, the sights rock-steady, thirty rounds exploding from the muzzle in one sustained burst. The windshield frosted over on the driver's side, not quite imploding, and Gallardo ditched the empty SMG, swinging the 12-gauge into target acquisition in a heartbeat.

One blast, and the limo was already swerving. A second, and he felt the driver lose control. Radial tires dug in on the passenger's side, while the others lifted off, losing contact with the earth. The limo toppled over on its side, a back door flying open on the driver's side, disgorging a limp bag of bones. The car rolled over its former occupant, crushing him flat, and continued through the rotation, coming to rest with its wheels in the air.

As Gallardo watched, a thread of flame crept along the limo's undercarriage, racing toward the fuel tank. When it blew, the car lighted up from one end to the other, but its armor-plated floorboards kept the worst of the explosion from immediately gutting the interior. Even so, it was only a matter of time, and Gallardo waited, watching the open doorway with his shotgun cocked and locked.

The first man out was no one he had ever seen before. The gunner didn't spot Gallardo standing in the shadows, failed to recognize his peril as he turned back toward the crippled limousine and reached inside. He strained against the weight of some invisible burden, rocking back on his heels. A pair of grasping hands came into view, followed by the arms, then a head.

The face belonged to Gomez, who cursed in Spanish, kicking out behind him with his one good foot. Another moment, and the gunner had him clear, dragging his boss away from the wreck before a secondary blast could scorch them both.

Nobody else got out.

Gallardo took his time and shot the *pistolero* in the back, a blast from fifteen feet that punched him through a sloppy cartwheel, past his commander in chief and into a heap on the grass.

Bernardo Gomez sat and watched his death approaching, fumbling underneath his jacket for a gun that had to have disappeared inside the limo, coming out empty-handed. He squinted through the drifting smoke, his eyes fixed on Gallardo's face.

"I know you, eh?"

"You ought to know a man, before you put a contract on his head."

"The gringo-lover."

"Suit yourself." The pump gun in his hands felt weight-less, like a toy, its muzzle centered on Gomez's chest.

"What happened to your rule of law?"

"It must have slipped my mind," Gallardo told him, squeezing off his first round as he spoke, working the slide and firing again while Gomez flopped on the grass like a stranded fish, repeating the action until his firing pin fell on an empty chamber.

Done—at least in one respect.

The sounds of battle told him he wasn't safe yet, by any means. He slotted half a dozen shells into the shotgun's magazine and walked back to retrieve the Uzi, reaching for a fresh mag in his belt.

Gallardo still had work to do. He couldn't let his guard down yet.

Not if he wanted to survive.

RIVERA'S ARMY PILOT had the helicopter's motor running when he reached the aircraft, rotors spinning fast enough to flatten out the grass for meters around. Rivera ducked his head, four soldiers on his heels as he pulled himself into the chopper, fumbling his way to the nearest seat and wrapping the safety belt around his waist.

Almost home.

Behind Rivera, Gomez's house went up in the mother of all explosions, nothing left to save in that inferno. The colonel cringed at the thought of being trapped inside there, how close he had come to the ultimate disaster.

Close, but he was still alive.

The small-arms fire was slackening around them, but Rivera didn't plan to stick around and find out who was winning. If Gomez and Dannecker managed to pull it out, they could scrape by without him. On the other hand, if they were already doomed—as the demolition of Gomez's house seemed to suggest—then Rivera didn't intend to get sucked down with his colleagues.

The last of his team piled in, a grim smile on his face. "The enemy helicopter, sir!"

"What about it?"

"Gone. A rocket from the ground." He grinned and clapped his hands together, finally pointing to the north. "On fire, I think."

Rivera felt his own smile coming on, suppressed it with an effort. "Very well." He slapped the pilot on his shoulder, leaning forward. "Hurry! Get us out of here!"

Their helicopter lifted off, painfully slow at first, causing Rivera to grind his teeth, but then they were gaining momentum, swinging away from the bonfire of Gomez's dream, sweeping over the dark forest beyond.

Toward safety, he hoped, and away from sudden death.

One thing was clear above all others in the colonel's mind.

It was time to cut and run.

MACK BOLAN SAW Grimaldi's chopper take the rocket hit, his stomach knotting painfully. Somehow, the Apache stayed aloft, unloading a last hellacious bombardment on the house before it roared out of sight, trailing smoke in its wake.

He offered up a silent prayer for Grimaldi's safety, then turned toward the source of the rocket. Two of the Bolivians were huddled in the shadow of a nearby hedge, one cradling the empty LAW rocket tube, his comrade brandishing an AK-47, scanning the hellgrounds for targets.

Bolan came in from their blind side, firing on the run. The rifleman never knew what hit him, 5.56 mm tumblers ripping through his flank and draping him across the thorny hedge before he could respond. His comrade swung toward the Executioner, raised the rocket launcher, suddenly remembering that it was empty, useless in his hands. He cursed in Spanish, dropped it and fumbled with a holster on his hip.

Too late.

The M-16 spit at him from a range of twenty feet, his body jerking as the bullets stitched a line across his chest and slammed him backward in a heap beside his lifeless comrade.

Two down for Jack, whatever happened next.

Suddenly he heard another helicopter revving up, closer at hand. Bolan ran toward the sound, drawing no fire on his way to the new target zone. Somewhere on his right, beyond the flaming shambles of the mansion, small arms still crackled in the night. There was no way of telling whether they had pinned down Gallardo, or if the defenders were simply firing at shadows, venting fear through their weapons.

The army helicopter was already airborne when Bolan came within range, swinging away from the house and the point where he stood. He chased the gunship with a burst from his assault rifle, knowing he couldn't trust the M-203 launcher to score a kill on a moving target at that range.

Whoever was on board the helicopter was slipping through his fingers as he stood there, watching helplessly.

The Executioner whirled at the sound of footsteps closing from behind him, his rifle leveled from the waist. Gallardo froze in his tracks, waiting for Bolan to recognize him in the split second before his finger tightened around the M-16's trigger.

"Who's that?" Gallardo asked him, nodding toward the chopper as it rumbled out of sight.

"No telling. It's a military helicopter, probably Rivera."

"Anyway, Bernardo didn't make it."

"Are you sure?"

"Dead sure."

And that was something, anyway.

"I think we've done the best we can," Bolan said. "Jack got hit. He's headed north, the last I saw. We ought to split."

"Suits me," the DEA agent answered. "I've seen everything I came to see."

Retreating toward the tree line, Bolan wished he could have said the same.

18

The crash, when it came, wasn't as bad as Grimaldi expected. He was skimming at treetop level when the engine choked and died from lack of fuel, and there was nothing he could do but fight the stick, coming down through the canopy, bracing himself for the impact to come.

And, in the end, the treetops saved him.

The topmost branches wouldn't hold him, the Apache boring in, nose down, to snap thicker branches, vines and creepers. When it stuck, Grimaldi was reminded of a landing on an aircraft carrier, the dragline suddenly arresting forward progress, so that he was thrown against his shoulder harness. The Apache dangled in darkness, fifty feet or more above the ground.

Terrific.

It took several moments longer for Grimaldi to decide the tree would hold his weight. The stricken chopper creaked and groaned around him, settling in its makeshift sling of vines and branches . . . but it held. The smoke was clearing out, it seemed, as if the fire had been blown out in flight, or at the point of impact. Waiting for the worst—the sound and heat of spreading flames—Grimaldi finally convinced himself that he was not about to fry.

Which left him with the problem of escaping from the crippled helicopter and regaining touch with Mother Earth.

The chopper weighed in excess of eight thousand pounds, without its armament. It was encouraging to know the tree would bear its weight, but Grimaldi hadn't lost touch with grim reality. He knew that anything—a straining limb, a sudden breeze—could shift the balance and send him plunging to the forest floor. The same was true for any movement he might make, but sitting still and waiting offered no alternative.

Taken to a farcical extreme, Grimaldi knew that he could sit there—hang there—in his harness until he died of thirst and hunger, waiting for the gunship to break free. More likely, someone would have marked the aircraft's progress, maybe seen the crash, and they would be en route to check it out. Tonight, in this vicinity, he was willing to bet that any hunting party would be hostile, either bound to Gomez or in league with state security.

And either way, captivity was just a prelude to death.

Grimaldi took his time releasing the shoulder harness, holding tight to one of the straps with his left hand to keep himself from dropping through the windshield. The Apache shifted slightly, and he let it settle once again before he twisted out of his seat, climbing hand over hand to the copilot's chair.

He rested there, almost within reach of the exit hatch, knowing he could touch the lever if he stretched out to his left.

No time like the present.

Grimaldi took it slow and easy, snagged the quick-release lever with his fingertips and gave a yank. The latch disengaged with a click, but he had to lean farther, giving the hatch a solid punch before it swung open and outward, banging against a branch outside.

The tricky part was coming next. To make his getaway, Grimaldi had to leave the relative security of his place, crawl through the hatch and find a solid perch outside. No simple matter, when any single move could be his last.

The hatch was just in front of him, perhaps six feet away, chest-level as he crouched against the empty seat. Beyond the open hatch was total darkness. The unknown.

Grimaldi timed his move, springing like a diver trying for Olympic gold. His hands and arms went through the hatchway first, his head and shoulders next. When he was halfway through the opening, the helicopter gave a scream of tortured metal and shifted radically. Grimaldi kicked free of the hatch, hands grasping at the darkness out in front of him—and snagging on a vine that felt like knotted rope.

Behind him, the Apache began to slide. It broke free a heartbeat later, scraping bark and snapping branches as it gained momentum, falling. Grimaldi almost lost his grip, felt something crack against his heel ... and then the vine gave way.

He gasped, as the world dropped out from underneath him. Clinging to the vine against all hope, he dropped twenty feet before he ran out of slack and the natural rope reeled him in. Grimaldi slammed against the tree trunk, slipped another yard or so and finally caught himself.

"Well, shit."

The chopper came to rest below him, settling with a crash that shook the tree from roots to upper branches. Grimaldi waited for the dust to settle and his pulse to stabilize before he started his descent, hand over hand.

It took him fifteen minutes in the darkness, creeping down the massive trunk, then picking his way around the Apache's twisted wreckage to reach solid ground. He had a penlight in his pocket and a compass on his flight vest, all he needed to point himself northwest, toward the highway.

Hiking through the dark, he kept his Beretta automatic in his hand, his finger on the trigger. He had seen and done too much to jump at shadows, even in the present circumstances, but he stayed alert. Along the way, he ditched his vest and webbing, skinned off the baggy jumpsuit, revealing jeans and T-shirt underneath.

Not quite the pilot, now, but still a warrior.

It took the best part of an hour to reach the highway. Standing on the grassy shoulder with his pistol drawn, Grimaldi felt ridiculous, as if he had been caught playing cowboys and Indians.

Start walking, right.

He covered half a mile, northbound, before he heard the sound of tires behind him, humming on the pavement. Turning to face the sound, he shifted hands with the Beretta and stuck out his right thumb in the international gesture.

Headlights blazed into his eyes. Grimaldi swallowed hard and cocked the automatic as he waited, saw the dark sedan swing over to the shoulder. A man on the passenger's side smiled as he cranked his window down.

"We can't keep meeting like this," Mack Bolan said.

A CIVILIAN JET WAITED for Rivera in La Paz. He could have left directly from the airport, but he had a stop to make, a team of his enforcers standing by, dressed in civilian clothes, to pack the jump seats in his armored limousine.

It was a short run to the downtown high rise where Rivera kept a penthouse home away from home. A flying wedge of bodyguards conveyed him to the elevator, two men staying in the lobby while the others joined him in the car.

Upstairs, Rivera wasted no time packing clothes. Instead he closed the bedroom door behind him, hunched inside his closet and opened a square safe set into the floor. A quarter-million dollars' worth of foreign currencies left room in the valise for his passports—all five of them—and a collection of documents verifying ownership of high-rent property in La Paz, Nassau, Miami and Paris—Rivera's walking papers.

Back in the elevator, Rivera felt his tension mounting. It had been a gamble, even coming here before he fled the city. It was unlikely that his enemies had returned from Sucre to La Paz so swiftly, but, then again, he had no clear idea of who his enemies were, or how many of them he faced. Suppose a contingent had been left behind in the de facto capital to watch his old haunts and report any movements?

Never mind.

It would take some time for Rivera to access his foreign accounts, fleeing as he was in the middle of the night, and a weekend at that. He needed traveling money, documents to facilitate his flight eastward, confusing the trail in case he was pursued.

He'd fly to Nassau first, where he would switch identities and catch another plane to Mexico City. From there, he was bound for London, another switch of planes and names, before proceeding to Switzerland. Once on neutral soil, he would have time to rest and consider his options, living under yet another identity while he sized up his choices.

The storm in Bolivia was too intense to last, but it had already doomed his career. Rivera understood that the exposure following the Sucre strike would leave his superiors no choice. They were practical men, politicians, and they would jettison any dead wood in an attempt to save themselves.

Rivera meant to get out, as the Yankees would say, while the getting was good.

The long drive back to the airport was nerve-racking, with Rivera constantly glancing behind him in search of a tail. It was impossible to say if they were being followed, but his driver displayed no concern, and the colonel tried to calm himself by concentrating on the next few hours.

The time would work to his advantage. Most or all of his superiors were home in bed, asleep by now, and it would be an hour or more before the first reports of violence filtered out of Sucre, longer still before the message reached La Paz. Rivera would be well away by then, before they started asking him for explanations or demanding that he move against the enemy.

It would be someone else's problem, and he was welcome to it. Hector Rivera was bailing out, with no apologies to anyone. He had done his best with what he had, and it was over. He had seen enough of war and killing for a lifetime.

It was time to rest, enjoy the fruits of his labor for a change.

They reached the airport without incident, used Rivera's rank to drive out on the tarmac in the limousine instead of passing through the terminal. His personal jet was on standby, ready to go, the crew on board and killing time while they waited for their passenger to arrive.

Rivera's soldiers covered him between the limo and the jet, but none of them joined him on board. They had served him well, fulfilled their purpose, but he didn't crave the attention that came from traveling with an armed entourage. Bodyguards were available anywhere, and Rivera trusted his other security precautions to cover him en route to Europe.

He couldn't see beyond the next few hours, but tomorrow would take care of itself.

His jet was cleared for takeoff, rolling out along the runway, lining up for the last dash to freedom. Rivera fastened his seat belt. This time tomorrow, he would be untouchable. Let Gomez and the others bear the heat, if they were even still alive.

Rivera didn't care. His new life lay before him like a banquet, waiting to be tasted.

THE WORD CAME IN TO STONY MAN at five past midnight, Eastern Standard Time. All holy hell had broken loose outside of Sucre, and it made the Zurich action pale by comparison. Bolivian troops were on the move, trying to contain the violence, but it was evident that they had gotten off the mark too late.

Aaron Kurtzman spent twenty minutes on the message he would send to Hal Brognola, weeding out supposition and speculation, hoping he might hear from Striker or Grimaldi first, but they were out of touch. His secondhand reports from spotters on the ground assured him that his people had escaped intact, but Kurtzman sensed that there was still too much confusion on the site to be sure. From what he heard, it could be days before some of the bodies were identified . . . if, in fact, they ever were.

And now, he had reports of the Apache helicopter being damaged—one source said destroyed—with no word from Grimaldi to lift the heavy pall of dread.

Each time his warriors took the field, Kurtzman mentally prepared himself for disaster. Wars weren't fought without casualties, and Stony Man had already suffered its share, dating back to the early days of the project, when Striker still operated under the code name of Colonel John Phoenix. It was inevitable, Kurtzman knew, that other members of the team would be wounded or killed in the future, but he would do everything within his power to forestall that moment.

Unfortunately, here and now, "everything within his power" boiled down to nothing at all.

Kurtzman knew that he could only watch and wait, but in the meantime, he would have to reach out for Brognola, keep him posted on late-breaking events. It was never pleasant, delivering bad news, but it came with the territory.

First, though, he would have to get the facts straight in his own mind. What, exactly, did he know?

The Gomez hideaway outside of Sucre was destroyed, thanks largely to Grimaldi's aerial attack; that much was obvious. Identifying casualties was something else, though Kurtzman had reports that told him Gomez was among the dead. No word, as yet, about Colonel Rivera, except that he was missing from La Paz and nowhere to be found.

It was little enough to start with, but Kurtzman kept hoping for the best, knowing that Striker and company had already overstayed their welcome in Bolivia. Guerrilla warfare was a matter of timing, above all else, and the longer a covert warrior remained in the field, the greater were his chances of being tagged—and eliminated—by the enemy.

Going on four days for Striker and Grimaldi, now. Too long. If they hadn't accomplished everything they hoped to, it was coming up on time for them to cut their losses and retreat. There was no shame in living through a battle, even when it went against you. No one made a clean sweep every time, and there was no such thing as final victory. Each triumph had to be recaptured periodically, lost ground regained.

And that meant taking risks.

He considered paging Barbara Price, decided he would raise Brognola first and get that hurdle out of the way. There was nothing Barbara could contribute at the moment, other than concern, and even that had limits. She couldn't reach out to Striker from the Farm and lift his burden, share the danger he was facing in Bolivia. Kurtzman would keep nothing from her, but she would have to wait her turn.

Whatever happened in Bolivia, the battle wasn't over yet. That much was clear to Kurtzman. Some of the primary targets had slipped past Phoenix Force in Zurich, and if there were other topflight survivors in La Paz, it meant the plot was still in motion—damaged, perhaps, but still viable.

And the hell of it was, they didn't even know the main thrust of that plot, to start with. The central focus still eluded him, but maybe Striker had a handle on the game by now.

Assuming he was able to report back when the smoke cleared.

At the moment, that was far from certain. Kurtzman kept his fingers crossed as he was reaching for the telephone.

Brognola answered on the second ring, no trace of drowsiness in his tone. "Hello?"

"Farmer Brown."

"What's the weather report?"

"Storm clouds lifting in the south, I'm told. No concrete word on losses yet. We're standing by."

"Our team?"

"Blank slate, so far. The word is, we lost our eye in the sky."

Brognola was silent for a moment, his voice solemn when he spoke again. "That's not confirmed?"

"Not yet. We're limited, you understand, in what we have an opportunity to ask."

"We need to think about evacuation, one way or another."

"I agree," Kurtzman said. "Selling it to Striker is another story."

"Do the best you can."

"I hope I get the chance."

"Amen."

The line went dead, and Kurtzman cradled the receiver. Barbara next, and he was relishing this call no more than the last.

There were times, he decided, when no news was bad news.

Like now.

"YOU TALK about a lucky shot," Grimaldi said. "He caught me broadside, circling. It couldn't happen again in a million years."

"Once is all it takes," Bolan reminded him, half-turned in his seat, glancing back at Grimaldi over his shoulder.

He was more relaxed now, with the team intact, despite their failure to achieve complete success. The military helicopter taking off meant one or more of their primary targets had escaped. Even in the midst of panic and chaos, Rivera's men would be more frightened of their leader than the unknown enemy. Bolan was willing to bet that none of them would dare to flee in the chopper while Rivera stayed behind.

But had he taken any other major players with him?

"We're confirmed on Gomez, right?" he asked Gallardo.

"Right as rain. I saw him, up close and personal. He's history, guys."

"What about Erdmann Junior?" Grimaldi asked. "What was his name?"

"Dannecker. I didn't see him anywhere," Bolan said. "If he's still alive, I'd bet he runs back to La Paz and looks for someplace to hide with his friends."

"If he has any left," Gallardo added.

"Never fear. We're still a long way from wiping out the Nazi presence in Bolivia. Remember, they've had fifty years to multiply."

"Like rats," Grimaldi said, a sour expression on his face.

"It's not our job to clean out the sewer," the Executioner reminded him. "Select excision, and out. We don't hang around and try to net the small fry."

"Even so."

"We have to figure that Rivera beat it," Bolan said.

"I should have nailed that chopper down," Grimaldi muttered.

"Let it go. You did your job."

"And then some," Gallardo said. "If you hadn't strafed those limos in the driveway, I'd have never made it to the house."

"We aim to please."

"What happens now?" Gallardo asked.

Bolan knew the answer to that one. "We split up. You've got a job to do, reports to file."

"I wouldn't be so sure."

"You'll be surprised, I think."

"And you?"

The Executioner caught Grimaldi's eyes; a silent signal passed between them. "We'll be moving on," he said. "I think we're finished here."

"You're kidding me." The federal agent was incredulous. "We've made some headway, sure, but when you talk about Bolivia, we've barely scratched the surface."

"Maybe next time," Bolan told him. "We've got business elsewhere."

"You're serious!"

They drove in silence after that, the miles unrolling. Bolan concentrated on the coming dawn and what would follow, where the new day would lead him. They had bet the limit in Bolivia and come out ahead of the game, but it was far from the clean sweep he had desired. The loose ends from Southern California had been tidied up, but in their place he had a new trail to pursue.

Rivera.

Logic told him that the colonel wouldn't linger in La Paz. It would be too much, trying to suppress the bad publicity from Sucre. Bailing out would be the only option left—but where would Hector go to ground?

Someplace where he had cash reserves, a place to hide, secure—as he supposed—from further harassment.

And where was that?

Bolan didn't have a clue, but it was something he could learn from Stony Man and the computer files that accessed every facet of daily life. Bank records. Travel documents. Identities. Deeds and securities.

It was virtually impossible to exist in modern society— even the third world—without leaving some kind of a paper trail. Rivera had the full resources of state security behind him, professional spies and forgers at his command, but any ruse could be unraveled with the right approach.

He thought of Kurtzman and smiled in the dim light from the dashboard.

They were on another trail, and it was warm. The enemy had managed to elude them once, but it was time to shuffle the cards for another deal.

Next time around, he thought, it just might be the dead man's hand.

*Don't miss the exciting conclusion
of the Terror Trilogy. Look for SuperBolan #37,*
Inferno, *in August.*

TAKE 'EM FREE
4 action-packed novels plus a mystery bonus
NO RISK
NO OBLIGATION TO BUY

Join Mack Bolan's latest mission in

THE TERROR TRILOGY

Beginning in June 1994, Gold Eagle brings you another action-packed three-book in-line continuity, the Terror Trilogy. Featured are THE EXECUTIONER, ABLE TEAM and PHOENIX FORCE as they battle neo-Nazis and Arab terrorists to prevent war in the Middle East.

Be sure to catch all the action of this gripping trilogy, starting in June and continuing through to August.

Available at your favorite retail outlet, or order your copy now:

Book I:	JUNE	FIRE BURST (THE EXECUTIONER #186)	$3.50 U.S. $3.99 CAN.	☐
Book II:	JULY	CLEANSING FLAME (THE EXECUTIONER #187)	$3.50 U.S. $3.99 CAN.	☐
Book III:	AUGUST	INFERNO (352-page MACK BOLAN)	$4.99 U.S.	☐

Total amount		$_____
Plus 75¢ postage ($1.00 in Canada)		$_____
Canadian residents add applicable federal and provincial taxes		
Total payable		$_____

To order, please send this form, along with your name, address, zip or postal code, and a check or money order for the total above, payable to Gold Eagle Books, to:

In the U.S.
Gold Eagle Books
3010 Walden Ave.
P. O. Box 9077
Buffalo, NY 14269-9077

In Canada
Gold Eagle Books
P. O. Box 636
Fort Erie, Ontario
L2A 5X3

GOLD EAGLE ®

TT94-2R